Praise for *Tales of B-Company*

What Other Writers Are Saying

Looking through his microscope, Chris has populated the now more tactile and detailed *Pennsylvania* world with unforgettable characters that live and breathe and leap from the page … As good or better than the original.

> —Michael Bunker, author of *The Pennsylvania Omnibus* and *Brother, Frankenstein*

Pourteau handles Military SciFi with a deft literary gift for both the regular and the heroic that reminds the reader of Bernard Cornwell. Brilliant in scope, nuanced in execution. Read this and enjoy.

> —Nick Cole, author of *The Wasteland Saga*, *Soda Pop Soldier*, and *The Red King*

Chris Pourteau's *Gelassenheit* will give you chills and will stick with you long after you've left its pages. "Magnificently tragic" is perhaps the way I know how to describe this first-person narrative … a must-study in terms of character development, tension, pace, and dialogue.

> —Eric Tozzi, author of *Phoenix Lights* and *The Scout*

With parallels to the original three day battle of Gettysburg … this thrilling military sci-fi adventure puts you back in

Bunker's world from the perspective of TRACE soldiers in their fight for freedom. [*Gettysburg*] is a fast-paced adventure that pulls you right into the battlefield.

—Ed Gosney, author of *Prometheus Stumbles*

We talk about writers' writers and readers' writers and Pourteau manages effortlessly to be both. He draws his characters with skill and one can appreciate and observe the techniques employed to do so. Yet he also manages to make them admirable and lovable, each with their own peccadilloes and strengths.

—Jennifer Ellis, author of *Reversal* and the *Derivatives of Displacement* books (review of *Susquehanna*)

Pourteau is at the top of his game. I didn't think this series could get better, but the third installment of B Company is exceptional. Pourteau has a cinematic style that pulls you into the story and refuses to turn you loose.

—Hank Garner, author of *Mulligan* and *The Seventh Son* (review of *Columbia*)

What Readers Are Saying

[*Gelassenheit*] was a riveting and enthralling story of one family's struggle between the old and the modern. It also features a searing psychological portrait of how each family member interprets their cultural beliefs.

—Chris F., Amazon reviewer (5-star review)

Heinlein meets Glen Cook. This fast paced short story ... keeps your eyes glued to the pages. Chris Pourteau writes a character driven, well-written sci-fi war story for all ages.

—Christopher B., Amazon reviewer (5-star review of *Gettysburg*)

I'm not usually a reader of sci-fi in any form but starting skimming this and then couldn't put it down. This is a story for anyone who enjoys adventure; a love of sci-fi is not required! The characters are so well developed; this author has a gift for making the reader know and like (or hate) the characters just through their demeanor and actions, and in such a short time.

—Supergenius, Amazon reviewer (5-star review of *Gettysburg*)

One thing I love about these stories is the female leadership of a resistance group. Captain Brenneman is one tough lady! She's smart, logical, efficient, cares about the men and women in her charge, and as we find out in this story, she is willing to make whatever personal sacrifices are necessary to ensure victory over Transport.

—VeggieLover, Amazon reviewer (5-star review of *Susquehanna*)

Susquehanna, the sequel to *Gettysburg*, does not disappoint. Beautifully written, with lots of edge-of-your-seat action carried out by well-rounded characters... I loved *Susquehanna* even more, and I can't wait to dig into the next story in the series. Top-notch writing here. Don't pass this series up.

—Missa C., Amazon reviewer (5-star review)

Chris Pourteau just gets better and better writing in this world. Crisp and engaging, his words bring you into the action and tension of the *Pennsylvania* universe with immediacy and drama. The B Company stories are great military tales, but are also stories of humanity and relationships torn in the midst of the ongoing conflict between the Transport Authority, TRACE and the rest of the population of New Pennsylvania.

—AnneHope, Amazon reviewer (5-star review of *Columbia*)

The stories grab you from the beginning and won't let go until the end and this story is no exception. Any cliffhangers or unanswered questions you might have had will be answered in [*Columbia*].

—Preston L., Amazon reviewer (5-star review)

Tales of
B-Company

The Complete Collection

by
Chris Pourteau
writing in the world of
Michael Bunker's *Pennsylvania*

Introduction by
Michael Bunker

Edited by
David Gatewood

This collection is for the fans of B-Company
Your enthusiasm, excitement, and love of these characters
Kept me writing about them

Contents

Introduction by Michael Bunker 1
Foreword by the Author 5

Gelassenheit 9
    Historical Note: *Gelassenheit* 35

Gettysburg 37
    The First Day 39
    The Second Day 65
    The Third Day 101
    Historical Note: *Gettysburg* 125

Susquehanna 129
    All Our Food Belong to Whom? 133
    The Ferryman..148
    Riverwalk...163
    Warpath 182
    Guns and Butter and Bourbon...217
    Historical Note: *Susquehanna* 227

Columbia 231
    A Little Night Work 235
    Obadiah's Orders...256
    The Tick-Tock of the Okcillium Clock 272

Up, Up, Up! 293

Legacy 323

Historical Note: *Columbia* 359

Acknowledgments 365

A Note to My Readers 369

About the Author 371

Introduction by Michael Bunker

Almost immediately after I published *The Pennsylvania Omnibus* in April 2014, I was very surprised to start receiving requests from fellow authors wanting to write stories in the world of New Pennsylvania. At one point I think there were more than twenty-five authors either writing or intending to write stories in the little sandbox I'd created. Of course, I instantly gave everyone who wanted to write in my world permission to do so, even telling them to sell their stories on Amazon if they wanted.

It's both humbling and a little frightening to know that other authors respect the fictional world you've built enough to want to explore it more deeply and add to its legend. I know some authors voice concerns about what will happen to the worlds they've created once they're opened up to what's commonly called "fan fiction," but I've never shared that concern. I've written fan fiction myself—*Osage Two Diamonds*, a commissioned novel written in the world of Kurt Vonnegut, and *The Silo Archipelago*, a novella written in the world of Hugh Howey's *Wool* are two examples—and I know there's no way that someone who loves an author's world and wants to explore it could do any lasting damage to that world. The whole concept that fan fiction might somehow have a negative impact on the original work, or on a reader's conception of that work, is foolishness to me.

Chris Pourteau and I became acquainted around the time *The Pennsylvania Omnibus* came out, and he asked my permission to write a story in the world of New Pennsylvania. I immediately said, "Yes!" I'd already read his debut novel, *Shadows Burned In*, and I'd really enjoyed it, so I knew he'd do a fantastic job with a *Pennsylvania* story. (And I'd have given him permission even if, for some reason, I hadn't enjoyed *Shadows Burned In*.) The fact that I'd seen so much natural talent and ability in his writing made me not only acquiesce to his request, but eagerly anticipate reading his take on the *Pennsylvania* world.

His first short story in the *Pennsylvania* universe was "Gelassenheit," published in the short story anthology *Tales from Pennsylvania*. The story is a terrific tale taking place a generation before the events of *The Pennsylvania Omnibus*. I loved the way Chris examined so many of the tensions and social and cultural conundrums of my own people (the Plain People) as they must interact with and relate to the world, while deftly tying together those examinations and infusing them into a story that accurately portrays the fictional world of *Pennsylvania* as I saw it. Needless to say, I was pleased and not at all surprised by the positive response Chris got from *Pennsylvania* fans who read his story.

Not long after that, Chris contacted me about writing a

longer story set in New Pennsylvania. I was thrilled to no end and very excited to learn that he was going to push that longer story out to the world in a series of parts, just as I'd done with the original *Pennsylvania* story. What I never expected—even though I was already impressed with the quality of his storytelling—was how expertly Chris would weave his "military thriller" approach into the *Pennsylvania* fabric.

I'm heavily influenced by the Russian literary tradition, so though my original story included war and battles, warfare is presented only as a backdrop to the story. Big concepts of warfare are discussed and some brief views of battle take place, but for the most part the war is *over there*. Much like Napoleon advancing on Moscow in *War and Peace*, the war between TRACE and Transport in *The Pennsylvania Omnibus*, though central to the plot, is not very explicit. It's a set piece. It represents and places emphasis on the rest of the story.

For his approach to the world of New Pennsylvania, Chris Pourteau has adopted a perspective more characteristic of American literature. Though he emphasizes the details of combat, he focuses on the very real human drama occurring between those comrades in arms fighting the battle ... *as they fight it*. I think this approach is really a game changer in the life of this fictional world. It elevates the whole. It's like a microscope that shows you that, on some chosen aspect of a larger subject, an entire world of life exists there too! A deeper and grittier world, with real events and consequences that roll outward, like the proverbial flap of the butterfly's wings, changing and affecting the world at large. Chris's approach gives greater texture to the whole. It's a fascinating mechanism to use this juxtaposition within the framework of the larger story, and I think Chris has pulled it off beautifully. I couldn't be more pleased with the product of his labors.

Chris has populated the now more tactile and detailed *Pennsylvania* world with unforgettable characters who live and breathe and leap from the page—characters for whom I began to care more deeply the more I read about them.

I'd like to leave you with this exhortation. Please do not read *Tales of B-Company*—compiled here from all its parts for your reading pleasure—with the idea that, because it's a tie-in or "fanfic novel," somehow it's intrinsically *less than* or inferior to the original. I've never seen it that way, and I hope you won't either. Far from it, in fact. In many ways, in my mind, what Chris has produced here, the book you're about to read, is on par with or better than my original *Pennsylvania* story. And it should be read as an expression of Chris Pourteau's own original and fantastic art—a piece of literature in its own right. I think it's that good, and I bet you will too.

Michael Bunker
May 2015

Foreword by the Author

If you're like me, when you buy a book, you probably don't purchase it for the foreword. Like the extras on the hill in *Monty Python and the Holy Grail*, you might already be standing up, waving your arms, and shouting, "Get on with it!" But if you'll indulge me a moment, I'd like to give you some background that, I hope, will enhance your reading experience of this collection.

Michael Bunker created a vital world of possibilities when he published his *Pennsylvania Omnibus*. Amish sci-fi? Um, okay. Sounds a little strange, but when you read it, it *works*. In fact, I found Michael's approach to be a totally original take on a familiar genre that I've loved my entire life—from *Star Trek* to *Star Wars* (yes, it's possible to like both) to Joe Haldeman's *The Forever War* and John Scalzi's *Old Man's War* books and beyond. "Totally original" isn't easy to do these days, but Michael pulled it off.

My story "Gelassenheit" in *Tales from Pennsylvania*, a compilation of short stories set in Michael's world, was my first toe-dipping in New Pennsylvania. Written in first person from the perspective of an Amishman (and father), the story looks at life under the Transport Authority some twenty-five years before the events in *The Pennsylvania Omnibus*. I wanted to study the inherent tensions between the Plain People in New Pennsylvania, who only want to live their life their way, and a government determined to enforce its will on its citizenry. I wondered: What might have occurred in the past to motivate *Pennsylvania*'s characters to rebel against Transport? But when I finished "Gelassenheit," one of the characters in the story wouldn't let me go. So I decided to write more about them.

I also wanted to update their story and bring them into Michael's contemporary world of New Pennsylvania. So I spun the hands of the clock ahead a quarter century for *Gettysburg*, the first of the B-Company tales. Weaned on military/adventure sci-fi and *Sgt. Fury and His Howling Commandos* World War II comic books as a kid—and, as an adult, being a huge fan of Bernard Cornwell's historical military fiction—I decided to create a band of TRACE commandos fighting the good fight against Transport. And I promoted my character from "Gelassenheit" to be their captain. Connection made. Let the fun begin!

Gettysburg and its sequels happen as a parallel storyline set at the same time as *Pennsylvania*. (In fact, some of Michael's characters make cameos in my B-Company stories, so keep an eye out, *Pennsylvania* fans.) I was so blown away by how well Michael and his readers received *Gettysburg* that I decided to write its first sequel, *Susquehanna*. That tale ended on a bit of a cliffhanger, and so *Columbia*—the third and final B-Company tale—was born. (Michael thinks I had a master plan for these stories, but honestly, one begat the next, so shhh, don't tell him otherwise.)

It isn't absolutely necessary for you to read *The Pennsylvania Omnibus* before reading this collection, but I highly recommend it. First, it's a great read and, as I mentioned, an innovative take on the sci-fi genre. And beyond that, if you've read *Brother, Frankenstein*, you know the story we pick up in *Pennsylvania* is part of the same universe.

But if you don't read *Brother, Frankenstein* or *Pennsylvania*, "Gelassenheit" should give you all the background you need to enjoy the three tales that follow. By the way, I mentioned above that "Gelassenheit" is told in the first person; *Gettysburg* and its sequels are written in the third person, and the reason for that is to give the reader a bird's-eye view of battle from the perspectives of different characters. I hope you don't find the switch too jarring.

One last thing—I originally published each of the B-Company tales separately, and with each, I included an afterword explaining the historical background for that particular story. For this compilation, I've kept those "historical notes" with their respective stories. However, I've collected the acknowledgments for those who helped me on the individual tales—artists, readers, editors—into one section at the very end of this collection.

So—I've delayed you long enough. I hope you enjoy my take on Michael Bunker's world of New Pennsylvania. Sit back, relax, and enjoy the ride.

Chris Pourteau

May 2015

GELASSENHEIT

"He wants to take our farm, Poppa!"

The words echo in my head as I sit here, waiting to learn the fate of my child. Words pointing out the path of God's will. A memory of an argument with Thomas, my son.

Thomas is sixteen years old. He questions everything, and this is as it should be. Never fear to question what is known. My father taught me that. But as with most young men his age, Thomas is slow to think and quick to anger.

Ah, I must apologize. I see by the look on your face that you have no idea what I'm talking about. I don't wish to burden you with this, but since we're both sitting here, awaiting the judgment of the Transport magistrate, perhaps you would listen to my story? It will help pass the time. Yes? I thank you for that. I'm alone here today, and though we're strangers, your presence brings me comfort.

I see by your clothing that you are not Amish. Please, there is no judgment when I say this. I simply point it out so that you understand why I explain things about myself. Things that, to another Plain Person, would seem unnecessary. I want you to understand what has happened. To truly know the tragedy that has befallen my family.

My name is Abram Brenneman. My family and I arrived in New Pennsylvania ... is it three years ago already? As you might have guessed, we were part of Transport's Emigration Incentive Program. We received the standard land grant—including livestock, seed, and building materials. In fact, we were one of the first twenty families granted land in the newest section of the AZ after Transport increased their recruitment efforts on Earth in 2090. We set up our homestead, planted our ground, raised our animals.

When I was younger, I lived in your world. A world where everything moves quickly, as if trying to catch up to itself. But it never seems to, does it? You fall asleep planning the next day and swear you'll take a moment for yourself or your family. And the next night, you fall asleep reciting recriminations for failing to do that. I remember the cycle well.

The life of the Amish is much slower. Our focus is on the task at hand. Milking the cow, sweeping the floor, enjoying a cold drink on a hot afternoon. We believe that God grants us the grace to experience these things. Some would call that lifestyle simple—and most of the time, they'd be right. But sometimes we Amish face complicated times. History has, on occasion, asked us to conform. Our way is to simply move on, away from that demand to compromise our values, until we find good soil again and can start over. We have learned to stay alert for such times. It's still difficult for me to accept that one of our own, a Plain Person, would have once more invited history to our doorstep.

But I'm getting ahead of myself.

Matthew Yoder is an elder in our community. I assume you know next to nothing about us, so let me explain: elders are ministers. They lead our community. They conduct worship services, prescribe the scope of the *ordnung*, our community's rules. They guide our spiritual development. It's important to understand this. Matthew's position made his proposition all the more shocking, and difficult to resist at the same time. Which brings me back to Thomas and our argument.

"He wants to take our farm, Poppa!"

We sit at the long table in our home, a simple wooden structure with three rooms: the common area (a dining room-kitchen-sitting room), a bedroom shared by the children, and the bedroom I share with my wife. I glance at Anne as she washes the dinner dishes. I see reflected in her eyes the conversation we often have regarding Thomas these days. *He is young, Abram,* her reassuring smile reminds me. *Too old to be so young in his thinking,* my eyes sigh back to hers.

Our daughter, Mary, sits across the room, sewing a quilt in the flickering candlelight. She uses two candles, an extravagance we allow her. She's always determined never to miss a stitch, and we want to encourage her industriousness. Even now I see her there in my mind's eye, beautiful and focused. The image of that simpler time—when a drought was my greatest worry—makes me want to weep openly.

"You assume too much," I say to Thomas. "He cannot take our farm. The government granted it to us. He cannot simply take it."

Thomas rolls his eyes. "He speaks for the Transport Authority! Or were you not listening, Poppa?" His fear and frustration drive him to his feet. I remain seated in his shadow. Sometimes strength comes from not having to demonstrate you have it. My father also taught me that.

"Lower your voice when speaking to me," I say quietly.

Thomas clicks his teeth together. He's trying to remain

calm but losing the battle with his glands. He's a young man. *Too old to be so young.* He stands in broiling silence, which grows uncomfortable.

"The proposal he offered is nothing our people haven't heard before," I say, to fill the empty air.

"He was not very pleasant about it," Anne says, wiping her hands dry. "That's a certainty."

I grant the point, saying, "I have found Matthew Yoder is rarely pleasant when it comes to an opportunity to make money from Transport." I'm venting a bit of my own distaste for the man. Matthew Yoder is what we refer to as money-Amish—what we call someone who lives our lifestyle but is more concerned with making money than most.

Thomas puts his hands on his hips and looks down at me. "Why shouldn't we modernize? Horse-drawn plows and wooden troughs bringing water from the river ... we could make more with better equipment, spend less time tilling the soil and more"—he looks around for evidence for his argument, then gestures at Mary—"more time quilting!"

His sister notices our conversation for the first time. "I would like that," Mary says simply. I smile at her innocence. I want to keep her that way forever.

This debate is as old as the Plain People. The tug of tradition against the push of progress. But some see embracing innovation as tantamount to surrendering our way of life. Nearly a century and a half ago, during the Second World War, we resisted serving in the military. In response, the U.S. government put the I-W Program in place as a way of placating those who saw the Amish as cowards. The program asked us to serve in factories on the home front, supporting our country but without compromising our commitment to pacifism. Many elders despised the program. Moving to large cities—being exposed to the allure of the fast life—permanently fenced off many of our young people from their Amish roots.

So when someone suggests that modernizing how we farm is a simple advance in technology, they rarely consider it from our perspective. How we raise crops, maintain livestock—these are not mere questions of technique or technology. Rarely can one man and his family maintain a large farm. He needs his neighbors. Sowing seeds promises to feed you next winter, but planting with others beside you nurtures your community's roots.

Modern equipment allows one man to do the work of many. Efficiency improves. Communities dissolve.

"So now you endorse Matthew's suggestion?" I ask, incredulous. Then I remember he is angry, not thinking. Anything he says now is meant to prove himself right, whether he be right or not.

"Better to modernize than lose the farm! Or maybe you just want us to run away ... like we always do!"

Ah, there it is. His glands again. My son is ready, quite literally, to beat plowshares into swords. "I will not explain again that which you know so well," I say. "I will only say this: we won't resist them should they come for the farm. We will simply move on. We will continue."

"Then we modernize!" My son slaps his hands on his thighs, a magistrate passing judgment.

I look at Anne, who sits down at the end of the table beside me. Her eyes are patient, always patient. It is, perhaps, the one quality I love most about her.

"No," I say, turning to face Thomas directly. I do not stand.

His jaws clench. His fists stretch the tendons of his strong forearms, flex the muscles built beside me in the fields since he could walk.

"You're not only an idiot, you're a coward!" He yanks the front door open and flees.

Now, though I'm older than Thomas, I'm still a man. My son has just called me a coward. I rise, my own mind giving way to fury. But patience puts her calming hand on mine.

"Let him go, Abram."

I turn furiously on Anne. She draws away, but her hand stays. Her patience is stronger than my anger. I sit back down.

"Is he right, Poppa? Will Elder Yoder take our farm?"

The quilt is set aside on Mary's lap. She looks worried. She idolizes Thomas. I try to keep my explanations simple, honest, and nonthreatening for my daughter's ears.

"He might," I say. "But I don't think it will come to that. There are others—Elder Noffsinger, the Benders—they'll also resist what Elder Yoder proposes."

Anne folds the dish towel neatly in squares and places it on the table. "Perhaps we should begin talking with them." At my raised eyebrow, she clarifies quickly, "About forming a new community."

I consider that. "We should certainly talk to the others, but honestly, if this is happening here—at Transport's behest—it's likely happening across the entire AZ. Transport would almost certainly enforce their new requirements on any new zone we raise. We might be simply delaying the inevitable."

Anne's lips grow thin. Not with anger, with concern. I see the same furrowed brow, the same worry I'd seen in Mary's face moments before. Anne is her daughter's mother. "And what is the inevitable?" she asks quietly.

"The choice Thomas laid out before us. You know as well as I that no one homesteads without Transport's approval. That's what the AZ is for, they'll say. We granted you land, handed you equipment and livestock, they'll say. This is what history has shown us."

"The Richmond Ruling?" Anne asks hopefully.

We won't find help there, and I say as much by shaking my head. As you might be aware, the Richmond Ruling only protects the Plain People from having BICE and TRID devices installed. The ruling proscribes as much as it prescribes our rights under Transport. One notable caveat specifically requires that the Amish make their case for not conforming, whenever the Authority identifies a need it considers important enough to warrant suspending their rights under the Ruling. In these situations, each case is then judged independently ... by a Transport magistrate. The most common result of such a proceeding is a judgment amounting to the application of eminent domain over the rights of the individual.

"Why don't we fight?"

Mary's question has the same innocence as before, when she said it would be nice if there were more time for quilting.

She has an earnest look on her face, the same kind of focus she gets when stitching.

"You know the answer to that, child," says Anne. "Violence is not our way. If God's will is that we should move on from here to preserve who we are, then that is what we'll do."

"What if God wants us to fight?"

I sigh. "Christ taught us to turn the other cheek, Mary. You know this."

"I remember a story," she says.

"Yes?"

"Of Jesus and the moneychangers in the temple," she says.

"Yes."

"Didn't he destroy their tables and drive them from the temple? Wasn't that violence?"

I pause in my answer. I know by doing so I seem as if I don't have an answer. But I don't want to patronize my daughter. Children tend to think in such black-and-white terms, so I must answer her in a way that she can understand and accept. But my answer must also be honest.

"Jesus restored God's temple to its holy purpose," I say. "It became again a house of worship rather than a bazaar for profit."

"So …" Again, the serious look. The furrowed brow. I can almost see her young brain carving a new path on its surface, learning to think. "So, violence is all right if its purpose is holy?"

"Violence is never all right," I say. I can hear the tension rising in my own voice. It's not meant for Mary, but it's directed at her. I've begun to fear that her assumption might be what Thomas is thinking too. Perhaps he considers himself a holy warrior. Perhaps he will do something stupid. But I should have known ... I should have known.

"Mary, that's enough for tonight," says the voice of patience.

"But Momma—"

"I said, that's enough. We have worship tomorrow, and Brother Lambright's farm is a long way from here. We'll need to get up earlier than usual."

"Yes, Momma." Mary stares down at the unfinished quilt in her lap. I remember being twelve and feeling responsible for upsetting my parents but unsure why it was my fault. Of course, it never was. She folds her quilting quietly and rises. "Good night, Momma. Good night, Poppa."

"Good night, Mary," I say. And then, because it's important she hears it right now: "I love you."

Halfway to her room, she stops and turns. "I love you too, Poppa. Will you ... will you look for Thomas? Is he okay?"

I feel tears catch in the back of my throat. While we've been debating theology, my son is out there, angry and alone. Perhaps I should have gone after him after all. My daughter has reminded me what being a good parent is.

"He'll be all right," Anne says. "He's just upset. He'll be back in time for worship."

Mary nods, but I see those arched eyebrows again. She wants to believe, but her worry overrules her. "Good night," she says again.

I watch her go into her room and slowly close the door. I consider the story of Jesus and the moneychangers and search for an answer to Mary's question: "Violence is all right if its purpose is holy?" I can come up with a half dozen rationalizations, but none that truly explain Our Lord's choice to physically overturn the tables and run the moneychangers out of the temple. These are not the actions of a meek man, I admit to myself. Perhaps His passion overruled His rational thought on that day, as Thomas's did tonight. As mine started to. Perhaps Mary is right, and there is an acceptable time for violence after all, if used for a holy purpose. But my faith cannot accept this. Then the irony hits me—the story of Jesus and the moneychangers comes to us from the Gospel according to Matthew.

The next day is Sunday. We're awake well before dawn to hitch up Maisy to the buggy for the long jaunt to Brother Lambright's farm. He is hosting worship services today. Every other Sunday a different family hosts. Thomas is beside me this morning, preparing for our journey. He jerks the girth of the harness roughly around Maisy's belly. She snorts her displeasure.

"Maisy is not trying to take our farm," I say quietly. He doesn't reply but pats her rump, murmuring to her softly as he loosens her girth strap a bit.

The ride to Brother Lambright's farm is long and mostly silent. Anne talks with Mary about the hymns they will likely sing today. I don't force a conversation with Thomas.

When we arrive, the men congregate in the barn to decide

who will preach today. As we mingle, Matthew approaches me.

"Good morning, Abram," he says.

"Good morning."

He places his hand on my arm, grasping my right hand in his to shake it. I want to pull away from this man who has caused such dissension in my own family. Instead I grasp his hand in return. Firmly.

"I feel like I might've stepped over the line yesterday," he says. "I wish to apologize if so. It was not my intent to threaten. That is not our way."

He is right, I think. It is not *our* way. However, I've had more than one occasion to question what Matthew Yoder's way is. I literally turn my head so my right eye focuses on him.

"Passions get the best of us sometimes," I say.

He nods, placated. "I was wondering—might I come over for dinner tonight? Let's start the conversation anew. I'll bring an apple pie and cider, if that's agreeable."

I consider it. Perhaps this is an opportunity to smooth everyone's feathers. To show Thomas what talking openly can do. And best of all, it was Matthew who offered it. I cannot say no and call myself a good father, or a good Amishman.

"Of course. I'll speak to Anne. Sundown?"

He smiles. "Sounds perfect."

Soon the sweet sound of singing from the *Ausbund*, our hymnbook, begins the formal worship service, and we men sit opposite the women on benches placed in Brother Lambright's front yard. Thomas sits beside me, straight backed and proud, and Mary sits next to her mother opposite us, a half-pint reflection of Anne's beauty.

Despite the various ministers who sermonized on several topics, I remember little else about the nearly three-hour service, save for one word: *gelassenheit*. It describes one of the core precepts of Amish society. In a way, it encapsulates all that we are. I have grown to hate it.

Elder Noffsinger is the speaker. "*Gelassenheit* is the glue that holds our community together," he says. He looks meaningfully across the open faces of the boys and girls on the benches and continues. "It's a 'death' or 'dying' of self. A willingness to subjugate the worldly desires of the individual to the needs of our community. An acknowledgment that for the community to succeed—to move forward and continue despite obstacles placed in its path—the individual must die to themselves and become something greater."

For most, this sermon is nothing new. I glance at my own children and see them fully engaged. Often, as it is with any religious service, ministers can drone on; worshippers can doze off. Some do that now as Noffsinger speaks. But not Thomas. Not Mary. I'm blessed with children able to see the relevance of a sermon in their own lives. Or, perhaps, *cursed* is a better word for it as I think back to yesterday. Even listening there on that bench, it caused me worry. How would Thomas hear this? If only I'd known then what would happen, I might have been able to stop it.

The rest of the service is a hazy cloud of hymns and homilies. Fellowship around bountiful tables of food afterward. A long ride home, though less silent this time.

"Poppa, did you hear what Elder Noffsinger said?" asks Thomas. "About sacrificing oneself for the benefit of the community?"

"I heard," I say.

"Did it mean anything to you after our … after our conversation last night?" I can hear in his voice that he's working to stay calm, rational, and I'm proud of him for that. He knows this will win his point faster than would calling me a coward again. I haven't raised an imbecile.

"Of course it did."

Anne and Mary sit behind us in the buggy. The road thumps beneath the wheels, rattling all of us. I feel Anne's hand on my back, perhaps to steady herself as the buggy clatters. Perhaps to steady me as I speak to my son.

"It meant that we must, each of us, do what is right for all of us," I say. "Not what we'd *wish* to do to satisfy our own desires. That includes the need to feel strong by conducting violence against those we perceive as having wronged us." Anne's hand squeezes my shoulder before releasing again. Maisy neighs, happy in the cool breeze.

Thomas looks away, muttering.

"If you would speak out loud, speak so we all might hear," I say.

He turns back to me, disgust on his face. "How our people have lasted so long, I'll never understand," he enunciates clearly.

I fear that is true, I think. The rest of the ride home is passed in silence. This time, I'm grateful for the quiet.

At first, Thomas is angry when he learns that Matthew has invited himself to dinner. Of course he is. But Anne, as is her gift, calms him down, and I wonder if he begins to see it as an opportunity to prove himself right. To show us all what Matthew Yoder is really all about. I'm willing to settle for that.

Mary, for her part, is happy to hear that Matthew will share our table. She offers to help her mother cook, something we usually have to coax her into doing. The entire family seems to embrace the opportunity to find a positive resolution to yesterday's discord, even if Thomas's motivations are less than peaceful.

There isn't much to talk about as the day passes. Although it's the Sabbath, Thomas and I spend the waning afternoon repairing a fence that had blown down earlier in the week. We Amish call this an "ox in the ditch" chore; while manual labor is generally frowned upon on worship days, sometimes it is necessary. Meanwhile, Anne prepares dinner, and Mary picks flowers behind the house for the table. Whatever I might think of him as money-Amish, Matthew is an elder in our community. We would be remiss if we did not host him with courtesy and share God's bounty with him.

As evening draws near, Thomas is still silent, simmering like the sun, and we both need to clean up before dinner. He takes his hat off to wipe his brow and look over the day's work. Together, we have finished repairing the fence.

"You did excellent work today, son," I say. I like knowing we mended the fence together. I feel closer to him for having accomplished it as father and son.

He hesitates, then, "Thank you, Poppa." He hesitates

again. I know the feeling well from being married. Is the fight over? Am I coldly courteous or has my heart softened? Do I speak the minimum expected or show the other person I still love them? "*We* did good work today," he says finally. "Together."

I smile at him and clap him on the shoulder. "Come. Time to clean up."

"We wouldn't want Elder Yoder to be offended," he says. There is sarcasm, but mostly his tone is playful. For my benefit, no doubt. He's trying.

As we approach the house, heaven wafts on the air. Pot roast, mashed potatoes, green beans, corn on the cob, biscuits made by rolling out the dough—not prefabricated from a can, like you might be used to—gravy for the roast. Mary has made Matthew a gift of muffins to take home with him, and she slaps her brother's hand away as he tries to take one. If Matthew is true to his word, we'll also have cider and apple pie for dessert. No doubt this will be a first test for Thomas to assess the elder's veracity. Will he at least bring to dinner what he promised?

No sooner has dusk fallen than I see Matthew's buggy, black against the sunset over the hill road. I let Anne know, and she and Mary rush to finish setting the table. I stand on the porch, puffing my pipe and watching his approach. Then I see that Matthew is not alone. It's not his wife or one of his sons with him. It's someone I don't recognize, a man.

In that moment, I know Thomas is right. Absolutely right. My heart sinks into my stomach. I'm no longer hungry for heaven.

"This is Sebastian Green," says Matthew by way of introduction.

I take the man's hand. It's obvious that he is with the Transport Authority. His imperious stance, his slightly condescending smile. Matthew has staged the man's clothes for him. Though not Amish, they are simple by Transport standards. And he isn't armed. Matthew was smart enough to see to that.

"I invited him to dinner," Matthew is saying. "I hope you don't mind. Here," he says, handing me a still-warm apple pie.

"Mr. Brenneman," says Green, hoisting a Mason jar full of cider in his free hand. He smiles. "I truly hope we can come to a mutual accommodation this evening."

I return the smile. It is the only weapon I can wield to protect my family. Glancing at Matthew, I say, "I wasn't aware tonight's dinner was for discussing business." I let it hang there until I'm satisfied they are both uncomfortable in the silence that follows. Then, "But, all things in their own time, no?"

I usher them into my home. Anne smiles and nods at Matthew as we enter. When she sees the stranger, her smile falters. Thomas looks bewildered; Mary, strangely distant and distracted. We sit at the long table as Anne recovers herself and gestures for Mary to help her add a sixth setting. I catch Thomas's gaze as we arrange ourselves, and I know he sees in my eyes the hardness that has settled around my heart. Either we will modernize our farm, or Transport will take it from us.

The clinking of silverware, the silent chewing, the occasional observation on the weather and the sermons earlier in the day. This is how dinner passes. The stranger, Green, says little. Afterward, Anne and Mary clear the table. Matthew invites me to the front yard for a pipe, and Green follows him like a puppy.

"Poppa, can I come?" asks Thomas. Since there are two of them, having two of us will make me feel better, so I allow it. I realize in that moment that I've begun thinking like that: *us* and *them*.

Matthew gets right to the point as soon as our pipes are lit. "This is how it is, Abram. There have been two rebellions in the last one hundred years, and the current conflict has left Transport short on resources. Many hearts and minds have turned away from the Authority, despite its knowing what's best for them. To regain the support of those citizens, we need to show them how much we really do care for their welfare. And we need your help to do that. For Earth. For New Pennsylvania. For all of us, really."

We? I think.

"But to do that, Mr. Brenneman, we need to feed people," offers Green, as if I don't know that people need to eat. "Both here and back on Earth."

I puff my pipe. "I'm happy to help feed anyone I can." This is true. This is Amish.

"That's good to hear," says Green. "The problem is, we need your farm—everyone's farms—to yield more, and yield it faster. We want to show citizens the Authority can care for them, so we have to do just that. We have an opportunity to encourage peace for everyone's sake. With your help, we can accomplish this."

I let that sink in. The night has settled down now, and the sky is clear. I note the vastness of the stars I can see, and I wonder, as always, at God's power, His generosity in placing them there, every night, for me to see.

"But you demand that we change the way we farm," says Thomas. "Don't you understand, how we choose to raise our crops is part of who we are?" He looks at Matthew with disgust. "You're no Amishman to ask this of us."

"Be careful how you speak to me, *junge*. I am an elder and not responsible to you."

Thomas snorts. "Clearly not. You're responsible to *him*." He gestures at Green.

"Thomas."

"Poppa ..." But then he reins himself in. He knows my position on the choice we have to make. He knows not to argue with me in front of others.

"Speak plainly, Matthew. You know my mind on this." I decide to give voice to Anne's suggestion. It never hurts to ask. "Is Transport at least willing to let us found another AZ with our traditions intact before they take back the land they gave us?" I say the last part, though they're really just extra words. I want Thomas to hear that Transport is not only taking our farm, but reneging on the promise it made. I want God's stars to hear it.

"Unfortunately, no," says Green. "All the Plain People in the AZ will be given the choice to modernize or move on. There are no current plans to form new zones."

"Move on?" My son's anger flares. This time I do nothing to squelch it. "Move on to where? The Wild Lands? We'll be eaten by those people!"

I'm sure you've heard the same stories we have about the Wild Lands. Cannibals. Thieves. A complete lack of law and order.

Matthew shrugs, and that simple gesture fills me with hatred for him. For all money-Amish. My feelings shame me. They are not Christ-like, but they churn inside me nevertheless. I begin to better understand what drove Our Lord to scour the temple with violence. No Amishman would ask this of us; Thomas is right about that as well. At least the Authority seems willing to let us go our way, if not to form a new AZ.

So, they damn us with either choice. If we stay, we modernize. If we go, we do so on our own, with no promise of a community to share our traditions. And yet, only one of those options ensures that we must give up who we are as a people.

"Gentlemen," I say the word with great effort, "thank you for coming to dinner. Your position is clear. And now, so is our choice."

Green seems to relax. Our decision is obvious to him. He knows enough about us to know that turning us out from the AZ is like ripping our hearts from us. No doubt this is the leverage he hoped to use to influence us to modernize. What saddens me is that he fails to realize how loathsome that choice is to us.

"How much time do we have until we must vacate the

land?" I ask.

Now Green is confused. Elder Yoder's face crumbles inward in defeat. No doubt this wrinkle will not play well with his Authority puppet masters. Knowing we Amish have complicated Transport's plans for a change gives me shameful pleasure.

"Two weeks," says Green. Now he seems irate too, terse. All business. "Another ship arrives from Earth in two weeks. We'll move a family in here at that time."

I puff my pipe. "Very well."

The two turn to go. Thomas is so angry now he can't speak at all, which is probably for the best. When we mount the porch, Anne and Mary are waiting. Anne's eyes search mine. I shake my head. She turns away, one hand covering her mouth. We have made our home here, raised our children. We have loved this land with seed and water and toil. And now we must leave it.

"What's happened, Poppa?" asks Mary. "What's going to happen?"

I cup her face in my rough right hand. "We will move on, Mary. We will continue." It's all I have to say. My heart is breaking for Anne, for all of us. I want to go to her, comfort her, be strengthened by her closeness.

Mary gets that distant look in her eyes again, then refocuses. "I almost forgot!" She runs into the house, then comes back out again with a bundle.

"Elder Yoder!" she calls. "Elder Yoder!"

Matthew has just released the brake on his buggy and resets it with a grimace. "Yes, child?"

Mary hands him up the bundle. "My muffins! You almost forgot them!"

Matthew is surprised as he reaches down to gather up the basket. Green's face is unreadable in the darkness.

"Why, thank you, child. Most kind," Matthew says. Mary returns his smile.

"She worked most of the morning on those," Anne sobs quietly behind me.

I wonder at my daughter's generosity under the present circumstances. I thank God for it. *One of us, at least, has remembered Our Savior's kind nature in the face of adversity*, I think.

The two men leave. By the time their silhouette has crested the hill road, Thomas storms past where we three stand quietly on the porch.

"Thomas! We have preparations to make! The decision is—"

"Damn your preparations, and damn your decision!" He strides off angrily, away from the house, just like last night. I feel so defeated—with him, with our situation—I cannot even find the strength to follow him.

"He will walk it off," says Anne. "Like last night."

I nod.

My memory of the next morning is blurry chaos. It begins with the low whine, ever closer, of a Transport airbus. By the time it's throwing up dust in front of my barn, the three of us are standing on the porch, watching. Thomas has still not returned.

Our animals neigh and cluck and moo their fear as the airbus lands. My daughter stands up straight, immovable. Anne clutches my arm and I take her hand. The ship expels soldiers into my front yard, led by Green. This time he's dressed less simply. There is braid on his shoulder.

I step off the porch as the airbus winds down its engine. "You told us we would have two weeks."

He strides through the dust, motioning his escort to unsling their weapons. I make sure I'm between them and my family. Is this to be a summary execution? All because we refused to upgrade our farming equipment?

"I'm not here for that," Green says. "Matthew Yoder is dead."

Anne gasps behind me. I, too, am dumbstruck. Then I hear her pleading, "No, no, no," and I know then I should've pursued Thomas last night.

"Stand aside," Green orders. His soldiers surround the porch.

"I don't know where my son is. He's not here." It is all I can think to say.

"I'm not here for him either."

I spread my hands. I don't understand.

"I'm here for her," he says.

Anne grabs the porch rail. I turn toward her, keeping myself between them.

"I didn't kill Elder Yoder," she says desperately.

Losing patience, Green says, "*Her.*" He points at Mary.

She sidles out from behind me, that defiant, distant look on her face.

"My daughter? Are you insane? She didn't murder Matthew!"

"Oh, but she did," says Green. "I found him dead on the floor of his home this morning. Vomit everywhere. And one half-eaten muffin in his hand. Poisoned."

I look at Mary and her eyes focus again.

"Child?"

"Oleander, Poppa. I baked it into the muffins."

She thinks I'm asking her how she did it. Anne collapses to the porch.

"My God, child." My voice is hoarse. "What have you done?"

Mary looks at me, knowing I'm disappointed, but determined to explain why everything is all right. "It's gelassenheit, Poppa."

"What?"

"*Gelassenheit*. Now you and Momma and ... Thomas ..." Her voice hitches on her brother's name. I see it in her eyes: she's committed murder for Thomas. She idolizes him. She thinks she's saved him from having to kill Matthew himself. She explains, "Now all the Plain People can grow crops how you want to. You can continue."

Anne moans her anguish. Mary thinks that killing one man—one moneychanger—will save us all. The black-and-white thinking of a twelve-year-old child.

"Oh, Mary ..."

My heart shatters.

"Stand aside!" Green is out of patience. Chambered rounds

punctuate his order.

I stand aside. Anne crawls toward Mary, wailing. I gather my wife into my arms, aware of the raised rifles around us. Even in my shock, I realize there is nothing we can do until we face the magistrate. I expect Mary to scream, to claw for her mother in return. Instead she walks silently toward Green, resolute and precise, as if doubling a stitch in her quilt. He grabs her by the arm and her kapp, its ties loose, falls into the dirt of the barnyard.

They take her aboard, and too soon the airbus is lifting off, its engines screaming. The echoing silence it leaves behind is broken only by a man yelling, "Mary! Mary!" Thomas runs across the field, reaching up as if to snatch the ship from the sky with his bare hands. Then we're all three on our knees together, sobbing on the porch.

And now I sit here with you on this bench, waiting to learn the fate of my child. She is being arraigned today. Anne is with Thomas, who is inconsolable. He blames himself for this, though I know I'm the only one to blame. I should have seen it coming. I should have stopped it.

I sit here thinking how, just two days ago, drought was my worst worry. Even yesterday, how small a problem it really was, in retrospect, to find a new home with good soil. But today, I am consumed by a single thought that keeps repeating, over and over in my mind.

Too young. Too young to be so old.

Historical Note: *Gelassenheit*

Gelassenheit is set in 2095, about a generation before the events of Michael Bunker's *Pennsylvania* and my own B-Company tales. I wanted to explore some of the history behind the events, already in motion, that Jed wakes up to when he arrives in New Pennsylvania in Michael's story. I was particularly interested in what might have motivated Dawn, Amos, and other former Plain People to choose the inherently violent path of armed rebellion in direct opposition to their Amish upbringing, a cornerstone of which is a commitment to pacifism.

Unlike Amos in *Pennsylvania*, Abram decides "to move on, to continue," based on what some might argue is a dogmatic adherence to tradition—a noble choice, but a choice that helps create the circumstances of the family's tragedy. Would Mary have acted as she did if her father had followed Thomas's advice to modernize? Even before Mary makes her own life-altering decision, Abram, by choosing to leave their community, sets the Brenneman family on a path that could destroy another fundamental aspect of who they are as a people. (In case it's not obvious, I prefer stories without simple, black-and-white choices; the grays are much more interesting to explore.) Was there really a *right* call here for Abram to make?

Being unfamiliar with the Amish culture, I read Steven M. Nolt's *A History of the Amish: Revised and Updated* to help me better understand the traditions of *Pennsylvania*'s Plain People. I also asked Michael Bunker some pointed questions about his own beliefs and experiences as a Plain Person, and he was very forthcoming, with great insights. I wanted to explore both our Englischer preconceptions about (and the actual, accepted role of) women in contemporary Amish society. And, again, I was fascinated by that question of whether or not it's better to move on and preserve tradition (farming techniques), despite losing part of oneself (community) in the process; or to stay, modernize, and preserve ties to the community. During our exchange on how the individual relates to his or her community in Amish society, Michael introduced me to the concept of *gelassenheit*. (Elder Noffsinger's definition is, verbatim, how Michael explained it to me.) Not only did Michael hand me the perfect title for my story, but he also showed me a way that Mary's actions could be absolutely consistent with Amish beliefs, albeit within the limited understanding of those beliefs by a twelve-year-old mind. Talk about exploring a gray area!

Chris Pourteau
November 2014

GETTYSBURG

The First Day

"You said it was undefended!"

Another triplet of lasers sliced the afternoon sky, landing somewhere behind their makeshift trench.

Lieutenant Sean Hatch shrugged. Difficult to do, head down in a ditch. "Oops."

Before his sergeant, nicknamed Stug, could snarl again, two more TRACE soldiers belly-crawled along the shallow ditch behind them, taking up position on their right.

"Hey guys," said Bracer. The huge machine gun on his back weighed him down, but he managed to huddle up under the embankment they were pressed against. "Nice fireworks, huh?"

"Oh, delightful," Stug groused in a fake high-society accent. It sounded particularly ludicrous coming from a soldier his size. "I seem to have forgotten the lounge chairs at home, wot? We'll have to watch from down here. Sorry, guv'nor."

Laser fire pop-pop-popped the earth on their left.

"Probably just as well," said Hatch. "I hate getting sunburned."

"Another spectacular intelligence failure," Hawkeye, the unit's spotter, said. "Why am I even surprised anymore?"

"The QB will *not* be happy," said Bracer.

"When is she ever?" asked Hatch.

"Good point."

"We can't just sit here," Stug said. He turned his head, looking up and down their long, narrow hidey-hole. It offered little cover, but for now at least the berm protected them. *If they flank us...*

"If they have drones, we're dead," deadpanned Bracer.

"They don't," said Hatch. "Or we'd be dead already. So there's that." He spit on his hand, stuck his fingers in the moist dirt, and wiped it across his face. The process, punctuated by occasional triplets of laser fire, took about thirty seconds. "How do I look?"

"Who said that?" Stug asked.

Hatch grinned and waited. Like clockwork, the next laser blasts popped overhead. Before the air stopped humming, his head was up, scanning the town's perimeter.

"Three count, sir," offered Hawkeye.

Hatch returned to cover, nodding his thanks to the spotter. "Okay, here's what I see. There's a guard post with one man in it firing on our position. No drones. Yet."

"One man?" Stug again. He was a big, brave brute of a man but tended to whine when more advanced weapons kept him from using his fists on the enemy. His griping came not from cowardice but from a frustrated need to beat Transport soldiers until they didn't need beating anymore.

Bracer understood his lieutenant's conclusion. "The three blasts we're hearing don't come from a choreographed squad of ballerinas firing with perfect timing, Sarge. One man, pew-pew-pew."

Hatch nodded. "And he's probably more scared than we are."

"Good," grinned Stug. "Looking forward to showing him what he's scared of."

"What do we do, Lieutenant?" Hawkeye wanted a plan. A good spotter is always more comfortable knowing a plan's details.

"Access your BICE," ordered Hatch. "Analyze the town and surrounding ground. Use the guard post as a reference point, find our position, and see what's around us. Stug's right. Eventually the Transporter with the itchy trigger finger will be reinforced and we'll be flanked. And if they have drones…"

No need to drive that point home again. Their own drones, hacked and reprogrammed for TRACE, were back with the QB. If Transport had drones here, the most Alpha Squad could likely do before dying for the cause would be to warn the rest of their company. And that assumed Transport didn't have active jamming in the area, a distinct possibility.

Hawkeye accessed his BICE device. The Beta Internet Chip Enhancement was a brain implant required by the Transport Authority. Among other things it allowed direct access to the Internet from inside a person's head. The spotter's eyes darted back and forth, ranging over GIS maps displayed on the backdrop of his brain. The terrain and town itself appeared in his mind like a dream, three-dimensional and vibrant. The Transport guard post was, of course, not a part of the public-domain data captured in the maps, but Hawkeye approximated its position with help from Hatch. He searched for better ground in his mind.

"Bracer, reposition twenty-five meters that way," Hatch said, pointing east, back in the direction the heavy-weapons man and his spotter had just crawled from. "Use the three-count rule and start returning fire. I want our Transport buddy firing in your direction when we move. We'll cover you once we get repositioned."

"Try not to get sunburned," suggested Stug helpfully.

"Love you too, Sarge," said Bracer. "Break out Betsy?"

Hatch shook his head. "No, small weapons only. We need to stay mobile."

Bracer nodded, moving off. The hundred-pound weight of the 18-millimeter heavy machine gun on his back made moving belly down in the mud awkward, but he managed.

"Lieutenant, I think I found something," said Hawkeye. "A water well about fifty meters to the west. With Bracer in his new position—"

"Crossfire. Got it. Move out. BICE me when you're in position. Go to local area network comms only. Let's take this bastard out," said Hatch.

Stug blew out his displeasure as Hawkeye moved west. "Doesn't look like I'm going to get to hit anyone."

"Day's young," said Hatch. "Feel free to charge him from the front, meathead."

The big man grimaced. "I'm a brute. Not stupid."

Three more shots overhead. These hit closer, frying grass ten feet behind them on the embankment. The Transport soldier, commonly called a "porter" by TRACE, was finally ranging in on them.

"Must be nice to fire laser rifles without a care for power," said Stug while they waited for their squadmates to reposition.

Hatch grunted. "Having an unlimited supply of okcillium cells to power your weapons will do that for you."

"Guess that's why we're here," said the burly sergeant. "Only it was *supposed* to be unguarded."

Hatch rolled his eyes. "Please stop saying that." He loved the big guy and would rather have Stug beside him in a bar fight than a whole squad of TRACE marines. But holy Christ, the man could get under his skin when the lasers started slicing. Nothing more grating on the nerves than a not-so-gentle giant with a nasal whine.

"Just sayin'."

"Well don't. That's an order."

Stug smacked his lips, then shut them.

"Bracer, in position," said a voice in their heads.

In battle, they turned off the option to see a projected image of the person communicating via the BICE. A voice inside your head was distracting enough; the speaker's holo projection on the screen of your mind would be downright deadly.

"Almost there," answered Hawkeye.

Three more pops. The grass on top of the embankment a foot in front of them exploded, kicking up clods of dirt.

Stug groaned. "I just washed this uniform."

Hatch stuck his head up, finding Hawkeye's water well as the spotter got into position. He quickly took in the tripartite lines of fire aimed at the guard post, then felt Stug's meaty hand on his belt. Before Hatch could threaten a reprimand, he was face down in the ditch as the laser fire kicked up more earth just inches above him.

"I said, I just washed this uniform," said Stug. "The last thing I need is your seared blood on it."

The lieutenant ignored him. "My count. Bracer, then us. Hawkeye, you're the kill shot."

"10-4," came back in unison.

Hatch turned to his sergeant. "If you want, I can have them

fire simultaneously so you can charge him."

Stug twisted his head like a dog seeing something curious. "If you want, I can count to three for you the next time you stick your head up, Lieutenant Hatch, sir. One-Mississippi style."

Hatch smiled. Mentally clicking his BICE channel to squad, he monotoned, "Three, two, one."

Automatic weapons fire from their right. One short burst from Bracer, then the sound of bullets hitting the concrete of the guard post. As soon as it ceased, the tip of a laser rifle poked through a slit in the guard post and fired in Bracer's direction again. *Pew-pew-pew.*

"Spotted," said Hawkeye in their heads.

Stug bellowed a long, yipping war whoop from deep in his gut as Hatch went up and over the lip of the embankment and dropped prone, firing a long burst from his rifle. More ineffective ricochets off the concrete protecting their enemy. But the porter moved to face the new threat and, for a moment only, became visible from the left.

A single shot.

Hawkeye whispered through the BICE. "Got him."

"Oh, good," the sergeant said. "Can I hit him now?"

"Do you ever get tired of playing comic relief?" Hatch asked. "Hawkeye, heatmap the area. We're near the outskirts of town, so try to distinguish any citizens as best you can and give me a threat assessment. Look for okcy signatures."

"Thank you, sir, I was awake that particular day of training," said Hawkeye, distracted. It was clear he'd started following the lieutenant's orders before they were given.

Bracer broke in. "Right flank is clear."

Stug blew out another breath. "Looking more and more like I'm not going to get to hit anyone today."

Hatch glanced down into the ditch. "Thanks for definitively answering my comic relief question. Now I no longer need wonder."

"Okay, it's a little hard to believe, but I'm not seeing any credible threat," sent Hawkeye. "A lot of heat signatures in homes, hunkered down. So far, no porters though."

Hatch pushed himself to his feet as Stug crawled up the embankment to stand beside him.

"That makes no sense," said the sergeant, all business now. "One soldier in that guard post, sure. But they've had plenty of time to bring up reinforcements since we engaged."

"Maybe his BICE malfunctioned and he had no way to call them?" wondered Bracer.

"Maybe they're on their way," replied Hawkeye. "Should Bravo Squad advance to our position?"

"No," Hatch said, mentally flipping a switch to bring them into the conference. "Bravo Squad, maintain position in the trees until further notice. Hawkeye likewise, and keep your eyes on the heat map. Bracer, you stay put too, and cover the approach to the town." Turning to Stug, he added, "Come on. You can punch the concrete or something."

They made their way the forty meters across the meadow to the guard post. A small bunker, really, meant to guard the old-style mud road that entered the town from the southwest. The road was still used by the more orthodox to ferry the goods grown in the nearby Amish Zone, an indulgence Transport allowed the local Plain People. Almost everyone else transported goods, and themselves, via Transport-regulated airbuses. Still, the positioning of the post commanded a wide and well-protected view of the western approach to the town.

While Stug inspected the dead porter, Hatch looked around the small post. It was Spartan, devoid of anything inside its concrete walls save for a chair and a half-eaten afternoon ration. Not that much else was necessary. Anything the soldier needed—area maps, duty rosters, tactical alerts—he would've accessed through his BICE.

"Laser rifle, three charge packs, two grenades," itemized Stug as he stripped the dead soldier of equipment. "BICE?"

Hatch nodded, so Stug took out his knife and moved to the back of the porter's skull. Some of the civilian leadership of TRACE found the practice distasteful, and others thought it disrespectful of the dead. But it was standard TRACE military policy to remove BICE implants from captured or killed Transport personnel whenever possible. Hackers later analyzed them, noting upgrades and operating system advances to improve the rebels' own hacking skills and equipment.

Stug went to work while Hatch surveyed the town through the bunker's rear port window. Gettysburg served as a hub in County Adams, New Pennsylvania, and was modeled after its namesake, its architecture simple and functional. Nearly the entire town's population was employed by the massive distribution center located there, so most of the buildings Hatch could see were homes and small businesses that supported their daily lives. Food grown in the nearby AZ was processed out to the rest of the planet, while refined goods were brought in from Earth and shipped via cargo ship to other settlements. TRACE insurgency in nearby Columbia— called "the City" by most, since it was the largest urban center of its kind in New Pennsylvania—had increased dramatically in recent years, so the Transport Authority had begun using smaller towns as strategic depots to support its war effort. In the case of Gettysburg, refined okcillium produced on Earth was brought through to supply the military's insatiable need for power cells to fuel its laser weapons.

And that's why TRACE was here. With no okcillium source of their own, the rebels raided whatever sources they could find for the rare and vital power source. Intelligence had reported that a new shipment of okcillium ore had just arrived in Gettysburg and that a military escort was almost nonexistent. The theory ran that policing the Wild Lands and rerouting troops to meet the heavy insurgency by TRACE in the City had resulted in an unguarded okcillium supply. Or maybe the Authority had decided a minimal military presence at a vital supply hub would keep rebel attention away from the town. But thanks to the ability of the SOMA—their supreme commander and administrator of the Southern Oklahoma Militia—to crack each new upgrade of BICE code the Authority threw at them, TRACE had learned of the okcillium shipment and sent two squads to probe the town's defenses.

"You done yet?"

"He must've been a vet," Stug grunted, nodding at the gray on the dead man's temples. "Lots of scar tissue to cut through." Another hiss of effort and the sergeant held up bloody fingers with the dead man's BICE chip clamped between them. "There."

Hatch nodded. "Bag the tag and let's go. This whole one-soldier-only thing is making me nervous. Too good to be true and all that."

At that moment, Hawkeye's voice whispered in their heads. "Dropship. Ten klicks."

Stug withdrew a plastic bag for the exhumed BICE as Hatch stood up.

"Bravo Squad, fortify and prepare to cover our retreat. Hawkeye, Bracer, we'll be out in five, four—"

"Bagged," reported Stug as he slung the dead porter's laser rifle over his shoulder.

The lieutenant motioned him out and covered his back as the big man lumbered across the distance to their embankment. *Seems longer going back*, thought Hatch, though he did so in protected mode, keeping his thoughts private, off their shared BICE channel. Once the sergeant was safely back in the ditch, Hatch followed.

"Thirty seconds," reported Hawkeye. "Only one that I can—damn it! Drones."

Transport drones zipped over the warehouses on the south side of town, zeroing in on the lieutenant as he leapt into the ditch.

"Alpha Squad, we've got your backs. Go, go, go!" said Lieutenant "Trick" Mason, Hatch's counterpart in Bravo Squad.

"Peel off," ordered Hatch, clipped and precise. "Bracer, go."

"Yes sir."

Standard operating procedure. The man with the heaviest weapon gets to run first.

It was the spotter's turn next. "Hawkeye."

"Lieutenant, I've got the eyes here, I should—"

"Were you awake the day they taught you to follow orders? Move!"

With no time to argue, the spotter dropped his omni-lens to his chest and ran for Bravo Squad and the safety of the trees.

Hatch could feel the white noise building in his brain. It was expected. Transport had learned how to aim a jamming signal at rebel BICEs to disrupt their communications, and they tended to deploy the strategy any time they were in range. No one, not even the SOMA, had yet figured out why only rebel implants were affected.

"Shut down BICEs, go to visual," sent Hatch as he followed Hawkeye, leaping over the ditch and running for the tree line. He powered down his BICE and felt the usual light nausea as its constant stream of information, projected in his mind, suddenly went dark and vacant. It almost felt like he'd lost his eyesight for a moment, and he half-stumbled. He saw Bracer go down on all fours as he succumbed to his own shutdown process, then watched the heavy-weapons man right himself again. The hundred pounds on his back slowed him down, but he resumed his loping, mad dash for Bravo Squad.

Precise laser strikes burned the plain behind Hatch. This was no lone soldier with a laser rifle. This was a dropship's gunner, whose sole purpose was to hit what he was aiming at from a moving air vehicle. The lieutenant quickened his step. Bracer made it to the trees and dove past the 18-millimeter machine gun deployed by Bravo Squad. It peppered the sky.

"Aim that bloody thing higher!" bellowed Stug as he, too, pounded through the tall grass and past the thundering *thrrrit-thrrrit-thrrrit* of Bravo's machine gun.

Hatch dove right, rolled, and popped upright again, the nausea all but gone. If he was lucky, between the threat of Bravo Squad and his own light feet, he might outmaneuver the dropship before it killed him.

The gravimetric servos keeping the enemy's ship in the air whined closer, broken up by the screech of its laser cannon. The dropship gunner and Bravo Squad's heavy-weapons man faced off like they were playing an old-fashioned game of chicken, each determined to force the other out of the firefight. Hatch saw the grass catch fire to his right as Hawkeye passed into the trees.

"Come on, officer, sir!" yelled Stug, his voice carrying incredibly over the mayhem. "I'm too old to have to train a new lou!"

Hatch ground his teeth, veering left. It was a mistake. His foot went deep into a smoking hole left by the tracking fire, and he stumbled jerkily, falling to his knees. As if hungry and aware of its prey's vulnerability, the dropship intensified its laser fire, the heat of a blast slicing the back of Hatch's leg. He collapsed forward, his face slamming into the charred dirt.

Distantly, he heard voices as time slowed down. Stug railing at Bravo Squad. Trick giving his troops orders. The almost calming flutter of the dropship engines. Slowly, painfully, he turned over onto his back. The first afternoon in July boasted the bluest sky he'd ever seen.

He heard a crack, a boom, and a long note warping up in scale, like a violin arcing upward from a low major to a high minor key. Then a Doppler shift in the pitch of the noise, and he knew the dropship was moving away from him. The laser fire had ceased. He turned his head and followed the Transport ship as it swooped back toward the town. Tracer fire from the 18-millimeter continued harassing the enemy ship as it limped away, still aloft but slowly descending.

Hands on him. Big hands.

"Now I have to sling you too?" whined the sergeant. For once, the gravelly, nasal voice sounded downright divine.

Hatch felt himself lifted like a five-pound sack of potatoes, then suddenly found he was looking at an upside-down canteen, two sonic grenades with their triggers pointing strangely upward, and the not insubstantial mass of Stug's ass. That's when he passed out.

Standing alone in the hastily erected field tent, the captain of Bestimmung Company—dubbed the QB by her soldiers—stared down at the hastily drawn map of the area. Normally, the Internet would've supplied any needed information via the BICE device, but they were under blackout conditions now. No unauthorized Internet traffic until further notice, lest the Authority tag an access attempt and run their location down like a hound treeing a possum.

That's a phrase Poppa might've used.

The thought came unbidden, an unwanted echo from the

past. Or at least, it *felt* unwanted. It always took a little time to get used to her inner voice again after shutting down the BICE. When the device was on, a channel of chatter buzzed in her head constantly, except during sleep. Someone was always asking for orders or giving them, discussions somewhere else required the QB's attention, or she'd be on the Internet researching and planning. Or, more rarely, she'd simply be escaping all the order-giving, researching, and planning by doing a little mindless surfing. It was during those times she popped Q and, usually, slept in a stupor. Sometimes it was the only way she slept.

But now, in the cavernous silence of her own head, that inner voice—the one that cajoled, encouraged, scolded, challenged, and oo-rahed her—was loud and clear. She'd thought of the voice as her only friend when she was detained by Transport as a child. On the days when Gutierrez would question her, she'd simply disconnect from reality, ignore him, and her inner voice would tell her everything would be okay. It would play games with her, distract her from his fumbling attempts to extract her cooperation. He was new at his job then, not very efficient, and she had been very young.

Now when the voice spoke, it just reminded her of that time. And thus it was unwanted.

You don't really believe that.

The QB jerked her head, as if she could knock the voice out of her ear and onto the floor. "I don't have time for this right now," she whispered.

Okay, that I'll grant you.

The tent flap pushed inward. Trick, of Bravo Squad.

"Captain, Stug—er, Sergeant Miller—is waiting outside."

She nodded, staring back at the map. Alpha Squad's spotter, Hawkeye, had drawn it for her based on the GIS surveys he'd pulled up during their firefight.

"Send him in."

Trick saluted and held the canvas flap aside for the lumbering Sergeant Miller. *Stug*, she reminded herself. The QB liked to encourage her soldiers' familiar names for one another, even used them herself on occasion. It promoted unit cohesion, made them fight harder for one another, like shield brothers in Ancient Greece. TRACE needed every advantage it could get in this war. Lord knew they had enough working against them. The odd realization struck her that no nickname had ever really stuck for Hatch. He was just "Hatch" to everyone.

"That'll be all, Lieutenant," she said, nodding her head. "Thank you."

As Bravo Squad's leader exited the tent, Stug came to attention. Not easy for someone of his height in the tiny space. He looked a bit like Atlas, recently relieved of the Earth on his shoulders, but still a bit hunched over and stiff. The top of his bald head brushed the tent's canvas.

"Sergeant," she acknowledged.

"Captain. Ma'am. QB." Stug winced at the slip.

Her inner voice smiled at his stuttering. It was rare for him to report to her; usually Hatch did. Clearly it made him uncomfortable.

And there it was again, her own familiar name among the troops. *The QB*. Her commanding officer had given it to her a long time ago. It supposedly referred to an old Earth sport, to the team leader, the quarterback, who called the plays on the field. She knew better. Once, when she'd come into conflict with the good colonel, he'd called her a princess, a Queen Bee. She'd taken some pride in that in the moment. Bucking authority was in her nature. It made her an original thinker, not always considered an asset by the military hierarchy. Later, she'd learned he'd meant Queen B. And the B wasn't shorthand for a buzzing insect.

But instead of fighting it, she'd made it her own, even encouraged its use by not stamping it out. And anyway, it was better than the other name they had for her. Old Granny. At 37, she was the oldest company commander in TRACE.

"Give me your report, Stug," she said, pushing past the memories.

The sergeant smiled at her use of his nickname. He actually stood up a little straighter, which only made him appear to be wearing the tent for a turban.

"Well, ma'am, we didn't get any further than the outskirts of the town when we hit the guard post. One man pinned us in a ditch till we took him out."

Succinct, to the point. Part of her liked the efficiency of it. Another part was frustrated by the lack of detail.

"Show me," she said, nodding at the map.

Stug came around. "Here's the ditch we were in. And here's the post. Bravo Squad was in this tree line, covering us. The dropship came from the town proper," he said, pointing to the map's eastern edge.

The tent was small and the sergeant was large. He still

smelled like battle. Sweaty and acrid, the heavy grit of weapons fire mixed with the sharp scorch of lasers. Ever since she was a child, men in uniform looming over her had filled her with fear. Even sometimes, like now, when the man was her subordinate and had no idea of the positive response he was evoking in her.

And never will, promised her inner voice.

Nodding solemnly, she moved around to the other side of the table, as if getting a better position to consider the strategic situation.

"How many drones?"

Stug stared at the map, as if doing so might show him their number on the paper.

"Unknown. Hawk said they were coming, but once the dropship got hit, we were outta there. Never made contact."

The QB factored that information into the battle assessment forming in her head.

"If we sent out our own drones to reconnoiter, maybe circle around the town, they could help us get a better picture," offered Stug.

Isn't that sweet? He's trying to be helpful, her inner voice said.

You're not, she responded.

"True. We could also lose the only advantage we have if they get shot down," she said patiently. "We have no idea of the size of the force inside the town. There could be an entire Transport division there, waiting for us."

There was silence for a moment. Stug shifted on his feet. His fold of turban tickled his dome.

"Do you have something to add, Sergeant?"

"Begging your pardon, ma'am." He was slow to start. He hated arguing with an officer. But he hated the right answer going unspoken even more. "But we *do* know there's not a division there."

The QB raised an eyebrow.

"If there was a division there, we wouldn't have made it back. We saw one man in a frontier guard post, one dropship with how many troops inside? Didn't get a chance to find out. And a handful of drones that never actually made it to the battlefield."

"Do go on."

"My guess? A platoon, maybe less, widely dispersed around the town. If the enemy was there in force, one man alone wouldn't have pinned us down for so long. They would've reinforced sooner. And they would've pressed the attack, not run for the hills because our gunner plinked one dropship's engine."

She looked down at the map again. "So what do you advise?"

Stug was flattered. He was used to being given an objective and told to take it with a handful of grunts. His opinion of strategy was not often asked.

"Our objectives are the warehouses, here and here," he said, pointing to the south side of town. "The big warehouse, of course, where the okcy shipment is. But it's insulated, protected by the squat, longer building to the south."

She nodded. Their original plan had been to simply walk in and take the okcillium from the large, multi-story warehouse, load up as much as they could, and steal away again. Like bank robbers racing a countdown before the cops arrived. Only in this case, the money was a precious mineral.

"We go in from the south and take the shorter warehouse," Stug said. "Stage the move on the taller one from there."

The QB glanced at the dimming shaft of light coming through the tent flap.

"We're almost out of daylight."

"A night raid might be better," the sergeant suggested.

She shook her head. "How would we see? They've proven they have jammers. We'd be fighting blind."

Stug shrugged.

In truth, he'd just confirmed a strategy she might've come up with on her own after studying the map closer. Bold, risky, with the promise of great reward. But it would be more of an even fight by daylight.

"One other thing, Captain," he said hesitantly.

"Yes?"

"We should send those drones out. Course them around the town's perimeter. Map the interior. Bring us back the big picture, load it up in the BICEs, set them to LAN access only. Keep them off the Internet. That way, at least, every soldier out there will have a tactically accurate situation to start with."

She grunted. "To start with. What's the old axiom from von Moltke? 'No battle plan survives contact with the enemy.'"

Stug shrugged a second time. "Better than nothing."

The captain smiled. "Ever practical, eh Stug?"

"Practical is my job." He stood up a little straighter still. "I'm a sergeant, ma'am."

The best I've got, she thought. "How's your lieutenant?"

"Hatch? Oh, he'll be fine," scoffed Stug. "Just got a little sunburned."

"Uh-huh. Can he walk?"

"As straight as he ever could," the big man said playfully. He was being familiar now, a bold move with his lieutenant's superior officer. She took it as a good sign of Hatch's health, so she let it pass. "The laser singed his panties—um, trousers, ma'am—but the leg burn is superficial. I'm not even sure why he passed out, really." He said this last in a teasing tone, one that promised Hatch wouldn't live down having fainted anytime soon.

"Good to hear." Nodding at the tent flap, she said, "You're dismissed, Sergeant."

Stug saluted and turned to go.

"Oh, and Sergeant?"

"Ma'am?"

"Send Trick back in."

"Yes, ma'am." He opened the tent flap, then halted, asking no one in particular, "When did it start to get dark?"

As he exited, the QB returned to the map. The short warehouse first. That would be the conduit to the second, larger storehouse it was connected to. They needed that okcillium. Badly. And if they could hold both buildings and the surrounding area long enough to load up the converted airships they were using to move the cargo, they'd have it.

She glanced over at her projectile-firing weapon. It had served TRACE well when no other option was available, but it was a relic to be sure. To compete with Transport, they needed better. They needed laser weaponry, and lots of it.

Or more to the point, they needed *power*. Manufacturing the laser weapons was easy—all you needed was a couple of 3-D printers. But you could print weapons all day and it would get you nowhere if you didn't have the okcillium to power them. And that's why these warehouses were so important.

There is an opportunity here, she thought.

Of course, even a warehouse full of okcillium wouldn't completely level the playing field. She knew that. Transport had always had more resources, more dropships, more drones, more everything—and it always would. Only in the area of BICE technology—thanks to the SOMA and his technological prowess—had TRACE been able to keep pace.

No, they couldn't match Transport's resources. But with that much okcillium, and the weapons it could power … they could come close.

Yes.

Lieutenant Mason entered the tent. Before he even announced himself, she motioned at the map.

"Stug thinks we should go in. The sooner the better."

The young lieutenant was silent for a moment.

"A bit blind, ma'am."

She nodded. "That's why I want you to send our drones out. Circumnavigate the town, stay to the woods and mountains as much as possible. I want a complete survey by morning."

Trick opened his mouth, then thought better of it.

"Speak, Lieutenant. No time for egos here."

He stared at the map. "We have half a dozen drones pieced together and programmed from how many skirmishes with

Transport? A lot of TRACE soldiers died so we could patch those things together."

She waited. She knew where he was going, but the argument needed to be made.

"We're taking an awful risk sending them out without ground support," Trick said. "If we lose them…"

The decision hung in the air for a moment.

"Our soldiers didn't die to create six museum pieces," the QB said patiently. "We have an asset. We need to use it."

Trick stood up straight. "And if we lose them?"

The QB took her eyes off the map and brought them directly to his. "Then we'll secure six more. We're not fighting a war for the vid cameras, Lieutenant. We're not saving dessert till after dinner. We're using every asset we have to bring Transport down and secure freedom for all of us. Caution is one thing. I'm not advocating recklessness. We've been lucky in victory of late, but time is not on our side. Eventually Transport will wear us down. With manpower, with resources, with the power curve to put more of both in the field than we can. We've been at war for a generation. Both sides are weary. But we're *older*, if you know what I mean."

This was the most she'd ever explained herself to a subordinate. It was uncomfortable but necessary, she thought. The whole war could turn on this one battle.

Trick stood up straighter. "Yes, ma'am."

She acknowledged his acceptance with a curt nod.

"Ma'am, one more thing."

"Yes?"

"Have you run this past Colonel Neville?"

She looked at him sharply.

His brows rose in defense. "I don't mean that the way it sounded. I mean—"

"You mean have I covered my ass?"

A bit sheepishly, he said, "Yes, ma'am."

She considered it, then, "No. Best to ask forgiveness on this one, not permission."

Trick exhaled. "Fortune favors the foolish, ma'am?"

"We'd best pray that's the case," she said. "Tonight, Lieutenant, by the book. Set pickets, two-man squads. Keep them inside the Umbrella. Send out the drones in pairs to recon the town's perimeter, two minutes apart. Close enough to reinforce should they encounter the enemy, but far enough from the other pairs so they can't all be taken out at once."

The lieutenant saluted. "Umbrella perimeter?"

"Keep it tight," she said. "Focused."

Powered by stored solar energy, the undetectable energy barrier that TRACE called "the Umbrella" would degrade quickly if too widely cast, but if focused in a tight dome, it would prevent any heat scans thrown their way from returning a signal. If the Umbrella did its job, a passing drone would only see one more area devoid of heat sigs. As long as the drone didn't come into visual range, it would never know they were there.

"Yes, ma'am."

"Briefing at dawn," the QB said. "And get some sleep. Tomorrow's likely to be a sunny day."

Trick paused. "Understood, ma'am."

As he left her tent, she looked down at the map. Such a

small town. Such a huge risk. And everything riding on her orders and the bravery of Bestimmung Company.

She prepared for bed and said a prayer she hadn't thought of in twenty-five years. Then she slept like a baby.

The Second Day

Hatch woke at oh-five-hundred, his left leg numb from resting on it all night. The laser burn still smarted on his right calf, so his choice of sleeping position hadn't really been an option.

"The ladies will love the scar," yawned Stug, sitting up on an elbow. "And you need all the help you can get."

"Says the upright-walking bulldog," Hatch replied, wincing as he sat up. "I hate getting shot."

"Grazed," corrected Stug. "Let's not be melodramatic."

"Hey, can you lovebirds keep it down when you go at it? Or get a room?" Bracer grumbled. "There's men trying to sleep here."

"Where?" Stug shot back.

"Okay, okay, we're all awake now," said Hatch. "The sun'll be up in half an hour. The QB wants us and the other squads at attention at oh-five-thirty. Eat hearty. Double-check your equipment. No FUBARs today, boys."

Stug lightly kicked at a snoring Hawkeye, who snorted and implied the sergeant's mother was less than virtuous. But he woke up.

After morning routine, the men of Alpha Squad were standing with their comrades from Bravo, Charlie, and Delta. As the QB exited her tent, Echo Squad, the heavy-weapons support unit, stepped into line. The twenty men and women of Bestimmung Company stood, wide-eyed and stock-still, in front of the QB and her aide.

"Good morning," she said, and was answered by a chorus of "Morning, ma'am."

"You've all been briefed by your squad leaders on the situation. Our knowns are these: Gettysburg holds a huge

67

supply of okcy. We need it. There's at least a dozen enemy soldiers guarding the town. We're making that assumption based on the one dropship Bravo Squad engaged yesterday. The enemy has drones. How many, we're not sure yet. The town is full of civilians.

"Our unknowns are everything else. There might be fewer Authority troops there than we think. There are likely a lot more. We have no idea where the sympathies of the civilians lie. They're employees of Transport, by and large. Will they obstruct us or open the city gates, metaphorically speaking? How much okcy is actually in the larger warehouse on the south side of town? To access it, we need to secure the smaller, cylindrical warehouse at the southern city limits. What's in that one? All unknowns. Questions?"

Trick raised his hand.

"Lieutenant Mason."

"What have our drones told us, ma'am? Have they mapped the town's interior?"

A slight grimace across the captain's face was all the frustration she showed her troops.

"Our drones have not returned."

Mumbling among the TRACE fighters. She raised her hand to quell it.

"Before you assume anything, here are the facts: at oh-three-hundred this morning, the first pair of drones surveying the town sent an alert signal to C&C. Apparently they contacted the enemy at some point because they evaded, which is standard operating procedure. Before they went off the grid, we sent them behind the mountains to the northeast. Each of the other pairs followed. They should have reemerged by oh-five-hundred. They have not."

Lieutenant "Charger" Freeman of Delta Squad raised a hand.

"Yes?"

"How does this affect our timetable, ma'am?"

The captain took a measured breath. "It doesn't."

More murmuring. Stug looked sideways at his lieutenant.

Hatch responded with an almost-imperceptible shrug. *Oops.*

"But ma'am," said Charger, "we'll be blind without those maps. And you just said we'll likely be outnumbered. We already know we're outgunned."

She nodded, granting the point. "We won't know the town's interior beyond the public GIS maps we already have. But we already know our target: the warehouses. And the fact that we're outgunned is precisely why we're going in. Without that okcy, we'll always be outgunned."

"Ma'am—" began Charger.

"More to the point," the QB continued, "the longer we delay, the more they reinforce. This isn't Medieval Europe on old Earth. We can't simply besiege the town until they raise their collective hands. Every moment we delay gives Transport an opportunity to reinforce. They already know we're here, and only a moron wouldn't know *why* we're here."

"So, then, we're not sure they know why we're here, ma'am?"

Stug was nothing if not sardonic. He received half-hearted giggles, even a grin from the QB, in response. It helped break the tension stoked by Charger's fears.

"Lieutenant Freeman, you're right to be concerned," the captain said, her quiet voice helping to snuff out the tittering. "But we have an opportunity here. This war has been going on as long as most of you have been in the world. It's true, TRACE has done well for a long time, since the SOMA broke the BICE codes. But we still lag behind the power curve. If we don't break out of this hit-and-run cycle, eventually Transport will bleed us dry. At the end of the day, it comes down to the mathematics of resources. We have to change that equation." She pointed at the ground beneath them. "*Here.*"

Charger looked straight at her, ruminating a moment, then nodded. "Yes, ma'am!" Emphatic. Committed.

"Reboot your BICEs, set them to LAN only. Until we hit Authority troops with jammers, we can at least coordinate squads. Stay *off* the Internet. No sense handing Transport our exact location, though I'm pretty sure they'll know where we are soon enough." Someone mouthed approval at that bit of black humor. "Any other questions?"

Silence. Then Stug raised his hand.

"Sergeant?"

"Do I get to hit someone today?"

More giggles in the ranks, though they were tentative, as if testing the waters that it was all right to find humor in such a serious moment.

This was a time to be a comrade as much as a leader, the captain decided. "It's been more than a day, hasn't it?" she said, putting grimness in her voice.

"Yes, ma'am," he gruffed. "That's a whole week in dog

years."

Open laughter now. Even Charger giggled quietly to herself.

"For better or worse," the QB said, "I imagine the answer to your question is yes." She sent a silent prompt to her aide, who snapped, "Ten-chun!"

The score of men and women immediately stood up straight, all joking silenced.

"Squad leaders to me. The rest of you, double-check weapons and sling extra ammo. You'll need it."

"Dismissed!" the aide said.

Lieutenants Hatch, Mason, Freeman, Lutz, and Gray joined the QB while the rest of Bestimmung Company prepared themselves for a fight. She kneeled on the ground, arranging rocks as landmarks and drawing a rough perimeter of the town with a stick. On the right side of the crude map, she stuck one small and one large rock. The warehouses. In the middle she placed an upright stick representing the guard post Alpha Squad had nullified yesterday. Behind the town she scattered sticks for mountains. While she could've drawn a 3-D image of the same plan using their BICE connection and shared it on their squad leader channel, the QB preferred battle plans she could touch. She was old-fashioned that way.

"Mason, you'll take Bravo Squad, supported by Gray's Echos, and secure the guard post by oh-nine-hundred. No doubt it'll be remanned, maybe even reinforced. Alpha Squad, once they've done that, we'll move up from the woods to the south, with support from Charger and Delta Squad, and probe the warehouses."

"*We*, ma'am?" Hatch already knew the answer, but he wanted it confirmed.

"I'll be attaching myself to your squad for the duration."

Well, there it was. Not a surprise and certainly not unprecedented, given the company's history. Still…

"Captain, if I may speak freely—"

"I'm going," she said. "Now speak freely, but make it fast. We're burning daylight."

Hatch took a breath. Dangerous territory. He admired her bravery. She set the standard for the unit. She was also too important to it to become an oo-rah poster model collecting laser holes.

"Strategically, we'd be better served with you coordinating from here, ma'am," Hatch said quietly. There was no ego here, no "nobody leads my squad but me." He was simply stating a fact.

"Coordinating how, Lieutenant?" she asked. "BICEs will be useless once the forward squads are in range of Transport jamming. And I've forgotten my smoke signal alphabet."

Hatch acknowledged the point with a nod. There was more to his concern than a simple consideration for military strategy, if he was honest with himself about it. There was the history between them. But best leave that unopened in the folder marked *Past and Done*. No time for it here.

"We're short on bodies as usual," she continued. Ever the tactician, she was aware his silence gave her the advantage to press forward. "We need everyone we can get on the front line today."

"Then the entire company is going in?" asked Gray, called

Smoker.

"Not quite," she answered. "Lieutenant Lutz and Charlie Squad will remain in reserve in the woods south of the town, behind Delta's tree line position, to preserve our flexibility. Once we probe the warehouses, we'll have a better sense of their numbers. Then we'll decide if and where to commit your squad."

The lithe lieutenant said, "Yes, ma'am. But I have a question. Why send Smoker with Trick to take the post? Wouldn't Echo's big guns be more useful supporting the attack on the warehouses?"

The question was reasonable. Echo's two chain guns fired four hundred rounds per minute, sustained. Each took two men to operate, one to aim and fire the weapon, the other to feed ammunition.

"I want them to think we're coming up the same slot we cleared yesterday," the captain answered. "Transport thinks we're a bunch of untrained rabble, even though it should know better by now. The stupid maneuver of a frontal assault across open ground should play right into their preconceptions about us. If we unroll the chains on their front door—"

"Diversion," said Hatch, "while we infiltrate the warehouses from the south."

The QB clicked her teeth, telling them all he'd gotten the correct answer. "Besides, we need to stay light. We have to take the first building and secure the second while Delta moves up and makes a landing zone for our converted airbuses to land and load." Itching to move, the QB slung her rifle to rest on her shoulder. "Any other questions?" Her tone made it clear they'd better be necessary.

There were none.

"All right, then. Trick, you and Smoker take that post by oh-nine-hundred. Let's go."

As the others moved out, Hatch lingered.

"Mary, you sure about this? You said it yourself: we have no idea what's really there. Want to call Neville for backup?"

She looked directly at him. Just for a moment, he saw the woman he'd known so intimately, if briefly. A woman who could melt your heart in the right light. Someone who had no business being called captain on soft evenings.

"I intend to, Sean. Right after Trick and Smoker take that guard post. By the time Neville arrives with reinforcements, we'll have secured that okcy. The good colonel can cover our retreat."

"And if there's a company or more of porters in that town?" he asked softly.

Her eyes flattened, taking on that computer-like, steely gaze she got when staring down the problem at hand. "Then it's going to be one long, hot day," she said.

"You did what?"

The colonel's voice grated in her head over the secure Internet channel.

"We've established a position on the left and are preparing to assault the facility," the QB sent back. "Sending you a packet now with the tactical situation."

The good news for her was, their Internet link could only be secured confidently for another thirty seconds. TRACE had built an algorithm into its Internet protocol to auto-countdown conversations carried on the Internet during a tactical situation. Every ten seconds, the detached feminine voice, known as Marlene for some unknown reason, helpfully reminded the parties their time was limited.

"*Twenty*," Marlene said. Which meant the colonel could only dress down the QB for another twenty seconds.

"Goddamn it, Captain, you should've informed me before moving on the town."

"Security protocol, sir, essential messages only. Transport might've hacked this line already."

"*Ten.*"

"You should've—"

"We need your other two companies and the converted cargo ships here as noted in Figure One's timeline."

"Captain, if this goes sideways—"

"*Communication terminated. Reestablish?*"

"Oh, hell no," the captain answered.

Trying not to eavesdrop and failing miserably, Hatch stood in the tree line gazing at the smaller of the two objectives: a two-story, cylindrical building. He was standing exactly where Bravo Squad had set up its machine gun yesterday to cover his own squad's retreat. Hatch felt an 18-millimeter caseless shell in the dirt beneath his boot. He bent over and picked it up. Rolling it between his fingers, he looked at it absently, considering their position. To his left, Bravo and Echo squads had just secured the guard post and turned it into a defensible anvil. Again, they'd found only one Transport soldier defending the bunker. Again, that Transport soldier had died. Echo's two chain guns were now deployed behind a makeshift berm facing east from the guard post, covering the town. Now, it was time to swing the hammer at the warehouses.

"Where the hell are they?" wondered Stug. "Can there really be that few of them?"

"The downside of having everything you need as a fighting force is that you don't have to innovate," said the captain.

"Sorry, ma'am, I'm just a sergeant. What does that mean, exactly?"

"It means," said Hatch, "that they're not the brightest military geniuses on the planet. They should've guarded the okcy with more troops to begin with. Now they're rationing out the soldiers they have here until help arrives."

But the big man shook his head. "Still doesn't make sense. They had all night to reinforce."

"And TRACE has been more active in the City lately."

Stug understood then. "The cops go where the crime is."

"By that logic," offered Charger, "the cops will be showing up here soon."

"Hell, they should've been here already," said Stug. "Okcy ain't cheap."

The QB nodded. "Which is why we can't stand around here talking about our good fortune all day." She looked at the sun halfway up the side of the hills behind the town. "It's oh-eight-thirty, give or take. Lieutenant Hatch, your squad will take point. Lieutenant Freeman, your squad will maintain vigilant support until Alpha is at the first building."

"You mean, ma'am, if we aren't killed, Delta Squad can come out of hiding?" asked Stug with a smirk.

Despite the grumbling from Delta Squad, the QB said, "Something like that."

"Ma'am," said Hatch, addressing the QB formally, as he always did in the company of others, "Might I suggest you hang back with Delta Squad until—"

"You can suggest it," she said, cutting him off again and immediately regretting it. She knew she was reacting to him the same way he was reacting to her. Anticipating arguments in conversations, overcompensating for the baggage they shared. At best, it was unprofessional and unbecoming of a soldier. At worst, it was damned dangerous and could get someone killed.

Clearing her throat, she said, "I appreciate your concern, Lieutenant." The daggers he'd been shooting her way softened and disappeared. "But the colonel is already polishing his gavel on this one." She turned to the two assembled squads, who were watching the two of them carefully.

No secrets in foxholes, her inner voice said.

"Let me make this clear. Lieutenant Hatch is in charge of Alpha Squad, and on all matters tactical, I'm placing myself under his orders."

Stug raised his eyebrows, which only made his forehead look like the grille on the front of an ancient automobile.

"But I reserve the right to make command decisions related to this mission," she continued.

Hatch blinked once, then nodded. "All right, let's go," he said. "Hawkeye's already scoped the advance. Stay low and use the rolling berms for the approach, just like yesterday."

"Remember, LAN only for comms, ladies," said Stug. "Er, and Captain. Ma'am."

With the sergeant on point, Alpha Squad humped it out of the trees and toward the long, silver warehouse, a.k.a. Objective One, on the outskirts of town. As they made their way to the buildings, the company hunkered down at each of the embankments while Hawkeye re-spotted. Each time he would communicate with Looker, Delta Squad's spotter, and once he confirmed the coast was clear, they would move up again. Before long, the silver warehouse was only fifteen meters from their present, gut-down position.

"Okay, I know I'm repeating myself, but this is too easy," Stug said. He lay on his back, his weapon clutched to his chest to protect it from the dewy grass. A whiny quality had begun to creep into his tactical assessment voice. A strange combination. "Where the hell are they?"

"Only one way to find out," said the QB, rising and running for Objective One's tin wall.

"Wait!" yelled Hatch, way too late. "Goddamn it!" He was up and over the berm and on her heels in seconds.

Stug spared a glance for Bracer, who was already lifting himself and his heavy weapon from their hiding place. "I bet she saves all the punching for herself, too."

Bracer murmured indistinctly as the sergeant helped him up. They dashed after their commanding officers. Hawkeye remained behind the embankment, throwing a quick look left and right through his omni-lens, scanning for threats as the other four ran across the open terrain. A quick check with Looker over the LAN told him there was still no sign of the enemy.

Hatch flattened himself against the tin wall and kneeled next to the QB.

"What was that about following my orders?" he asked.

"I didn't hear any orders," she replied.

"Well, hear *this* one," he said as Stug and Bracer joined them. "You will not move from our tactical position unless I say so. Understood? Captain, ma'am?"

Who the hell does he think he is? her inner voice raged. But she remembered their agreement and knew he had every right to be angry.

After a breath: "Understood."

"Movement in town," said Hawkeye over the comms. "Heat signatures with okcy readings moving toward the big warehouse."

"About time," grunted Stug.

"How many, Corporal?" asked the captain.

"I see six so far. No drones. Yet," answered Hawkeye.

"Echo, chain three bursts over Objective Two," said the captain.

"*Over* the warehouse, ma'am?" came the reply.

"Did I stutter? We need to minimize civilian casualties whenever possible. See if we can warn those half a dozen porters off."

"Understood."

Three bursts from each chain gun thwacked the atmosphere. The bullets fired so fast, they sounded like three long, loud whips cracking together. Somewhere beyond the town, 250 new holes pockmarked the mountainside.

"Corporal?"

"They've stopped. For now, ma'am," he said.

She looked at Hatch. It was his show from here.

"Stug, you're first in. If you survive, I'll follow you with Bracer." Then, after a moment: "And the QB."

"Sure ... send in the bald guy," gruffed Stug, no whine evident in his voice now. The odds of getting to hit someone had just significantly improved. He opened the door and, crouching, went in. Not waiting for his sergeant to call it clear, Hatch folded in right behind him.

The warehouse was long and flat, with a curved, almost elliptical roof. Though morning sunlight streamed in its windows, the interior was dim. Dust hung in the air, defying gravity.

Stug took up position behind the nearest cargo crate, Hatch on his heels. Their three-count recon of the interior—as far as they could see, anyway—revealed a whole lot of nothing. The lieutenant motioned Stug forward to a second crate about twenty meters farther in, then took up a guard position to cover the advance. When the sergeant reached his cover without incident, Hatch accessed the company-wide comm channel.

"Alpha Squad to my position. Hawkeye, join us."

As the QB and Bracer entered the warehouse and Alpha's spotter made his way, berm by berm, to their position, Stug stole a glance over his cover. What he saw made him wrinkle his forehead again.

"There's nothing in here," he sent to Alpha Squad. "This place is full of jack. Wait, no—he's gone too."

"Cut the commentary," said Hatch. "Once we—"

"Porters on the move again," said Looker from the tree line. "They're inside Objective Two."

"Orders, ma'am?" clicked in Echo's Lieutenant Gray.

"Hold your position," said the QB.

Bracer and Hawkeye had both joined Hatch and the captain inside. The spotter followed SOP and scanned the interior of the warehouse they'd taken.

"Nothing but a handful of these cargo containers. Not so much as a rat chewing on one, according to heat sigs," he said.

"Drones!" barked Looker. "Sweeping around from the ... at least ... orders?" His report was broken up by the all-too-familiar fuzzing of their comm system by Transport jammers.

"Delta Squad, come in," tried the captain. She knew better, but... "Bravo, Echo squads, respond."

Nothing but static.

"Reduce your comms to minimum," she ordered. "I want them kept on, voice only, in case someone takes out that jammer. For now, we're on our own."

"Secure the warehouse," Hatch said. "Bracer, get up to the second floor and deploy at the window with the best fire arcs on Objective Two. Hawkeye, go with Bracer. See if you can get any heat sigs on Two from his position. Stug, get over to the door, the one beneath Bracer's position. I want eyes there."

"And what are my orders, Lieutenant?" asked the QB, emphasizing his rank.

"You watch my ass," he replied, observing the deployment of his men. He failed to notice the rare look of amusement that briefly lit up her face.

"I see movement over there," called Hawkeye. Objective One's size and shape amplified his voice. "They're fortifying."

"Of course they're fortifying," answered Stug from the side of his mouth. He never took his gaze from the window that looked out on the larger building some twenty meters away.

"I'm more worried about those drones," said Bracer, locking his 18-millimeter gun in its tripod. He'd already broken out the window overlooking the kill zone between the buildings. Now he surveyed that still-empty space with his machine gun barrel.

Rapid fire erupted from the tree line where Delta Squad was emplaced. The Authority drones had engaged, and the *thritt-thritt-thritt* of Delta's machine gun responded.

"So much for my B-grade vid plot hope that those were actually our drones returning," sulked Stug. "We're flanked."

Hatch sidled up to position on the opposite side of the door from the sergeant. "That's one way to put it," he said. Between the two of them, their vision arcs covered the sidewalk connecting the two objectives. They were positioned directly below Bracer and Hawkeye, whose vista view guarded the same approach.

Stug began to thump his left index finger to a beat only he could hear, an old song from a long time ago. It made him smile, and his lieutenant caught the expression.

"Well?" asked Hatch.

Tap-tap-tap-tap-tap. "Should we stay or should we go

now?" the big man half-sang.

Hatch turned to the QB. "Well, Captain? We seem to be standing on that blurry line between strategic goal and tactical execution."

"Hawkeye, what are you seeing over there?" asked the QB.

There was silence while the spotter completed a second survey of Objective Two. "They're in there, but shielded," he said.

"Neoprene suits?" asked the captain. Halfway through the war, both sides had quickly discovered that one way to hide their heat signatures was by wearing neoprene skinsuits, which masked the body heat of the wearer. The temperate climate on New Pennsylvania made the suits impractical most of the time, though.

"Nope," said Hawkeye. "You're not gonna believe this—I think they've built glass into the walls."

Another masking strategy, though TRACE had never run into it on this scale. Enterprising war patrons in the tech industry had long ago adapted infrared wavelengths to pass through most walls by modulating them closer to radio wavelengths. But glass distorted those wavelengths just enough to filter out the part of the spectrum used to spot heat-producing sources. Sometimes before an urban engagement, Transport soldiers would even carry body shields made of glass to mask their heat signatures, then discard them once the battle started.

"I can see something now and then, when someone moves behind a window, though," Hawkeye continued. "They're definitely in there."

"Gotta hand it to Transport," said Hatch. "They planned that building from the ground up. Literally."

The captain thought about it. If they stayed, Transport would eventually tighten the noose on the smaller warehouse, killing them all. If they moved, at least they could retain the initiative and not simply wait to die. It wasn't the first time they'd faced this situation. Her response was what she named B-Company's shark strategy: keep moving or die.

"We go," she said.

Hatch glanced back at her approvingly. This was why they called her the QB. She was daring and didn't mind making a tough call that overrode an ineffective strategy. Their colonel thought of it as impetuous. But Hatch and his squad had recognized it long ago as courage.

The firefight outside intensified. Delta Squad had drawn off the drones. Now was their chance to move in the open.

"Bracer, lay down suppressing fire. Hawkeye, stay with him and watch our backs." Hatch stared at Stug and smirked. "You go first."

"Again. I go first *again*," the sergeant grumbled unconvincingly. "It's the price I pay for refusing to become an officer. And fair enough, I might add." It was an old joke between two old friends.

"As for you," began Hatch, turning to his captain. Then he stopped. He'd almost told her to stay put. In the flash of a few seconds, he questioned himself as to why. If she were any other soldier, he'd have ordered her to charge the no man's land with Stug and cover the sergeant's left while Bracer's machine gun pinned down anything to the right and front. That was the correct tactical answer here. Baggage notwithstanding. "As for you, go with Stug. Pin down the left. I'll coordinate with the boys up top and follow."

A loud explosion erupted behind them, in the open ground between their building and the tree line. Delta Squad was getting hammered hard in the woods. Everyone inside the warehouse held their breath a moment. Then *thritt-thritt-thritt*, followed by another blast, smaller and grinding. Drones were known for their silence. Except when they died.

"That's one down," said Stug.

"We need to move," said the captain. She knew, like everyone else, that Delta Squad wouldn't last much longer against the drones.

"Right. Bracer, count it."

"Three!" barked the heavy-weapons man.

Laser blasts outside, followed by the *thritt-thritt-thritt* of Delta's gun. It was crazy to think it, but to Hatch, the machine gun sounded the slightest bit desperate.

"Two!"

They could hear Echo's chain guns now, opening up on the left from the fortified position at the guard post. Probably trying to keep more porters from entering the primary objective. The captain prayed there were no civilians in the way.

"One!"

Bracer opened up with his machine gun, one long chug of rapid fire. He blasted the windows first to force the porters' heads down, then traced a line of bullet holes along the right outer wall of Objective Two to warn away any would-be heroes that might be around the corner.

Hatch yanked the door and Stug charged, a bull moose with his head down and screaming a war whoop better suited to charging a hill somewhere in history. The QB followed, aiming at the window opposite them on the left, shattering its panes inward.

"Report!" shouted Hatch, straining to be heard over Bracer's continuous fire.

"Suppression successful, sir. Heads are down," said Hawkeye.

Hatch leapt after the others and sprinted for the second warehouse. Stug was flat-backed against it now, under the window and preparing a sonic grenade. Some brave porter had kicked the door open and was tracking the QB's steps with his laser rifle. Hatch took aim on the run and put him down as the captain reached Stug.

The sergeant pulled her down and away from the window, and Hatch dived for their position as the sonic grenade detonated. There was no sound, none at all. The grenade blasted its area of effect with sound attuned to a spectrum beyond human hearing. The frequency of the silent sonic boom temporarily overwhelmed the inner ear of any target within range, spiraling them into vertigo and knocking them off their feet.

Hatch squat-ran to the door now blocked by the porter he'd shot, who still breathed but could do little else. Bracer ceased fire for a moment while Hawkeye called down through their broken window, "Drones! Go, go, go!"

He could feel Stug moving behind him, but there was no

time to let the sergeant by. Stepping over the moaning soldier, Hatch elbowed the door open, bringing his weapon to bear and moving through. He could see three soldiers to his left, obviously stationed at the window prior to Stug's pineapple toss, clutching their heads, weapons dropped. Lasers blasted the wall behind him, and he dived and rolled forward to kneel behind a shipping crate. He popped his rifle around the right side of the crate and sent an otherwise useless barrage of bullets at his attackers, hoping to make them duck and cover.

Stug was in now and, instantly assessing the situation, moved to cover behind a crate just inside and to the right of the door. The QB was on his tail, briefly trying to decide whose crate to hide behind.

"Get the hell down!" shouted Hatch. In his mind, he did his best imitation of Stug's whine, bemoaning how little time it took being off the front lines for an officer's instincts to atrophy.

She ducked and dived for Stug's crate in time to avoid a laser blast that took out the door they'd just passed through.

Outside, they could hear Bracer's fire resuming, marking the wide walls of the warehouse they were in. Then the first of the drones came through the door.

Hatch turned his weapon around, keenly aware that the porters—knowing the TRACE fighters were being attacked from behind—could simply charge their position. Hopefully Stug would think of that too and keep the human enemy pinned while Hatch dispatched the mechanical threat.

"Stop!" yelled the QB. "Don't fire!"

The lieutenant's index finger twitched over the trigger as a second drone whooshed through the open doorway.

"They're ours!"

As if aiming to prove her right, the two drones—with scorched hulls and nattering servos—flew over their heads and straight at the porters' position.

Hatch gawped while Stug whooped, "I knew it! My whole life *is* a B-grade vid plot!"

Suddenly a blast came from the left, its heat scorching the plastic container and melting Hatch's sleeve to the crate in the process; apparently one of the soldiers felled by the sonic grenade was back in action. Hatch rolled left first, ripping the sleeve now slagged to the crate, then back right, and leveled his weapon. First the upright threat went down permanently, then the two still on the ground died.

One drone screamed mechanical death as laser fire enveloped it from two sides. Its partner passed its position, twisted in midair, and targeted the porters, immolating one and injuring another before it, too, was destroyed. But Stug was up and whooping again, charging straight for the two remaining porters. Having turned to meet the threat from the drones, they were now out of position, away from the cover of their makeshift pillbox of crates. By the time they turned to meet the terrifying sound of Stug's roar, he was already on top of them. He cracked one on the chin with his rifle butt and ducked when the second fired wildly over his head.

"Okay, now I'm mad!" Stug screamed at the young Transport soldier, whose shocked expression seemed to likewise freeze the rest of his body. The sergeant knocked away the porter's laser with a backhanded swipe of his own weapon, then pulled his right fist back and buried it in the center of the man's face with a satisfying, bone-smashing crunch.

"Finally!" the big man exulted. He returned his attention to the first porter and dealt him a similar blow. "Two-fer!" he gloated.

Both porters hit the ground with a pleasingly solid thud.

Except for the wheezing pop of their downed drones, all was suddenly quiet inside Objective Two. Stug looked around, slinging his weapon into its ready-fire position. Smoke drifted from the drones. One of the men he'd just flattened moaned quietly, out of it.

Glancing upward, the sergeant surveyed the second and third floors of the warehouse but found none of the enemy. "Well that was refreshing, if short-lived. We really should draw these fun times out more."

Hatch stood up and whistled as the captain moved to his side. She, too, was captivated by what she saw, her rifle hanging loosely at her side. Crate after crate filled the warehouse, ready for shipping. Crate after crate of okcillium.

Delta Squad had lost two men: their heavy-weapons expert and their spotter, who were often positioned close together. The drones that had initially attacked from the right had indeed been Transport. TRACE's own drones—the five that were left from the recon mission launched the night before—had returned in time to combine arms with Delta and send the Transport drones limping off, three shy of their original six attack force. By the end of the engagement, TRACE had lost all five of its remaining drones, two of them protecting Alpha Squad inside Objective Two.

The QB left Bravo and Echo squads in their original position at the town's perimeter to watch for enemy intervention, then pulled the rest of her squads in to secure the second warehouse. Stug continued to grouse about how easy the whole thing had been, and no one was disagreeing. Still, they had okcillium to move. More okcillium than they'd ever hoped to see in one lifetime.

Colonel Neville arrived within half an hour of B-Company's securing the objectives. After very publicly admonishing the captain, he oversaw preparation of the landing site for the converted airbuses that would ferry away as much okcillium as possible before Transport counterattacked and retook the town. Once loading began, Neville's principal contribution was to stand around and look imperious.

After taking the big warehouse, they'd found Transport's BICE jammer on one of the upper floors. Rather than destroy it, they'd pulled its okcillium battery and turned over the equipment to Neville's communications specialists for later disassembly and examination. Having the use of their BICEs back had made coordinating the loading of their prize that much easier, but still, moving that much okcillium onto the cargo ships took the better part of the afternoon.

As the loading continued, Hatch approached the QB. "You

did good here today," he said, smiling and brandishing a laser rifle retrieved from a fallen porter. "This haul might push the war home for us."

The captain tilted her head noncommittally. She'd always had trouble taking praise graciously. In a way, she preferred the kind of reprimand Neville had given her several hours before. She kindled the end of a cigar she'd commandeered from Stug, who always smoked one after surviving a firefight. Gave him good luck for the next one, he claimed.

"Once Pook and the others make the weapons and okcy batteries, I'll relax a little," she replied. Pook Rayburn, proprietor of Merrill's Grocery Supply in the City, and his cohorts in the resistance could manufacture new laser weapons using 3-D printers. And now that they had the critical component—okcillium—they could also make power sources for them. "I'm with Stug, though," she continued. "Too easy."

Exasperated, Hatch replied, "Maybe, for *once*, it's supposed to be easy. Maybe, for once, we don't have to barely make it, barely survive. Maybe luck was on our side."

She winced and shook her head as if to clear it, and he knew why instantly. Hatch could see others doing the same thing, their hands going to their ears as they mentally switched off their links.

The jamming was back. And that meant so was Transport.

A crate crashed onto a ramp as two TRACE soldiers succumbed to the vertigo caused by the jamming. Granulated okcillium spilled onto the ground like crystallized black gold.

"Move it, people!" Neville was saying. "Get those cargo ships out of here!"

A final broadcast to all TRACE soldiers indicated multiple gunships and dropships inbound from the City. Then the warning fritzed out to static.

The captain looked at her former lover. "You were saying?"

"*Crap*. Alpha Squad!" Hatch bellowed, adjusting once again to coordinating his command with his voice. "Prepare to defend those ships!"

Stug spit out his stub of cigar. "Knew it," he said to no one.

They could hear Echo's chain guns spinning hot bullets into the sky from their position at the guard post. The first of the converted airbuses fired up its engines as explosions thundered outside. Transport was here. In force.

To cover the landing zone, the QB moved Alpha, Charlie, and what was left of Delta squad to the second-story windows of the warehouse. They barely had time to set up their 18-millimeter guns before Transport drones were plinking them with laser fire. Delta, having lost its gunner, stood in support of the other two squads, helping to direct fire and occasionally pot-shotting at drones with their rifles. Fortunately, the late afternoon sun was behind them and not in their eyes.

Two TRACE cargo ships were in the air. To Hatch they seemed heavy, like lumbering elephants, standing still and swaying on a lazy morning. In contrast, Transport's advance drones were quick and nimble, swarming like hornets, stinging the tough skins of the cargo ships with laser fire. The drones seemed uncoordinated at first, but as the first gunships bore down on the warehouses, Transport's drone attack became more effective. What had been useless laser fire against reinforced hulls was now aimed at vulnerable engines.

The TRACE cargo ship farthest from the battle was the primary target. The magnetic servos of its anti-gravity engines squealed and sputtered, the nose of the craft pointed toward escape. But now enemy lasers were finding their marks. The cargo ship, bloated with okcillium, began a slow arc downward.

The QB stood and stared as the ship plummeted with its precious cargo. It hit the ground with more force than a bomb exploding, shaking them all through the building's superstructure. A great plume of earth and okcillium dust burst upward as the ship broke apart. The captain's mouth opened in simple disbelief. Not only had they lost the okcillium, but four TRACE soldiers had also just perished in the crash.

Despite her earlier sarcasm, she'd almost allowed herself to believe they could get away with it. That TRACE could pull this off, steal a vital resource right out from under the noses of Transport in the City. A deed worthy of the kind of David and Goliath tale historians loved using to capture a child's imagination. But now those hopes were going up in smoke. Transport had shifted its attention away from the warehouses and was now concentrating fire on the four remaining cargo ships.

Hatch was shouting at her, but she couldn't hear him. Her ears seemed closed off, filled up with some kind of resin that stopped all sound save for the thud of her racing heart.

He slapped her hard across the face.

"We have to get out of here! Now, while their focus is elsewhere!"

She swung her head around sharply, saying half-dreamily,

"But the okcy—"

"That battle's done!" replied Hatch. "Either those ships make it or they don't. We can't help them anymore." Seeing the look in her eyes—a look as close to hopelessness as he'd ever seen there—made him stop and take a breath. More softly, he said, "We have to preserve as much of TRACE as we can. For the next battle. B-Company needs its captain now, Mary." He directed her attention below, where Neville and his staff were fleeing the warehouse on foot. If they followed the plan, they'd be regrouping deep in the woods southeast of town. "*You* have to get us out of here," he said.

She stared at him in shock a moment longer. Then the iron-willed focus that made her the QB filled her eyes, as if the spirit of a warrior long dead had repossessed her body to do what needed doing.

"All squads, retire in good order!" she shouted. "Get to the rendezvous point in the woods as best you can! Go!"

The remaining members of Delta Squad helped pack up the others' deployed machine guns in record time. In less than a minute, they were preparing to dash across the open space to the first warehouse. Charlie and Delta squads hoofed it first, covered by Alpha. They met little resistance, since Transport was targeting the remaining cargo vessels.

The captain, however, turned away from her retreating squads, heading west along the wall of the long warehouse.

"Where the hell..." But then Hatch knew. She still had two squads deployed to the west, assuming they still survived at all. He hadn't heard the chain guns in a while now. With their BICEs jammed, the only way to get them out was to tell them to leave—in person. Maybe they would've recognized the chaos for the defeat it was and bugged out already, but maybe they'd stand and fight and cover the retreat for everyone else. Knowing Smoker and Trick like he did, Hatch bet on the latter.

"Come on, boys, we're not done yet," he growled. "Hawkeye, take point. Stug and I will follow. Bracer, try and keep up."

The sounds of battle were mostly behind them now, beyond the warehouses and pursuing the bulk of the retreating TRACE fighters. Intermittent heat sig reports from Hawkeye suggested Transport soldiers were occupying the town in force but were going door to door, slowly checking the homes for rebels.

Making their way to the guard post was remarkably uneventful. Transport appeared to simply ignore the mosquitoes nipping at them from the west, instead concentrating all their energy on spoiling TRACE's plans for stealing the okcillium.

Remarkably strategic thinking for Transport, thought Hatch.

When Alpha Squad arrived at the guard post, they discovered why the chain guns had gone silent. One was destroyed, the other out of ammunition. The two squads had each lost half their number. Everyone left was injured but mobile.

"Leave them," Hatch heard the QB order as he approached.

"But, ma'am, we can't afford to abandon these guns," Smoker said, wiping her brow, but only smearing the grease and dirt covering her face.

"I appreciate your being so conscientious, Lieutenant Gray, but preserving our *human* resources is my priority now," answered the captain. All hint of her earlier hesitation was gone, along with the sting in her cheek from Hatch's insubordinate slap. She was settled into herself again. She was the QB.

"Yes, ma'am," answered Smoker. "You heard her," she said, addressing both squads. Trick, nursing a left arm dangling loosely at his side, didn't object. "Grab what you can, we're falling back."

Hatch deployed Alpha Squad to watch the town as they prepared to bug out, but Transport wasn't pursuing. No doubt the Authority was feeling flush with victory. Dusk was falling like a shroud around the mountains to the east. He could still see smoke and hear occasional weapons discharge beyond the warehouses, but nothing alive moved.

His captain moved up next to him and followed his gaze to the smoking horizon. She was tempted to slip her fingers into his, to squeeze his hand once just to feel the reassurance of human contact in the wake of what had happened here today. How many TRACE soldiers had died? And for what? Had even a single cargo ship escaped Transport's grasp? Or was their sole achievement the okcillium dust that now fertilized the fields around Gettysburg? But Mary resisted the urge to touch him. Her soldiers couldn't see her need for solace. As their commander, she should stand beyond the touch of despair.

The QB surveyed them as they slung packs and loaded the last of their ammunition. In the waning light of a day made hazy by tons of spilled okcillium, the members of Bestimmung Company appeared tired, dirty, and defeated. But their captain knew better. A shower and rest would remove the grime and fatigue. And they had never been defeated as a unit. She rejected the notion that they'd been defeated here today. B-Company was hers. In fact, it was *her*. Struck down to their knees, they would rise again. Regroup. As long as she stayed strong, they too would survive.

"Time to move out, ma'am?" asked Smoker.

She simply nodded, her energy spent. Then in a determined voice she added, "Time to move forward."

To reduce the odds of running across Transport patrols, the remnants of B-Company marched a line directly away from Gettysburg and at a forty-five-degree angle to their ultimate objective in the woods. It was possible that Neville's remaining troops had evaded their Transport pursuers and would rendezvous after midnight as planned at the designated rally point, but the QB wasn't taking any chances. They'd approach from the southwest after walking two klicks in the opposite direction.

At the point of the turn, Smoker's sergeant, nicknamed Brick, fell first to his knees, then onto his face. Exhaustion and blood loss. Stug offered to carry him, but the captain refused. They'd stop here, camp off-trail thirty meters into the woods, and rejoin the others at the rally point at dawn. Everyone needed the rest.

The captain personally tended to Brick's wounds while the others set up camp. Unlike Stug, Echo Squad's second was a modestly built man, more agile than thick. His nickname was an ironic ode to his ability to hold anyone at arm's length, no matter how strong his opponent, through some inner-strength discipline he called Zenkwondo. He'd even bested Stug that way.

"Prop up his legs," suggested Hatch.

She nodded, glancing at the jagged hole in the ashen sergeant's right leg. A tourniquet wrapped just below the knee and a makeshift bandage stanched the flow. Still, the bandage was pregnant with blood. Wiping Brick's sweating brow, the captain said, "We should've stopped sooner."

Hatch almost bit her head off. He was tired too, and he didn't have the patience for being needed right now. But he stopped, reminding himself that this was her command. One of her sergeants was dying, and there was little she could do about it but comfort him. And the others—they'd been bright-faced and eager, if the slightest bit frightened, when they'd gathered at dawn. Now, a third of their original number was dead. And whether Charlie and Delta squads had escaped was anyone's guess.

Thinking it best to ignore her, Hatch said, "Hey, I just noticed something." He shook his head. Battle still banged his eardrums, but his mind had lost that low-grade buzzing sound from earlier in the day. "We must've cleared the range of their jammers."

The QB nodded. "A while back. They're all off chasing the rabbits in the woods."

"Should we try to establish contact with Neville? Find out the final score?"

The captain shook her head. "LAN only. Stay off the Internet. We're in no shape to receive a Transport hunting party. We're off grid for the night."

"Brick needs aid. If we don't—"

"Brick's dead," she said, palming over his open, lifeless eyes. "Have Stug strip him and distribute his equipment." Her voice had taken on that tinny, monotone, autopilot quality. She was stony, immovable. "Detail a burial in the woods, but don't bother digging too deep. Everyone needs their rest tonight," she said, rising and walking into the woods away from camp.

Hatch watched her go. Sometimes he hated her coldness more than the war itself.

His tone stiff with boot camp formality, he said, "Yes, *ma'am.*"

The Third Day

Stug had earned his physicality by being raised on an Amish farm. He was moving hay bales with his father before he could read. His name had been Joseph Miller then, and his affinity for the animals they raised and ultimately slaughtered remained one of the cruel ironies of his love-hate relationship with his childhood. Like so many others of his generation, the sergeant had abandoned his upbringing to fight Transport. His shunning by his parents for that choice made his obsession with punching the enemy into unconsciousness all the more personally satisfying.

On the farm, they had never had fewer than two dogs at a time. He decided, one Sunday afternoon when he was a boy, that the reason he loved the dogs so fiercely was because he was never required to kill them. All the affection for animals he couldn't afford to feel for the family's livestock, he invested in their dogs. And to this day, dogs held a special place in the big man's heart.

So when his sleeping self heard barking in the distance, his family dogs returned from memory and entered his dreams. Sloppy and drooling, Jonah's goofy pant-grin made him smile as he lay on the hard ground of the woods outside Gettysburg. Young Joseph and his dog were chasing away a raccoon from Momma's apple pie in the window. The overlapping, train-like echo of Jonah's braying spoiled his momentary joy with a longing homesickness. Until his dream-self remembered he wasn't twelve anymore. And he wasn't just dreaming about his old hound.

Stug's eyes snapped open. He rolled to his side, cocking his ear in the air. Blinking sleep and sore muscles away, he felt the sticks and leaves drop off his body into the dirt. Two soldiers from Smoker's squad had stood up from their picket duty and were staring northeast.

Baaaaaroooooooorrr. Baaaaaroooooooorrr.

"Alert the camp!" Stug whispered. "Up, up, up!"

The others stirred, stiff from battle, but urgent and alert nonetheless. Hatch sat up, wincing at his still-smarting injury from the first day's skirmish. He'd rested on his left leg again, and it tingled with lingering sleep.

"Dogs," said Stug, not waiting for the question.

Hatch massaged his leg briefly as the others began moving. "Hawkeye, crack the sleep out of your eyes and give us a range," he mumbled groggily.

Smoker and Trick were already gathering essentials, leaving behind what few luxury items they'd had.

Baaaaaroooooooorrr.

The captain snapped a clip into her automatic rifle, leaving a captured Transport laser still slung across her back.

"Two hundred meters," said Hawkeye calmly.

"Why the hell dogs?" asked Smoker.

"Brush party," said the QB. "All the high-tech gear is chasing down Neville. Hell, they probably didn't even expect to find anything in this direction."

"Can we analyze the enemy's application of low-tech resources later?" Hatch and his tingling, aching legs were in no mood. "By now they'll have our heat sigs. It's only a matter of time before they overrun us with drones or dropships."

Grabbing her rifle as the others gathered around, Smoker said, "We'll never outrun either one. We should set up a defensive perimeter and—"

"—die," finished Stug. "We're in a clearing with trees and poison ivy for defense."

Hatch nodded severely. "It always comes down to the math."

Baaaaaroooooooorrr.

"One hundred fifty meters," said Hawkeye, less calmly this time.

"We don't have time to debate," insisted Bracer. "Dig in or run?"

The captain turned and looked southwest, seeming to sniff the wind as if she were a bloodhound herself. Then, with the same frostiness she'd had the night before, she said, "We run. Follow me."

The eight members of B-Company tramped through the undergrowth. No one bothered trying to hide their trail.

The fauna seemed to be on Transport's side. Vines and nettles grabbed at the commandos' legs, slowing them down. The injured fighters struggled the most, yanking and pulling through the undergrowth. One, then another stumbled, and their comrades bent to help them up.

"BICEs still up," noted Hatch.

"Keep the LAN online," said the captain. "Everyone tie in to Hawkeye's omni-lens." The hunting party following them was indeed likely an afterthought by Transport command. No advanced transportation, no BICE jammer. A party sent to flush out any birds that might be hiding in the bushes. The QB switched on her Internet feed.

"Warning," Marlene said in their heads. *"Internet accessed.*

This is a tactical situation. Recommend you—"

"Shut up, Marlene," said the captain, using the official shorthand that deactivated the warning system.

Baaaaaroooooooorrr.

"One hundred twenty-five meters," said Hawkeye.

Everyone quickened their pace.

Only half watching the terrain, the captain misstepped, twisting her ankle. Hatch reached down without stopping and dragged her back to her feet, and she stumbled forward. She was in pain but kept moving, step-dragging until she could put some weight on her ankle again. She'd been distracted momentarily by scanning the local map she'd projected in her head. Pulling up the map was why she'd needed the Internet. She knew they were close, but how close was the question.

Ah, there it is, said her inner voice. Dragging Hatch with her, the QB jagged suddenly left. The others followed.

"I take it you have an objective?" Hatch asked.

She ignored him. They were close.

The dogs barked savagely. They could smell the sweat and fear of their quarry on the wind.

"One hundred ten meters," Alpha's spotter dutifully reported.

The captain angled right and pushed her way through a last wall of wild vines to find what she was looking for.

"What is this, a deer trail?" wondered Stug.

Baaaaaroooooooorrr.

Much closer now.

"This way!"

Unobstructed, she led them in a loping run away from the

town along the wide, rutted road. Hard from lack of rain, the cuts in the dried mud seemed determined to trip them up.

"What the—?"

Stug had merely voiced the question on everyone's lips as they came to a sudden halt. The road had dead-ended at a towering wall of debris. It looked like a dozen high rises had come crashing down here, then been shaped into a jagged superstructure jutting skyward. Made from the tons of transported debris from Earth's destroyed cities, the wall was piled high and irregular, reaching hundreds of feet upward at schizophrenic angles.

"You've led us to the wall around the AZ?" asked Smoker. "Why?"

Hatch didn't blame her for the desperation in her voice. *What a perfect backdrop for a firing squad*, he thought to himself. He barely remembered to keep it off the unit channel.

"All walls have holes," said the QB, as if that answered Smoker's question. "Start finding this one's."

Smoker merely stared at Trick, then Hatch. Her eyes didn't need the LAN to speak her mind to her fellow lieutenants. *She's gone mad*, they said. *We're all dead.*

One hundred meters up the hard-packed mud road, the dogs burst from the woods. Four of them, followed by their handlers. It was hard to tell who was controlling whom.

Vines and ivy had crawled up and around the rubble of the wall, trying to reclaim the space for Mother Nature. *Fitting*, thought the captain, *for a wall surrounding the Amish Zone.* She stared at her officers, who stared back at her.

"Get your goddamned hands in the ivy and find me a

breach!" she ordered.

Despite their doubts, Smoker and everyone else obeyed instantly.

The bloodhounds strained at their leashes. Breaking out of the thick woods, Transport soldiers appeared behind them. The handlers kneeled down to their charges.

As he felt beneath the living camouflage along the wall, Stug said, "They're about to—"

"Don't say it!" ordered Hatch.

"—release the hounds."

"Here!" yelled Hawkeye. The spotter had found a man-sized gap at the bottom of the wall. If they dropped their equipment first, they could pass through, if slowly.

Stug pulled out a sonic grenade. "Go!" he ordered everyone, regardless of rank.

"Sergeant—" began the QB.

The dogs were braying as they leapt forward. They spread out as a pack does when approaching a trapped quarry.

"*Go!*" Hatch echoed, kneeling to a firing position.

"Everyone, through the breach! Help Bracer with that eighteen!" ordered the captain.

The Authority soldiers, assuming they had the rebels boxed in, were in no hurry. They fell far behind the bloodhounds. At a dead run, the dogs would be on the TRACE fighters in seconds.

Hatch took aim.

"No, wait, chief," said Stug.

There was a quality in the giant's voice Hatch rarely heard. Against his better judgment, he hesitated.

The hounds were already too close; the sergeant couldn't get them with the grenade without also being in the blast radius himself. He stood, cocked his arm, flicked his thumb, and let the grenade fly, aiming for a spot about twenty meters out.

"I'd plug your ears if I were you," he growled to Hatch.

The grenade fell behind the charging hounds, but its silent explosion caught them from behind. To avoid being flattened themselves, Hatch and Stug covered their ears and fell backward, knocking their companions into the concrete and steel and rebar of the wall.

Their balance blasted, the hounds went down hard, yelping and bruised by the petrified ruts in the road. The Transport soldiers behind them scattered left and right for cover, one firing uselessly over the heads of the rebels trying to crawl through to the AZ.

Hatch righted himself to find that all but Bracer, the QB, and Stug had made it through to the other side. The handlers, incensed that their hounds might've been injured, took aim at the remaining commandos. Hatch flattened himself among the rubble.

"Okay with you if I shoot the guys with the leashes?" he asked Stug as he sighted down the barrel.

"By all—"

Hatch fired a brace of bullets, causing the enemy to return fire, wild and shaky with fear. Having established the range and wind, Hatch fired once, twice, and a third time with precision. With each shot, a Transport soldier, leash in one hand and weapon in the other, fell to the ground.

Pulled from the other side, Bracer went through. The QB ordered Hatch and Stug to follow, then dived through the rubble herself. The hounds howled in their confusion and pain, contorting on the mud road.

"You're fatter, you go," said Hatch.

For once not arguing, the sergeant handed his rifle carefully through the gap, mindful of sliding it through the dust and dirt. Flipping on his back, he squeezed through the hole, with the help of a long, cursing haul from the AZ side. His wide shoulders barely let him through.

The few veterans in the Transport ranks advanced more boldly than before. Laser fire scorched the debris around him as Hatch turned and crawled to the opening. First his rifle went through, then his body. With arms extended, he was yanked out the other side.

"Get him out of the way," the QB said. "Be quick about it."

His men hauled Hatch away from the wall. The others tossed rocks and refuse toward the gap, packing it quickly.

The QB nodded to Smoker, who like her captain held one of the captured laser rifles. The two women positioned themselves at opposite angles to the wall and took aim above the breach. From the Amish side, the wall had been smoothed over with concrete, like an old rebar-skeletoned sidewalk from the now-destroyed suburbs of old Earth.

"*Now.*"

Both fired their lasers in a long, continuous burst at the packed debris over the hole. There was no effect at first. But slowly the molecules of the concrete coating began to heat up, then disrupt. In less than thirty seconds, the hole was plugged.

"That won't last long," said Stug.

"It won't matter anyway," observed Hawkeye. "They'll have dropships coming from the City soon enough."

"Let's go," said the QB, slinging her laser across her back. Favoring her ankle but unflagging, she led them into the interior of the AZ.

The rutted road was less overgrown and better cared for on this side of the wall. As the soldiers slogged along, few had time to notice. Being hunted like escaped prisoners had already sapped what meager reserves a fitful night's sleep had rebuilt.

"We need to get off the road," said the captain. "Hawkeye's right. Those ships will be coming."

"I didn't think Transport could enter the AZ without permission," said Smoker.

"Like getting a form signed would stop 'em," groused Stug.

Now that they were beyond the wall some 150 meters, the QB led them at a perpendicular angle to the road and back into the woods. Their pace slowed as their path grew thick again. And with her adrenaline fading, the throbbing pain in the captain's ankle demanded notice. But she gritted her teeth and led them deeper into the zone. After half an hour's broken march, they came into a clearing, where her ankle failed at last. She tumbled to the ground, cursing.

Hatch knelt beside her and spoke quietly so the others couldn't overhear. "Mary, that's enough for now."

Through a clenched jaw, she said, "They'll be coming. Transport."

The lieutenant shook his head. "They'd have been here already. Our heat sigs are obvious. They must've written us off, at least for now. Maybe they really are negotiating the politics of our extraction with the elders in the AZ. Hell, I dunno. But I think we can afford a rest."

"We need to keep—"

"Mary!" His whispered urgency cowed her stubbornness. "If they come, whether they catch us here or a mile from here won't really matter, will it? You need a rest."

Her energy drained, her will to fight as low as it had ever been, she nodded wearily.

Hatch stood up. "Hawkeye, climb the tallest tree you can find within fifty meters. Keep an eye on the wall." As the spotter nodded and turned to carry out his orders, the lieutenant said, "Smoker, Trick, can you range for half a klick toward the interior and report back?"

"That's not necessary," said the QB.

"Captain—"

"I know exactly where we are," she finished.

Trick asked, "How can that be, ma'am? I know we've all got the GIS maps, but thanks to the Ruling, the AZ isn't part of the public record." The principal purpose for the Richmond Ruling had been to exempt the Plain People on New Pennsylvania from having electronic devices—TRIDs and BICEs—installed. But one of the subparagraphs, one few paid attention to, exempted the AZ's interior from grid surveys by Transport. Not many people believed the Authority actually kept its end of the bargain on that point, but at least the zone wasn't on the official maps accessible by the public. "Unless the SOMA passed along intel—"

"Nothing so nefarious, Lieutenant. I was raised here."

Hatch did a double take. It was the first he'd heard of that little fact. "You?"

She turned to him. "Why so shocked, Lieutenant Hatch?"

"Yeah, why so shocked?" asked Stug. "I was raised plain too."

The sergeant's tone was defensive, challenging his superior to make something of it. But Hatch just shook his head, laughing to himself. The irony of two of B-Company's best fighters—one with the iron will of a billy goat, the other the strength of a bear—raised as plain folk could not be denied.

"Guess that whole pacifist thing fell through, eh?" he said.

Neither his captain nor his sergeant was laughing.

"Lieutenant," said Stug with barely repressed anger, which in such a large man was somehow more frightening than all-out rage, "all due respect—but try not to speak about things when you don't know anything about them. Sir."

Hatch stared at his old friend. He'd really hit a nerve. "Stug, I—"

"We don't need to go ranging, ma'am," cut in Smoker.

"Lieutenant?"

"*They've* found *us*."

Rifles came to ready positions, but when Smoker nodded in the direction of the threat, she did so without raising her own. Coming toward them were two men wearing simple clothing and sporting long beards, which wisped in the light warm breeze as they walked. Both were shaded by broad-brimmed, flat hats, and they seemed to have no qualms about approaching the heavily armed soldiers.

"Weapons down," said the QB simply as the plain men approached.

"Good morning," the older man said. He removed his hat, shaded his eyes, and noted the position of the sun. "Although, it *is* getting along a bit." Replacing his hat, he said, "I'm Paul Noffsinger, one of the elders here in the AZ. Welcome." He held out his hand.

Every member of B-Company stared at it. They weren't sure of protocol. And one or two were just a little wary of touching the hand of what were, to some, near-mythical people.

The QB moved forward. "Mary," she said shaking his hand firmly. "Captain Mary Brenneman."

The second man stepped forward. He didn't offer his hand.

"That's an Amish name," he said simply. Direct, as if stating the current temperature for everyone's edification. "Are you Amish, Ms. Brenneman?"

She stared just as directly at him. "And who are you, sir, if I might ask?"

"Name's Shetler," he said. Each syllable was cut sharply.

Noffsinger stepped forward. "Aaron, is that tone necessary? These people are tired and could use a good meal." The fact that they were TRACE soldiers recently in battle and clearly on the run from the Authority hung unspoken in the air.

"If we feed them, we could incur Transport's wrath," said Shetler.

"And if we don't, we could incur God's," responded Noffsinger with a sigh that said they'd had a score of such conversations. "Come," he said, motioning to the soldiers, who stood awkwardly, unsure how to act around such pious people. "We have food. It isn't far."

Shortly after noon, they were sitting in Paul Noffsinger's barn and wolfing down a hastily prepared meal of fresh vegetables, warm bread, and jerked beef. The curious community had gathered as word spread of their arrival. Out of respect for Amish traditions, the QB had made her troops stack their weapons and packs against one of the horse stalls, though she was careful to keep them in plain sight.

"We know about what happened in Gettysburg," said Noffsinger. "It was ... unfortunate."

Smoker stopped eating. "Unfortunate?" She sounded insulted.

"*Lieutenant*," the QB admonished. "Elder Noffsinger," she said, drawing the conversation away from the previous day's events, "you are the minister here?"

He nodded, glancing once at Smoker. "One of them."

"The Amish have multiple preachers speak when they worship," explained Stug for the group's benefit. "Services can last for hours."

"That sounds awful," said Trick without thinking. He looked up sharply. "Sorry."

The captain gave him the eye, then said to Noffsinger, "I

think I knew your father. He was also a minister?"

Noffsinger sat back. "Yes, yes he was. You *are* Amish, then," he said, confirming something for himself. "And *that* Mary Brenneman."

"Used to be. Not anymore," she said around the beef she was chewing.

"Oh yes, she used to be one of us," said a new voice entering the barn. A large man approached. All heads turned from the table. "But now she's shunned."

Stug couldn't hide the surprise on his face. Hatch smelled the electricity in the air. Noffsinger, who'd suspected the truth and had only now seen it confirmed, stood up from the table.

"Marcus, your suspicions seem to have been proven correct," Noffsinger said, his hands coming up to placate the other man. "But it is also true that, at times, we help TRACE. *Many* of their fighters are formerly of the AZ. We have never used that fact as a litmus test for our willingness to provide succor."

"None have ever shamed us as she and her family did," the new man—Marcus—said, his anger growing. "We should turn her and her rebel friends over to Transport immediately."

Stug began to stand up, but Hatch put his hand on the sergeant's thick forearm. They shared a look, and the lieutenant merely shook his head.

"Who are you?" asked Mary.

"Marcus Yoder," he said. His eyes dared her to remember.

The QB looked down at the table briefly, then stood. "We must leave. Elder Noffsinger, everyone," she said, casting her eyes across the stunned onlookers, "on behalf of TRACE and the SOMA, thank you for your hospitality. You've given us aid when we needed it most. Blessings upon you and all in the AZ."

Hatch started to rise.

"Oh, no, please stay," said Yoder, his words dripping with crocodile honey. "You look tired. No need to rush off. I called my cousin, Donavan, with Transport. They'll be here shortly."

"Sonofa—" Stug rose as one with the others to retrieve their weapons.

"Marcus!" Noffsinger gasped. "You had no right—"

"*I have every right!*" Yoder exploded. "After what she did to my family? *Every right!*"

B-Company was already slinging their gear when they heard the whine of the first airships in the distance. Everyone in the barn began to talk at once as violence threatened to erupt all around them.

"Hurry up, people!" said Hatch.

"Elder Noffsinger, my apologies for what I have brought down on your head," said the QB quickly. "You must evacuate this barn, with all your people. We must make our stand here."

"No!" said Noffsinger. "We cannot condone your committing violence here! This is our home, our land!"

"See? It's in her nature. Like her stubborn father, her hot-headed brother," said Yoder, venom in his voice. "She poisons us all with her very presence."

The captain looked to be at a loss. Obviously, the Amish were not clearing out, and yet to run now with her fellow soldiers would be committing pointless suicide. Fortifying the barn would at least give them the opportunity to take a few of the Authority with them.

Then all the TRACE fighters in the barn shook their heads simultaneously.

"Was that what I think it was?" asked Stug.

Another ping resounded in their skulls. Someone was trying to contact their BICEs.

"No sense hiding now," said Hatch, connecting to the Internet.

"—*extraction from your present location. Captain Brenneman, please respond. This is Lieutenant Norwich of Stillen Company. Our orders are to conduct your extraction from your present location...*"

Stug's baritone whooped so loud it filled the barn from stalls to hayloft. "They're ours!"

"No!" shouted Yoder. "Transport is on the way! I will not allow—"

"Marcus! Quiet yourself," said Noffsinger, visibly perturbed by how events had unfolded. "You're already in trouble with the elders. Try not to compound it."

Admonished, the other man glared daggers at B-Company's captain but said nothing more.

Noffsinger turned to her. "It is good that God has provided your deliverance, Mary Brenneman. For if it were left up to me..." His hands showed that he had no idea what his decision would've been.

"I understand, Elder," she said.

Heralded by the babble of livestock, the airbuses were landing in the barnyard.

"No time for long goodbyes, ma'am," said Hatch, with a

wry grin. "Your deliverance awaits."

"Go," she ordered, and the others began to move out. Turning to Noffsinger, she said, "Don't punish him harshly, Elder. And if Transport gives you a hard time, say we merely held you hostage until you fed us and we could get away. It's what they'll say anyway, when they spin this battle for the public."

"Go now," he said to her. "And may God bless."

The ride to the TRACE safe zone provided a final release of tension for the eight survivors of Gettysburg. Crammed into one airbus, the exhausted and overfed members of Bestimmung Company held loosely to the straps keeping them in their seats, their heads lolling. When they landed, the airbus opened to a busy camp. In one corner, one of the cargo ships full of okcillium sat, scorched but intact.

"At least one of 'em got away," breathed Stug. They had all stopped to stare at the ship sitting on the ground, looking like nothing so much as a beaten-down prizefighter. The same question was in all their minds, and they hardly needed their BICEs to share it.

"Was it worth it?" asked Smoker.

"I guess we'll find out," replied their captain.

She went straight to Colonel Neville's tent to make her report. He and half his command had managed to rendezvous in the woods and evade Transport, but he'd lost the other half, along with four cargo ships, six drones, and the personal arms and equipment of every soldier who'd died. In return, he'd gained one shipload of precious okcillium, a score of laser rifles, and further disdain for the costly tactics of Mary Brenneman. The debriefing wasn't pleasant.

While their captain was being upbraided, the remaining members of B-Company reunited. Charlie and Delta squads were like inverse images of one another. Charlie had helped cover TRACE's retreat from Gettysburg but had hardly seen any real action. As a result, the squad had lost no one. Delta Squad was a different story. Charger and her troops had held the tree line against Transport's flanking drones, then continued the fight when the Authority had taken the field in force. In the end, they'd lost all but one: their sergeant. Everyone called her Pusher. She held her head up but talked to no one in the camp, silent tears tracking randomly down her cheeks. Still in shock, she seemed like a mother who'd just been told that her children had died in a senseless accident.

Hatch sat across the table from the QB in what passed for a lounge in the rebel camp. The waitress had left them each a bourbon, neat, and walked away.

"Bad?"

She shrugged. "Some would say not bad enough. Pusher might say that."

He shook his head. "I doubt it. She's grieving. Let her do it. Try not to take it personally."

Her eyes met his with a look that assured him there was no other way to take it. She was in command. These were her troops. Her orders had led them to their deaths.

"What'd Neville say?" he asked.

Again a shrug. "The usual. I bit off more than I could chew. I should've waited for his backup to get there. By moving early, I tipped off Transport. The usual."

"Or ... had we not moved when we did, the Authority might've had the entire town reinforced by the time he got there and we'd have come up with bupkis. It wasn't your fault the intel was wrong and we bumped into Transport on the first day. Command should've known a warehouse full of unguarded okcy was too good to be true. The only question after we made contact was how quickly to move. I think you made the right call."

She slugged the bourbon back. "Command seems to agree with you. I'm still here."

Hatch smiled. "Good. You should be. And Neville?"

She reached over, took his glass, and slugged it back too. "So's he."

Less happy now, Hatch nodded to the waitress. "The next time you want a double, just order one."

She twisted her mouth at him.

"So, in the AZ, I gotta ask. How did you know that hole was in the wall?"

Mary shrugged. "I played around there when I was little. All the kids did. There are holes all along the wall, though Transport tries to keep them plugged up. I figured if we looked hard enough, we'd find one."

"And Yoder? What was he going on about?"

Her face went flat. She'd known it was coming, and that it would come from Hatch. As close as they'd once been, she'd never shared her history with him, the circumstances of her life that had led her to join the resistance. Her shunning by the Plain People. And she didn't feel inclined to share it now.

"It's not something I talk about. I've tried to forget it ever happened."

A laugh if there ever was one, her inner voice said.

The waitress set down their drinks and walked away.

"Oh, come on, Mary," he urged. "It's just you and me here now."

"I was young and stupid, Lieutenant," she said. She used his rank to let him know their personal connection wasn't going to work here.

He took his glass in hand and sipped it. "Have it your way, Captain."

She immediately regretted the distance she heard in his voice. The distance she'd put there. But she didn't want to talk about her life in the AZ.

Ever, her inner voice confirmed.

"It's just not something I want to relive, Sean," she said. "But I appreciate your concern."

Hatch finished off the bourbon. "I care about you, Mary. You know that. Whatever our ranks."

She nodded. She knew.

"Hey, you know what tomorrow is?" he asked.

"It's not today," she replied. "That's a start."

"It's the Fourth of July."

She stared at him, uncomprehending.

"It's an old holiday back on Earth. Independence Day."

"Ah. How ironic." Her voice bled sarcasm.

"Don't say that!" Hatch said. Sometimes her defeatism,

though it was rare, really got to him. Maybe its rarity was why it hit him so hard. She was a rock. Most of the time.

"I'm sorry, Sean. I guess I just don't feel much like celebrating."

Hatch nodded. He got that.

Pusher walked through the door. She looked around, spotted them, and headed straight for their table. Mary braced herself. She'd seen this before. The release of grief by assigning blame. Blame that Mary thought might even be justified. Every tactical situation was different, a complex web of opportunities and decisions. All a soldier had was her training and her gut instincts and a dubious relationship with the Almighty. A small quiver of arrows, really, when it came down to it. "I did the best with what I had" often fell flat with those asked to pay the price for her decisions, good or bad.

The sergeant stopped at their table but didn't sit down. Everyone in the lounge went quiet and watched.

"I lost my squad yesterday, ma'am," Pusher said. There were no tears. Just a clenched jaw holding them back. "I lost Charger. I lost them all."

"Yes, you did," said Mary. She wanted to harden up, to be the QB. But something about the pools of anguish staring from Pusher's stony face wouldn't let her. She had to take this as a person, not a soldier. Death was never impersonal.

"I just wanted to say, I'm proud to serve under you, Captain Brenneman. I'm proud of what we did. I'm proud of my soldiers. I'm proud of my lieutenant. I'm proud that they died for something worth dying for."

Mary stood up. Standing was required to honor the woman

in front of her, who was stock-still and looking her captain straight in the eye. Standing was necessary to pay proper respect to the dead.

"I'm proud to have you in my command," she replied solemnly.

Pusher reached out her hand and Mary took it. The sergeant saluted and walked away.

When Mary sat back down, she did all she could to hide her emotions. To reestablish the mask of the QB. The old trick. The muscle memory of command.

Hatch pushed her bourbon toward her, but she let it sit.

"And that's the difference between you and Neville," he said simply. "That's the difference between being a leader and being in command."

Mary was unable to catch it, so a single tear bled down the curve of her cheek. She quickly wiped it away.

"And now what?" she asked, her voice hitched.

"It's like I told you when the heat was on. Now, we have to get ready for the next battle. Bestimmung Company still needs its captain, Mary."

She picked up the bourbon, rolled its weight around in her hand. She took the shot in one slug, its smoky tingle burning the back of her throat.

"Well," she said, "I'm still here."

Historical Note: *Gettysburg*

The American Civil War has always seemed like a Shakespearean tragedy to me. Its five acts spanned 1861 to 1865, and its two sides were matched as inverse images of one another, seemingly fated to fight an extended, bitter conflict. The Confederacy had better leaders, more élan early in the war, and—whatever our modern perception of its rationale for secession (the catch-all concept is "states' rights superseding federal authority"; the most obvious expression of those rights involved the continuation of slavery as a cheap labor force, something the South considered vital to its economy)—an absolute belief bordering on religious fervor in the rightness of the Southern cause. In other words, the Confederacy was more motivated to fight and—thanks to the quality of its military leadership—more capable of doing so effectively, despite obvious but willfully ignored strategic disadvantages.

The Union, on the other hand, had everything else. A larger population from which to draw soldiery, a mature industrial base, a more thoroughly developed transportation system, a better-equipped navy—which it put to good use in strangling Southern trade from abroad—and President Abraham Lincoln, whose force of will is often credited for our having a cohesive United States today. What the Union lacked early on was effective military leadership, and that simple fact extended the pain of the conflict—the crucible of the American character—much longer than it should have lasted. In an ironic twist worthy of the Bard, a week after the start of the bombardment of Fort Sumter on April 12, 1861, then-U.S. Army Col. Robert E. Lee was offered command of the Union army. But this was a day after Lee's beloved Virginia seceded and he demurred, saying he could never march against his home state. In Lee, the Confederacy found a brilliant, daring leader for its own army, and some consider him the greatest military commander in American history. His greatest blunder was the Battle of Gettysburg.

The battle is called the "high-water mark" of the Confederacy because it represented the culmination of a rare offensive campaign by a Confederate army and the South's last real threat to Northern soil. Losing the battle began the long descent of Southern fortunes that ended at Appomattox Court House on April 9, 1865, almost four years to the day since hostilities began. Until July 1863, the Confederate army had won (or, in some cases, fought to a draw) every major engagement of the war. In the North, the political will to continue the fight was waning, as evidenced by draft riots and Copperheads (Northerners favoring an immediate peace with the Confederacy). Had the Confederacy won at Gettysburg, many historians have suggested we might well have two American nations today.

When Michael Bunker created the world of *Pennsylvania*, he brought forward to his land of New Pennsylvania many of the artifacts and familiar places of old Earth. I decided to have fun with that notion. It wasn't so hard to imagine that folks who immigrated to this new land—named for a state in the old world—would also bring their town names with them, perhaps even naming a town Gettysburg. And what if fate and history conspired to create circumstances that resonated with events more than 250 years in that world's past? Instead of Confederates looking for shoes and bumping into Union cavalry, let's have TRACE looking for okcillium and bumping into a platoon of Transport soldiers. Yeah, that's the ticket!

I had a lot of fun reimagining aspects of the battle as elements of my story. I just gave one Easter egg away with the shoes/okcillium example, so I won't give away any more. But if you know the battle, maybe you'll find and crack open some more of those eggs. I hope you enjoy their discovery. And if you're not a history buff like me, it's cool; I hope you enjoy the story for what I primarily intended it to be: a tale of adventure, bravery, and catastrophe—much like the Civil War itself.

Chris Pourteau

September 2014

SUSQUEHANNA

All Our Food Belong to Whom?

"Swing and a miss!"

One of the bar patrons thought she was a comedienne.

Stug's momentum carried him through, and he caught himself against the bar. It shuddered under his bulk but it held. He could feel Garza, the loudmouth sergeant from A Company, moving behind him. So Stug played possum, stayed prone.

"What's wrong, Miller?" Garza said in that annoyingly smooth Spanish accent of his. "Too much to drink? Or are you just getting old?"

Stug actually considered the question as he prepared to push himself up. Then he shrugged internally. He didn't think he understood the concept *too much to drink*. And as for getting old? So what if he was in his early thirties? So maybe he woke with a few more pops and aches in the morning. They had yet to slow him down.

"Just stay right there, Garza," he slurred without turning around. "And I'll show you the difference a little experience makes."

Stug flexed. The bar groaned. Garza centered himself.

In one smooth motion, Stug thrust himself up and back, right into Garza's center mass, forcing air and surprise from the younger man. They both flew backward, their audience of soldiers parting around them like the Red Sea before Moses. Garza landed on his back on a wooden table, and their combined weight was too much for its shoddy workmanship. They appeared to hover in the air for a moment, then rode the splintered tabletop to the floor, crashing hard. Beneath Stug's bulk, Garza took the worst of it. He wheezed, lungs aching.

"Man, you even *moan* with an accent," Stug said.

Someone laughed.

"What the hell is going on here?"

The laughter tapered off quickly. Bodies moved aside as others pushed through. Someone—sounded like the comedienne—groaned her disappointment.

Captain Martin Seamus of A Company and Lieutenant Sean Hatch of B Company's Alpha Squad pushed their way through the ring of soldiers surrounding the two men. Stug and Garza lay on the floor, one looking slightly confused, the other still remembering how to breathe again.

"Sergeants, I asked a question," said Seamus.

"Nothing, sir," wheezed Garza, rolling the bigger man off him. "Just a little fun."

"Fun?" Seamus cast his eyes around. Not one, but *two* tables were flattened. Three chairs broken. He'd obviously arrived at this particular party a little late. And the bartender, a young corporal with freckles on her cheeks, looked justifiably annoyed and terrified at the same time. In his peripheral vision, Seamus noticed someone reluctantly tapping a uni bracelet against someone else's—no doubt settling a bet. "You two thick apes destroy half the Rock Slide, and you call that fun?"

By now, both of the combatants were attempting to get to their feet.

"Sergeant Miller, explain yourself," grumbled Hatch.

Failing to answer, Stug merely stood in a Zen-like state, swaying softly to a breeze only he could feel.

"Sergeant Miller!"

The big man blinked in surprise, as if he'd just been reminded that he was, in fact, alive. "*What?*" he answered, annoyed. Then, thinking better of his attitude, he added, "Nothing."

"What?"

"It's what Garza said. Nothing." He burped. "Beg pardon. Sir."

"Lieutenant…" began Seamus, at his wit's end.

"Sir, if I may." Hatch used the voice he preferred when trying to demonstrate to a superior officer his clear understanding of the military code of conduct. To his unsteady sergeant, he said, "Consider yourself on report, Miller."

"Report? Just for having a little fun?"

"Now we're back to fun," said Seamus. "I thought it was *nothing.*"

Stug glanced at the bartender, then leered at the captain and winked. "Even a little nothing can be fun with the right person." Sneering at his opponent, he said, "I wasn't talking about you, Garza."

"Report it is," said Hatch, grabbing Stug by the arm and attempting to drag him out of the Slide. *It's like moving a cargo container full of okcy one-handed*, he thought. "Captain Seamus, might I assume the same for your lunkheaded Spaniard?"

The captain frowned, debating internally, then nodded.

"Thank you, sir. Now, if you don't mind, I'll get my man to his bunk."

"What about my bar?" called the freckle-faced bartender after them.

Hatch ignored her. The crowd parted, joking and laughing, as he lugged his burly friend out. Stug was muttering incoherently under his breath, difficult to hear over all the noise.

"What'd you say, meathead?"

"I said, why'd you have to be such an ass? Report? Whassup with that?"

"Because if I hadn't taken control of the situation, you idiot, Seamus might've given you worse," explained Hatch. "As it is, you get a mark on a piece of paper. Assuming I remember to file it."

A soldier held the door for them as they made their way outside and into the cool October air.

"Ah," said Stug. "Well, in that case, thanks for being such an ass."

"Oh, it was my pleasure."

Pound. Pound. Pound.

The inside of Stug's head felt like the timing drum on an ancient Roman warship, its skin stretched to the limit by the constant beat of the *pausarius*, the officer who kept the men on the benches hard at their oars. And only one thin membrane for a drumhead to receive the drummer's abuse.

On top of that, some demented bastard was shining a light in his eyes. He didn't remember getting captured. So why was he being tortured?

Pound. Pound. Pound.

Now he understood Garza's concept. In a hazy, half-remembered, not-sure-you-didn't-dream-it-up kind of way. Maybe it *was* possible to drink too much.

I am *getting old*, Stug thought.

"If you don't turn off that light, I'm going to snuff it out," he growled at the tormentor standing over him. "And you won't like how."

Instead, the man holding the flashlight said, "Get up, vampire."

Stug snarled and came up off his cot, lunging at the glare and the shadowy figure holding it. The man slid left easily, jerking the light ahead of the sergeant, who pursued it like a kitten with a new toy. Finally realizing he'd been tricked, Stug stopped in his tracks.

"You're lucky I'm not Transport," said Hatch. "Or you'd be dead."

Mostly upright but swaying, Stug turned quickly to face his friend. He immediately regretted the movement. His hand went to his forehead. Had his brain just sloshed in its fastenings?

Pound. Pound. Pound.

He almost fell backward, then steadied himself on his feet.

"*You're* lucky I'm still drunk," said Stug. "Or you'd be flat. Turn off that torch from hell. Please."

Hatch snapped off the flashlight. "The QB wants us in a briefing at oh-six-hundred," he said. "Get some coffee in you and wipe the drool off your chin."

Stug mechanically passed a lazy backhand across his stubble. Even that change in equilibrium made him sway a bit more. "What time is it now?"

"Oh-five-thirty," said Hatch.

The sergeant gave him a disbelieving look. "You mean I could've slept for another..." He paused. Even the simplest math seems like rocket science when you're drunk. "Twenty-five minutes?"

Hatch snorted. "You're already on report, as soon as I get around to filling out the paperwork. Want to be a corporal again, too?"

Stug, tottering on his thick legs, gave the impression he was considering it. His hand rubbed over his sweating bald head, the simple movement almost sending him backward again. "Might be worth it."

"Well, feel free to hit the bag again. But I wouldn't want her mad at *me*."

Stug swayed in cloudy contemplation. "I've seen her mad at you," he allowed, finally finding his balance. "Okay, I'll sober up. Damn it."

Hatch grinned, enjoying the thought of his sergeant's

difficult road ahead. "Coffee's over there. I'll roust the others."

Bracer and Hawkeye had imbibed significantly less than their sergeant the night before. Both were in their fatigues before Stug had finished half a cup of coffee.

"Feeling all right this morning, Sergeant?" asked Bracer, putting on his jacket. "You look a bit peaked after tangling with Garza."

Stug gazed over the brim of his steaming cup of non-alcoholic beverage at the other man. His stare seemed to consider whether or not Bracer was secretly giving orders to the Roman officer pounding the inside of his skull. He didn't say a word, but a low rumbling came from the back of his throat.

Bracer had passed tactics with flying colors. He knew when to retreat.

"All right ladies, let's go. It's quick chow this morning. Captain's waiting," said Hatch.

Walking across the compound in the pre-dawn darkness, Hatch watched the almost constant bustle of activity. Even in the dead of night, silence and stillness were rare. He observed the TRACE soldiers on the wall, some of them manning emplaced 18-millimeter machine guns like the one Bracer carried into combat. There were twelve positioned around the pentagonal walls of Little Gibraltar, the island fortress which TRACE cells south of the City had come to call home. Its walls were overgrown with strategically interlaced vines that hid their stony sides. Tall red cedar and pine trees hugged the outer walls, as if Mother Nature embraced the rebel stronghold in her protective arms.

Part town, part base, part fort, Little Gibraltar sat squarely on an island in the middle of the Susquehanna River. Some said God Himself had skipped a huge stone along the length of the river, commanding it to land here. The river was named for the Susquehanna that flowed through the heart of Old Pennsylvania back on Earth. It had been a route for exploration and trade on the Old Planet, first for the Native Americans, then for the Europeans who'd displaced them.

The chow line was moving a little quicker than usual this morning, Hatch noticed. Then he saw why. One splat of eggs, two pieces of bacon, one piece of bread, one cup of coffee. No fruit.

"We're on half rations," Bracer said, stealing the words from the lieutenant's thoughts.

Stug groaned. Despite his behemoth stature and generally affable nature, the man had the annoying whine of a five-year-old boy who's been told he can't have a second cookie. It was most maddening when it surfaced in the middle of combat. The threat of death had a way of accentuating the big man's complaints in a way that wrapped a fist around Hatch's spine and squeezed.

"I'll never get sober on bird feed," the sergeant complained.

As the line moved along, Hatch turned back and thumped the sergeant's belly with the back of his hand. "You might get a little thinner, though."

Stug sneered. "Women like me this way."

"Women like you?" Bracer asked playfully.

The sergeant moved forward in line, holding out his tray to the server. "If I weren't still drunk…"

"A cloudy day," said Hawkeye, glancing up. He was always the first to notice anything that might obscure visibility or limit line of sight.

Hatch looked up at the sky as he made his way to a bench. One cloudy day wasn't a problem. Two cloudy days were worrisome. Three cloudy days could kill them.

Little Gibraltar was protected by a huge version of the Umbrella, a solar-powered energy shield used by TRACE companies to protect base camps from prying Transport eyes. The name for the system was a bit of a misnomer, since the Umbrella was modulated to allow infrared light from scouting drones to penetrate its dome—it just wasn't allowed to return to its source after pinging a target. In short, scans could enter the Umbrella, but they couldn't get out. So unless a drone or dropship flew directly overhead or spotted the machine guns on the fortress's carefully camouflaged walls, Transport would never see them. Unfortunately, the solar batteries that powered the Umbrella could only store sixty hours of energy, give or take—that meant that three days of dark clouds would cause the system's power to fail. And with its camouflage gone, Little Gibraltar would be exposed.

"It'll blow over," Stug mumbled, stabbing his two pieces of fatback bacon and stuffing the greasy taste of heaven into his mouth. "No rain today," he mumbled. "Can't smell it." His head still pulsed, but now that he'd begun eating, the Roman officer had been replaced by a little drummer boy banging on a tin can.

Hatch glanced up again. Except for the ominous clouds, the skies were clear. Transport rarely flew aircraft down the Susquehanna or over the tear-shaped isle of Little Gibraltar, which was why the resistance had chosen it for their base. Located some twelve miles downstream from the City, the island was off the Authority's main flight paths, but close enough for quick access to the Amish Zone, where TRACE got most of its food.

Though the pacifistic Plain People refused to fight directly in TRACE's generations-long war against Transport, they often supported the struggle in less direct ways. The Amish had known the iron boot of intolerance for six hundred years, so they were sympathetic to the rebels' fight against the Authority's tyranny. The eggs, milk, bacon, jerked beef, fresh fruit, and vegetables that flowed covertly to the island came directly from them. Without it, TRACE soldiers would starve or be forced to requisition food from the smaller homesteads of New Pennsylvania, and that would likely breed resentment in the very population they were fighting to free.

The food was brought west across the plain from the AZ by wagon in the dead of night. Moving the supplies by airbus would have been far too visible to Transport, even if no flight plans were filed. Newly manufactured weapons and other technical goods also arrived under the cover of darkness, although these came down the Susquehanna from the City.

It was the SOMA himself who had suggested the strategy of moving supplies and materiel the old-fashioned way, by wagon and ferry. All of this was illegal, of course, since movement was strictly regulated by Transport, but the irony of subverting the Authority's control by low-tech means had only enhanced the SOMA's legend among his TRACE soldiers.

The fact that they were on half rations told Hatch that the food, at least, had come into short supply—and that was a problem even more pressing than three cloudy days in a row. Little Gibraltar was a vital link in the supply chain that fed TRACE's entire resistance network. A great deal of food passed through the fort on its way to soldiers in other theaters of the war, so if Little Gibraltar was feeling the pinch, so was the rest of TRACE.

The fort was a distribution hub for materiel as well, including laser weapons manufactured via 3-D printers in the City and powered by the okcillium secured in the Battle of Gettysburg three months earlier. His own squad was armed with the modern weapons now, though they also carried old-fashioned .50-caliber sidearms on their hips. His people had worked with advanced technology long enough to know how little they could trust it.

"You through yet?" asked Stug, breaking Hatch's concentration. "We're due with the QB in two minutes." The sergeant must be sobering up at last; he could tell time again.

"Well. We don't want to start the day on the wrong foot, do we?" asked the lieutenant sarcastically.

Alpha Squad took their seats at the briefing. Bravo, Charlie, Delta, and Echo squads were already there. Hatch assessed them as the other companies gathered.

There were a lot of new faces in the room. Bestimmung Company had absorbed soldiers from other units to fill its own ranks, depleted after Gettysburg; some had seen action in theaters as far west as the Great Shelf. Other changes had happened internally. Sergeant Emma "Pusher" Ellis, who'd lost her entire squad covering the retreat of the rest of the company from Gettysburg, now played mother to Echo Squad, which carried B Company's two heavy chain guns.

"Ten-hut!"

Everyone stood as Colonel Obadiah Neville entered the room. He commanded the three assembled companies. Behind him came his company commanders, including B Company's Captain Mary Brenneman. The good colonel had dubbed her his own personal "Queen Bitch" for her less-than-respectful attitude toward him. But in admiration for her ability to make quick decisions in the field, decisions that had saved their lives many times, her troops in B Company had shortened the nickname to "QB."

Hatch observed her demeanor. To anyone else, she had a subdued air about her, but he knew better. They'd been lovers once, and he knew her better than anyone else in the room. Her face was flat, a particular expression she wore when she focused in combat. But her right hand flexed and wiped ever so surreptitiously on her uniform. She was sweating. She was excited. Something was up.

"At ease," said Neville, producing the superior air he always did when addressing his command. "Be seated, ladies and gentleman."

After the scraping of chairs subsided, he put his hands behind his back.

"Who does he think he is, Montgomery?" whispered Stug to the air. "He needs a cheesy moustache—"

"Shhh." Hatch wanted to hear what was incoming. If Mary was excited, he was excited. *Some things never change*, he thought, amusing himself.

"I assume you all had enough to eat this morning?" asked Neville slyly.

Some big grunt from the back took the bait. "Not really, sir."

"Precisely why we're here, soldier," answered the colonel, stabbing at the air to make his point. "*Precisely*. My aide is sending you a map of the area. Note the highlighted routes, which the Amish use to cart food to the river. Note also the big X approximately halfway between here and the Zone. That's the last known location of yesterday's weekly shipment from the Amish. Ladies and gentlemen..." He paused, loving the drama. "Someone has stolen our supplies."

As the map data entered his BICE, Hatch examined the terrain in his mind. It was made up mostly of slow-rising hills, and the tall trees of the wilderness shielded the wagonloads of supplies coming from the AZ. A small, thin band of river wound its way westward from the Zone to empty into the Susquehanna. The X the colonel referred to marked a valley. If someone was going to steal TRACE's food, that would be the place to do it.

"Six Amish wagoners met our squad at Shenks Landing this morning, where they were to transfer their cargo. Highwaymen had waylaid them in that valley and set them afoot."

"'Set them afoot'?" whispered Hawkeye with a grin.

"Highwaymen?" added Stug. "Waylaid?"

Hatch shushed them with a flat cut of his hand at the air. Everyone knew Neville liked to speak in anachronistic terms when giving a situation report. They all assumed it added to his sense of self-importance as a historical military figure. But the men never tired of poking fun.

"Our job, ladies and gentlemen, is to find that food," continued Neville. "We just yesterday shipped most of our stores out to other resistance cells. We were expecting resupply this morning. If we don't find that shipment, we will soon feel hunger's feral bite, I'm afraid." Despite the serious situation, Neville smiled at his own pun. He then turned—slowly, almost reluctantly it seemed—to the leader of Bestimmung Company. "Captain?" he said, sitting down.

The QB rose. Unlike her commanding officer, her stance was relaxed and unposed. She simply stood up straight.

"B Company has been ordered to the X on your maps," she said. "We'll ferry across to Shenks Landing and hump it from there. We leave in an hour."

She sat back down.

"Well, that was anticlimactic," muttered Stug.

Hatch knew why. She was anxious to move. Talk of waylayings and puttings afoot was, to her, merely wasting time with words.

Neville stood back up. "Yes, well then. As Captain Brenneman said, B Company marches in an hour. We've already sent a squad to escort the unfortunate Amish wagoners back to the AZ via a different route."

"Those wagoners who were previously waylaid and set afoot," whispered Stug. Hatch rolled his eyes. Sometimes the big guy just didn't know when to shut up.

"Any questions?" asked Neville.

"How much food did we lose, sir?"

"Three wagonloads."

Some gasps met that proclamation.

"Any idea who the highwaymen are, sir?" asked the underfed grunt in the back.

Kiss-ass, thought Stug.

"No, Private. The darkness hid them well. We suspect Transport, but we have no evidentiary support for that."

"Why would Transport hork our supplies? That makes no sense," whispered Hawkeye, ever the forward observer of the obvious.

Hatch shrugged. He'd given up trying to understand how incompetence passed for strategic thinking a long time ago.

The QB stood. "If there's nothing else?"

Colonel Neville looked sideways at her but said nothing. One hand, halfway into the air, went back down.

"Yes, well then," said the colonel. "Dismissed." While B Company roused itself for duty, he added, "Captain, if I might have a word."

Hatch knew what was coming. The QB would be receiving a short but wordy lecture on briefing protocol and the importance of ceremony in impressing the frontline troops.

Some things never change, he thought again, less pleased this time.

The Ferryman

When B Company's twenty soldiers reached Shenks Landing on the riverbank, they found an old man of nearly seventy years dressed in thick clothes and a dark, heavy jacket. The air had grown chilly with winter's approach. Like the old man, they too were outfitted for marching in the cold.

"Name's Sticks," he said.

"I like it," noted Echo Squad's Lieutenant Gray, nicknamed Smoker.

The old man regarded her for a moment, his face a bit askew. "Someone who reads a lot named me Sticks. It stuck."

"Of course it did," said Stug.

The QB nodded a greeting. "Well, Mr. Sticks—"

"No Mister, just Sticks," corrected the old man.

The captain took a deep breath. "All right then, *Sticks*, there's a valley about six klicks—six kilometers—inland from the river. We need to get there. You're aware of the location?"

"Oh sure! Your commando buddies that took the AZers home asked me about it. I know right where you need to go. And *why*," he winked.

Mary turned her head slightly, assessing him. Missing most of his teeth, the man had the predatory, piercing eyes of someone who would mete out information slowly, and with each bit expect a slightly larger sum of unis. Whether the information was reliable or not was irrelevant to his type, because he'd be long gone and likely untrackable before the mark noticed they'd been had.

The QB shrugged mentally, her inner voice prodding, *Nothing ventured...*

"You know about the stolen supplies, then," she fished.

"Oh sure! Food from the AZers comes through here all the time. Who do you think freights it across the river to your little Alamo over there?"

"Little Gibraltar," corrected Smoker.

"Whatever," dismissed the old man. "You can call it TRACE Castle for all I care." To the captain, he said, "Here's what I also know. You start footin' around through the woods with all these commando types, whistlin' tunes of freedom and such, and you'll never find that food."

"What do you mean?" asked Pusher, stepping up beside Smoker. Gray was her lieutenant now. Even in conversations, Pusher felt compelled to have her back.

"I mean, the people you want'll scurry like roaches when you flip the light on. This ain't like no Transport warehouse, just sits there and waits for you to take it. Oh sure, I heard about that. And your company, Captain, ma'am. But you go tromping through the roughs with an army..." Sticks waved his arms like a flock of birds taking flight. "I wouldn't take more'n three or four of you if you want any chance of them showin'. Plus me, o'course."

"You're our *guide*?" asked Stug. "You don't look like you could make it six klicks through the weeds to me."

Sticks turned to him. "I'll still be walking the New Penn wilds long after you've collapsed for lack of the half a pig it must take to feed you every day, thickneck."

Hatch laughed out loud at Stug's confused expression. He could tell the big man wasn't sure if he should punch the old man or pat him on the head.

"Just who are we looking for?" pressed the QB.

"Is it Transport making off with the food?" asked Smoker.

The captain gave Smoker a sour expression. *Never hand a salesman information he can sell right back to you*, it said.

"Oh sure! That's it," he said, cackling. "*Transport*. What ignoramus came up with that idea?"

"His name's Obadiah," Stug supplied.

"Oba-what-a, now?"

"Back on point," said the QB. "If not Transport, who?"

Sticks squinted at her, perhaps assessing how many unis the info was worth. Then he shrugged to himself, committed to his course.

"You probably heard of 'em. Most folks call 'em Wild Ones."

"The cannibals?" said Smoker.

"Why would cannibals steal..." Stug smacked his lips. "Wait—what have the Amish been feeding us?"

There was amusement among the company, and Sticks's cackle cut through it like nails scratching metal.

But the QB was getting irritated. She knew exactly who the

Wild Ones were. Opportunists trying to survive. Something between homesteaders and scavengers. But she never really believed the cannibal story. Did she?

"So, you're telling us Wild Ones have suddenly started stealing our shipments from the AZ," she said. "Why?"

Sticks gestured like he didn't know or didn't care. Or both. "Times are hard," was all he said.

Time to make a decision is what it is, her inner voice fumed. "Right, then. Hatch, you and Alpha Squad are with me. Bracer, leave your 18-millimeter with the company," she said, eyeing the hundred-pound machine gun on Bracer's back. "We'll need to stay light and mobile. Trick, I'm leaving you in brevet command of B Company." Trick stood a little taller, proud of the unexpected, if temporary, field promotion. "I want you to stay on this side of the river but out of sight," the QB continued. "Secure Shenks Landing, but outfit for aerial recon flights by Transport. Once you've secured the area, give Colonel Neville a situation report."

Trick raised an eyebrow. "Shouldn't you, as commanding officer, make the report before you go?"

"As of ten seconds ago, you're commanding officer, remember?" she said. "The more time we waste making reports, the less likely we'll get those supplies back." *Plus,* her inner voice added, *the good colonel prefers the sound of male voices calling him 'sir.'* For the sake of military discipline, she kept her commentary off the company's BICE channel.

"Very well, ma'am," Trick said, his manner reflecting an acceptance that his was the lot of a subordinate officer. Then, paying forward the love, he ordered his sergeant to break out the camouflage nets. They'd set up a perimeter around the ferry landing and protect themselves from Transport eyes in the sky by stringing the nets between the stout trees near the river's edge. A portable Umbrella, solar powered and cast atop the camouflage, would shield them from infrared scans.

"Five of you? You're takin' too many," Sticks said to the captain. "They'll hide in the woods."

"We work in squads," said the QB matter-of-factly. She didn't explain further, and Sticks merely shrugged again. What did he care?

"We taking the raft?" asked Stug.

"T'ain't a raft," said Sticks. "That's a pole barge. Only way to get up the Pesky." He winked, "That's what I call the little strip of river that goes east. And no, we ain't takin' it. Only an idiot poles the river during the day." He jerked his thumb over his shoulder at the sky. "Too many eyes. Only pole the river at night. Daytime, we rough it cross country and let the trees keep our secret."

"Then let's get moving," the captain said.

As Alpha Squad prepared to move out, the QB stared across the river for a moment toward Little Gibraltar. It was well hidden, even from her knowing eyes. The soldiers behind its walls would be eating another half meal in six hours. Before much longer, they'd be down to quarter rations. And if the island dried up as the supply hub for the entire TRACE network in the south, well—once the roots die, the limbs soon follow. Restoring the food shipments from the AZ was vital if the resistance itself was to survive.

"Let's go," she said. "Bellies are rumbling."

The ferryman led them east away from the river and beneath the canopy of thick trees that painted the landscape of New Pennsylvania. With fall coming on, their cover from spying eyes above was less than it would've been just a few weeks before, but it would do. They followed a well-worn path Sticks knew by heart, though the trail itself felt erratic. But, Mary soon realized, there was a method to the old man's madness. He favored the broad-leafed maples over the cedar and pine trees for the better cover they provided, and sometimes walking under their protection required a bit of meandering.

Mary also noticed bluebells along the path, and the little girl still sitting inside her soul longed to reach down and pluck one, to draw its fragrance into her lungs. But she settled for noting their beauty in her mind only—off-channel, of course—and moving on.

Pesky Creek, as Sticks named it, was deeper than it looked. They noticed schools of large shad fish swimming in the clear water. The second time they spotted them, Stug's stomach grumbled. Two hours passed swiftly, marked by furtive glances upward by Hawkeye and random slaps by Stug. For a man born on an Amish farm, Stug had little tolerance for bugs.

"How long till we get to these thieves?" he asked, punctuating his question with a whack at his neck. "I'm in the mood to punch something bigger."

"Not long at all," cackled Sticks, striding over a final gathering of weeds and wildflowers into a clearing.

B Company unslung their laser rifles. The mid-morning sun shone bright and warm on the site where the Amish deliverymen had been ambushed. Fifty feet in front of them, one of the three missing wagons stood on its side, a wheel shattered and strewn among the weeds. According to the reports Mary got back at the camp, none of the half a dozen Amish drivers had been hurt; the scavengers had merely pointed them at the river and told them to get moving. The Wild Ones must've overturned the wagon afterward. *Why?*

"Why would they trash the wagon?" wondered Bracer, echoing Mary's thoughts. "Why not pack off the supplies in the buggy that brought 'em?"

"Wild Ones are sorta like the Amish," explained Sticks. "Very practical. Maybe the wagon was damaged in the fight with the drivers."

"The Amish don't fight," said Hatch.

"Okay, good point," said Sticks, shutting up. He had the air of a man who'd been caught in a lie, Hatch thought. His faith in the ferryman had been thin before. It now evaporated entirely.

Cautious now, the lieutenant said, "Hawkeye, heat sig the clearing. Give me a one-hundred-foot radius around us, too."

The spotter put his omni-lens to his eye and scanned for heat signatures, making a 360-degree arc across the wagon and surrounding tall grass.

"Looks clear," he reported. "A few animals in the underbrush."

"I still don't understand the wagon," said Bracer.

Sticks fidgeted nervously.

"I do," answered Stug, walking across the open ground. When he reached the overturned wagon, he pointed at the bolster beneath the driver's seat, then to the axle near it. "Laser fire." Now that he was closer, the sergeant noticed random foodstuffs strewn about. Dropped in a hurry, looked like.

"Lasers?" Hawkeye asked the question that had popped into everyone's heads. "When the hell did the Wild Ones get lasers? Hell, *we* just got lasers!" The spotter wrapped both arms protectively around his weapon.

"T'weren't them with the lasers," said Sticks finally.

"Transport?" Bracer's tone wondered what the Authority would want with a bunch of scavengers.

"Looks like it." The QB jerked her head toward the far side of the clearing. The weeds and grass had been flattened by the antigravity engines of some kind of air vessel. "But where are the bodies? It's not likely the scavengers won the skirmish, much less took no casualties."

"You shouldn't underestimate 'em," said Sticks. "They won. Or there'd be bodies."

Hatch understood. "They take their dead and wounded with them." He rounded on the ferryman. "You knew about this. Why didn't you tell us?"

The old man regarded him. "We weren't sure you'd come if you really thought Transport was involved. A few salvagers? Well, you'd come to that party for sure."

"We?"

Sticks closed his mouth.

"Hawkeye," Hatch said, glaring at the old man, "scan the hills with your omni-lens for heat sigs. Find out if there are eyes on us."

The spotter acknowledged the order.

Stug wandered over to the landing site. "It was a dropship all right," he said, recognizing the landing pattern.

He found arrows cut by hand from tree limbs and tipped with flint points. A knife of quartz, jagged and hand-sized, was embedded in the earth. And there was blood. Whatever else had happened here, the Wild Ones—armed only with handmade weapons—had chased off a much more advanced Transport dropship armed with a state-of-the-art Gatling laser. The Amishman in him appreciated the irony. The soldier in him was impressed as hell.

"Well?"

"Nothing, sir." But no sooner had Hawkeye said it than he held up a hand. "Wait. I see ten, maybe fifteen in the tree line of that hill." The others followed the direction of his lens to a wooded hill a hundred yards to the north. "I didn't see them at first. They ... they're masking their signatures somehow. Their heat sigs are human-shaped, but it takes closer inspection to see them."

"What are they doing?" asked the QB.

Hawkeye shrugged. "Looks like they're watching us watching them."

A feeling crept up the back of Hatch's neck. "They're just standing there?"

"Yep."

"*Crap*. Stug—"

As he turned to his sergeant, the behemoth who loved bar fights already had his hands in the air. Beyond him, emerging from the tall grass beyond the dropship's landing zone, at least fifteen Wild Ones approached in a semicircle, surrounding Stug.

"Sir," said Hawkeye, still observing the people on the hill, "they're starting to move this way. It's like they don't even care if we see them."

"Hawk," Bracer said, tapping his spotter on the shoulder. When Hawkeye turned an irritated eye on him, the heavy-weapons man jerked his head at Stug.

"Oh."

Hatch watched the QB for how to play it. But she followed Stug's lead. Her laser rifle hung swaying by its strap at her side as she raised her hands in the air.

"And you call yourself a spotter," fumed Hatch, raising his own.

Hawkeye shrugged. "Looked clear." The point man's dark humor, as old as warfare.

"Uh-huh." *You sure about this?* Hatch asked, aiming his BICE chatter at the back of the QB's head.

Do you see the missing food? she answered. *Assuming we could even mow them down without biting it ourselves, how would we find it?*

She had a point.

As the circle closed in, the soldiers of B Company formed a tight circle of their own, their backs to one another. If it turned ugly—uglier—they wanted their laser rifles pointing out, not in.

Covered in mud, the Wild Ones stopped ten feet away from them. A few of them held body shields made of glass, obviously pilfered from Authority troops at some point. The resistance fighters were now completely surrounded by muddy scavengers with spears, bows, and knives made of quartz. All just as deadly as lasers in close quarters.

One of the Wild Ones stepped forward. He was older, with a thick beard and a long rifle slung across his back. He was chewing some kind of green plant and didn't seem worried about offending anyone with the green spittle mucking up his beard. The man considered the QB admiringly, then Hatch and the others. When his eyes landed on Stug, he backed up half a step.

Sticks walked out to meet him. "Like we agreed, eh?"

"Agreeing yes, you and us," said the muddy man with the gooey green beard. He withdrew a bag that clinked as he handed it over. "Much more money you," he said.

"Much more money me, indeed!" replied Sticks.

"Sonofa—"

"Now, now, Sergeant," said the ferryman. "Why get paid once when twice is twice as nice?"

"That's the last time TRACE will pay you for anything," said the QB quietly. Hatch knew that tone. The calm before a storm.

"Oh, I dunno," said Sticks. "Wait and see. This ain't a trap. It's an opportunity."

"I'd like an opportunity," Stug scoffed, moving toward him. "Want to know what I'd like an opportunity for?"

The large, muddy man stepped between Sticks and the sergeant. The ferryman darted out of the way as Stug's grip found the scavenger's shoulders. But the older man dropped straight down, pulling Stug off balance. He fell forward, and the Wild One lifted with his legs, shouldering the big man in the gut. Surprised by the maneuver, Stug went airborne. He hit the ground hard, flattening the grass, then recovered and rolled up on one knee. The other man, a big, green, beardy grin on his face, stood ready to catch and flip him again. Stug hesitated, knowing he'd underestimated his opponent once already. The muddy man knew how to wrestle. But Stug wasn't prone to making the same mistake twice.

The Wild Ones aimed their weapons at the sergeant.

"Sure, hide behind your sticks and arrows. Big man with backup."

"Shutting it, Man Mountain," the muddy man said, his green grin fading. "Or flipping again, that's me."

"Stug, stand down," Hatch said.

Stug exhaled his fury, retreating a half step but no more.

"Ferryman going now."

"Oh, sure! I'm not one to overstay a welcome, no sir!" Turning to the QB, the near-toothless river man said with clear satisfaction, "I told you not to underestimate them." Then the menace in his voice was gone, replaced by a happy-go-lucky tone. "But no one listens to me, no sir! Well, y'all have a nice parlay now, ya hear? I wager I'll be seein' you again!" In a moment, Sticks had faded into the grass, a gummy whistle his herald.

The Wild One doing all the talking then turned to the QB. "Being leader here?" he asked.

"I'm in command, yes." The captain imbued a threat in her voice that her raised arms didn't much support. "Captain

Mary Brenneman."

"Name being Goa Eeguls," he said. "Needing to talking, we. Putting arms down now, you. Keeping hands from triggers. Or sticking you, that's us."

"Yes, we need to discuss where our food is," the QB said carefully, trying to establish some measure of power equity in the conversation.

Eeguls smiled, the green spittle making a bright curve in his beard. "Not knowing already? All your food belonging us."

Riverwalk

The Wild Ones escorted them out of the clearing. And strangely—an assessment everyone shared via BICE—the scavengers didn't demand the soldiers turn over their weapons. Like Sticks, their captors kept the trees overhead as often as possible, and in short order, the party passed over the wooded hill, picking up the group Hawkeye had spotted earlier. Within half an hour, they'd entered a short box canyon and followed a well-worn path to a cap rock resembling a thumb pointing at the sky. Below it, a camp nestled into the cliffs overlooking Pesky Creek.

The QB was fascinated as they passed into the community itself. *That's the word for it,* her inner voice said. *Not camp. Community.*

The Wild Ones had adapted the rock formations to form dwellings. Sheets of stone served as roofs for apartments, and caverns had become rooms. Naturally occurring gaps in the vertical rock of the cave walls formed windows fronting a common area. This central open space framed a foyer of flat stone structures where children played and adults tanned skins and tended fires with meat roasting over them. Stug's stomach began to growl again.

"I sure hope that's not people," he whispered to Hatch. The lieutenant passed him a glance that said, *Me too.*

"Walking this way, Man Mountain," Eeguls said, waving them past the children who stopped their play to gawk in fear and awe at the bulky soldiers passing by. Most of the children were captivated by the laser rifles; their simple, sleek industrial plastic was undoubtedly a stark contrast to the bumpy weapons of stone and wood they were used to seeing. Several of them stared openly at Stug, perhaps wondering if, as Eeguls had suggested, he'd come to life from the stone around them, a real, live Man Mountain.

Then Mary noticed a girl of about ten or twelve years old watching them from one of the cookfires. The girl refused to turn her eyes away, staring up defiantly at the uniformed, hard-cast woman walking by. Mary attempted a smile for her, perhaps seeing a reflection through time in the young girl's face. But the girl's eyes, so young to be so old, returned no kindness. Rather, their flinty flatness dared the stranger to make trouble for her people.

Not so very different, you and I, thought Mary to herself, her smile saddening at the corners. The girl's gaze tracked her warily as the soldiers of B Company moved deeper into the settlement.

They came to a formation stretching upward to a second floor. A graying man, cleaner cut than the others around him, sat working a huge knife along a piece of wood as he talked to other Wild Ones hunched in a circle. Their conversation quieted as the QB and her soldiers approached.

The gray man put the knife down and stood up from the group. He watched them approach, acknowledging Eeguls, who stopped before him and bowed slightly.

"Bringing them like you asking," said Eeguls.

"Appreciated," said the gray man. He gestured to the woman sitting next to him, and she handed Eeguls a leather satchel. "All the tobac you can chew."

"Many and much more thanks," said Eeguls, opening the bag and staring inside. He stuck his nose in and took a big whiff. As he looked back at the QB, the green spittle-smile stretched across his beard. "Easy-peasy." Then his face turned serious. "Being nice. Or getting the pointy end. Understanding?"

The captain's lips formed a thin line. "Understanding." Outwardly she was calm, even relaxed. To her squad, the QB sent *Stay alert, stay frosty* via BICE.

Eeguls nodded and, with one last gesture of respect to the gray man, wandered off into the camouflage of his community. Mary noted how the children jumped excitedly around him, a wizened wizard returning from the wide world with stories to tell.

"My name's Logan," said the gray man. "Please, sit down."

The QB regarded him coolly. That he was in charge was obvious from his easy, relaxed bearing. *The inverse of Obadiah Neville*, her inner voice said. A slight, knowing gaze played around his eyes, which she read as his acknowledgment that they were equals here. She sensed no threat, though the scavengers around them were well armed with knives, bows, and a few long rifles like the one Eeguls had carried.

"Mary Brenneman, captain of the Free Forces of New Pennsylvania," she returned. "You probably know us better as TRACE. And I prefer to stand." Her men followed her lead. All stood at an easy parade rest, hands resting casually near their weapons.

Logan shrugged. "Suit yourself. But it's harder to eat standing up." He returned himself to a seated, cross-legged position.

"Nice knife," the QB said, measuring the blade with her eyes.

The gray man picked up the machete-like knife he'd been whittling with when they'd arrived. Its twenty-inch blade made it seem more like a short sword of the ancient world, but its clipped point defined it technically as a knife. Silver sunlight reflected off the steel, a clear sign that it was diligently cared for, though its rough edge showed it was sharpened and used often.

"Thanks. It's called a Bowie knife. Named after a famous knife-fighter from a long time ago. Handed down in my family since God knows when."

He sheathed it. *Probably to show he means us no harm,* the QB guessed. She didn't relax an inch.

"I know who you are, by the way," he continued. "And, obviously, why you're here."

Stug's stomach growled.

"Does that gut of yours ever shut up?" Bracer whispered.

"Only when its mouth is full."

Logan overheard and chuckled. It was a good-natured

sound. Nevertheless, the QB maintained her vigilance.

"Your men are hungry, Captain. Please, sit and eat. After all, we're the ones who took your supplies. We should at least offer you a meal, no?"

He was trying to be humorous, but the QB's face showed she was in no mood for joking. Still, she considered it. If they were truly here to parlay, as Sticks had suggested, then maybe they shouldn't refuse the hospitality.

Nothing more important than getting those supplies back, her inner voice reminded her.

"If we wanted you dead," Logan said in all sincerity, "you'd already be that way. And we certainly wouldn't have let you keep your weapons."

He makes a good point, Hatch sent via BICE.

"Very well, then," said the QB, nodding permission to her soldiers. Two of them took up position on either side of her, as the space allowed, before sitting down. Even on their butts, Alpha Squad had arranged themselves tactically, in case events took a wrong turn. Stug sat directly behind the captain, a blocker protecting his quarterback.

Several Wild Ones brought over small baskets of food. Roasted deer, cooked carrots and potatoes, even fresh bread and churned butter. Not overly generous portions, but fresh and hot. Stug's gut groaned louder than ever at nirvana's nearness.

"Since you know why we're here, would you please tell me why you took our food?" asked the QB.

"Eat first," said Logan easily. "Else we'll never hear one another over the mountain's stomach begging to be fed."

Another ten or fifteen minutes won't matter, suggested Hatch in her head.

"Thank you," she acknowledged, taking a bite of the roast deer. Making small talk, she said, "Obviously, this is more than a camping ground. I thought the scavengers were supposed to be migratory."

"We prefer the term salvagers," Logan corrected her. "Moving around is becoming more dangerous by the day." Motioning to the stone buildings around them, he said, "We call this place Bedrock."

While her men chowed down, the QB took a few moments to assess the situation. For the squad's benefit, she used their shared channel. *Obviously, this is where they live.* She cast her eyes around again to confirm the camp wasn't transient. This place had been their captors' home for a while. *That we haven't been harmed and still have our weapons suggests they want something for the food. Else they'd have killed us outright rather than risk losing it to us in a fight.*

Agreed, sent back Hatch.

They took a big risk bringing us here, noted Hawkeye. *Showing us the location of this place without even putting blindfolds on us.*

The captain clicked an acknowledgment in her head. *We need to figure out what they want.*

Logan smiled at the seemingly quiet squad. "Sharing thoughts on why you're here, I imagine," he said.

Mary barely avoided showing her surprise. Stug laughed out loud, a muted greasy sound. He'd never had much of a poker face.

"I used to be a TRACE espionage agent," Logan said, rescuing them from their sudden paranoia. "I infiltrated places like this village all the time. Many years ago, before the SOMA even broke the BICE codes." He wiped a piece of bread in the deer grease and took a bite.

That explains a lot, sent Hatch on the channel. *Better spoken than most of these folks, better educated. More strategically minded.*

He took us without a shot and has us eating a meal with him in minutes, sent Bracer. *Gotta admire that.*

"How did you end up with these—with the Wild Ones?" the QB asked. Scavengers they might be, but they didn't refer to themselves as such, as Logan himself had said. Negotiations 101. Speak to the other party on their own terms.

"I wanted a simpler life. I got tired of the constant battles. And the constant losing."

That was something Mary understood. Despite TRACE's long-term success in the war with Transport—the resistance still existed, after all—they were perennially behind the power curve. Until now. Though they'd technically been routed at Gettysburg, the rebels had still come away with a cargo ship full of okcillium. Now most of their fighters were on an equal footing with the Authority, at least in terms of weaponry. Time and resources were not on their side, however.

"So this is your home now?" she asked.

Logan nodded. "For many years. But it's not like it used to be. Transport is now actively trying to eradicate the Wild Ones. Before, they ignored us. We existed technically outside the law, but no one really cared. Now, we're another thumb in the Authority's eye. They're even losing patience with the Amish since the AZers are such reliable, if covert, supporters of the resistance. No one is safe now. No one."

"Why are we here, Mr. Logan?" the captain asked.

"No 'mister,'" he said. "We don't use titles here. Of any kind."

Stug grunted.

"You have an opinion, Sergeant?" asked Logan.

"Clearly you're their leader," said the big man. "So you have a hierarchy."

"We have functional, practical relationships. These people asked me to guide them a long time ago. I have done so. But I claim no title for the honor."

"You haven't answered my question," said the QB. She tapped her rifle. "You've left us our weapons. You've brought us here in apparent friendship and fed us. What are you buttering us up for?"

Logan laughed out loud again. "Direct! I like that. And you couldn't have chosen a more apt way to phrase your question."

The QB raised an eyebrow.

"Are you familiar with the phrase 'guns and butter'?" asked Logan.

The captain turned to Hawkeye, who was like a human encyclopedia when it came to military trivia.

"It's a phrase from the Old Planet," he said. "It refers to a government's need to strike a balance between buying enough food to feed its citizens and enough weapons to defend them. Too little of one, you have a revolution. Too little of the other, you get conquered."

"My God," said Logan. "Did he come out of the box like that?"

Stug chuckled.

"Okay, so you've taught me a new phrase," said the QB. "How does it apply here?"

Logan smiled at her from under his brows, finally ready to share his secret. "I have butter," he said, winking. "I need guns."

Neville will serve you up with a side *of butter is what he'll do,* said Hatch in her head as they marched.

Logan had given them their space to talk over whether or not they'd help him. His plan was to go to the City and, with their help, steal the guns the Wild Ones needed directly from Transport. The plan was bold, something the QB liked. But it was also dangerous and something Neville would never approve of. Worse, in Hatch's eyes, Logan refused to take any Wild Ones with them. Should things go sideways, he wanted no trace of their involvement, lest Transport exact revenge by finding and exterminating Bedrock.

More than anything else, what had convinced the QB to help the salvagers was Logan's willingness to explain his people's needs while leaving B Company armed and dangerous among their children. Hatch had tried to convince her otherwise, something no one else would've dared, but with no success so far. And since the plan required they wait until darkness to enter the City, they had spent most of the day debating it. Now, as they marched beneath the trees in the late afternoon sun, Hatch attempted one last time to convince her what a mistake this was.

I wish you'd stop trying to change my mind, she said on the private comm channel she'd opened with him. *We need that food. And what he's proposing will arm an ally for us. I don't see a downside.*

Then you're damned shortsighted, replied Hatch. He touched her arm, and they let the rest of Alpha Squad buffer the distance between themselves and Logan. He looked directly into her eyes and sent, *Have you considered that arming these people with advanced weapons might not be a good idea? An ally today. An enemy tomorrow, maybe.*

She had considered it, yes. He was right, of course. In politics, allies became enemies faster than drunken porters traded bedfellows at a City brothel. But that didn't change TRACE's need for those supplies.

I'm worried about TRACE soldiers starving today, she replied. *If by arming the Wild Ones we can weaken Transport one iota, I'll not only hand them the weapons, I'll load them myself. Besides, Logan has pledged security for future shipments from the AZ.* Out loud, staring hard into his eyes, she said, "I'll ask one last time, Sean. Do you support me or not?"

Her voice, as usual, had its intended effect.

Sighing, he said, "Always."

Finally, the debate was over. They hurried to catch up to the others as they neared the banks of the Susquehanna.

"Here we are," said Logan ahead of them. When the QB saw where his finger pointed, she felt like he'd shown her the punch line to a day-long joke.

The smile on Sticks's face was broad and disturbing in its toothlessness. "Told ya I'd be seein' ya again!"

"Seriously?" Bracer couldn't believe it himself.

"Oh sure! Gimme lip!" Sticks said. "And after I set it up so nice for you to get all your supplies back."

Hatch glanced guardedly at the QB. *Still think this is a good idea?*

In answer, and after only a moment's hesitation, she stepped onto the old man's ferry. It was a small side-wheeler with a bridge and aft quarters, a smaller version of the historic riverboats from the Old Planet. Her soldiers followed her. The waterline barely rose as they climbed aboard; the ferry was used to carrying cargo heavier even than Stug.

Trick approached the dock. He'd done a good job hiding the rest of Bestimmung Company. Until they came out from under their camouflaged canopies, the stillness on the banks around the docks had been broken only by the croaking of frogs and the ballet of water dancers.

"Captain, looks like you're not done with your trip yet," said Brevet-Captain Mason.

"Right, Lieutenant. Come aboard. I'll brief you."

As Trick stepped onto the ferry, he didn't think he liked what he saw in Hatch's body language. And after the QB introduced Logan and explained the plan to secure the Transport weapons from Columbia, he was sure of it.

"The only way to get these people their weapons is to break into Transport's *armory*? Inside the City?"

"Unless you have a better idea," said the QB. "I'm all ears."

"Can't we just smuggle guns out from Pook?"

"And power them how?" asked the captain. "TRACE will never release the okcy we took at Gettysburg for that purpose. The only cache of laser rifles with batteries this side of the Great Ridge is in Columbia."

Trick admitted he had no better option for securing weapons for the salvagers. He wasn't happy, she knew, but he'd follow her orders.

"Once we're away and committed, Logan's people will deliver the supplies to you. Expect a flat barge to come down the creek, loaded with what's left from the three wagons. It should be here in six hours. Secure it and have Charlie and Delta squads escort it to the island. Hold this position with Bravo and Echo until we return, or until oh-four-hundred, whichever comes first."

Trick acknowledged her order. "But what do I tell Neville? He's due an update at sundown. I fended him off earlier, but he'll want details on your progress."

"Tell him you don't have any. He'll believe that. He's used to my mavericking."

Trick nodded reluctantly. She had no doubt he planned to practice his report before giving it. Or that he was uncomfortable lying to a superior officer. Even Neville.

"We could take the food from these people," Pusher said, stepping onto the ferry. "It's ours by right, and we have the firepower."

The QB stared Pusher square in the face—really for the first time since the day after the battle that had taken the lives of her squadmates. That day they'd both stood in the bar, consoling one another with words of salt and steel.

"Sure, we could do that," the captain replied. Her voice carried. She wanted Logan to hear, to understand why, exactly, TRACE was willing to help. "And make a new enemy. Or, we have the chance to make an ally instead, and impede Transport in the process. It's a no-brainer, Sergeant Ellis."

Pusher said, "I know. I just wanted to hear you say it, ma'am. I like to know what I'm fighting for and why these days. It makes a difference."

Mary understood Pusher's need to know. Specifically, her need to know that their objective was worth the cost. Something Pusher, as much as anyone, understood personally. The damnable thing about it was, you never knew the cost till fate had exacted it.

"And I'd like to go with," said Pusher.

The QB observed her for a moment. "Why?"

The question was simple and direct, its tenor unforgiving. As it needed to be.

The sergeant paused before answering.

"Is it because you have one of those 'I lost my squad and I feel guilty' death wishes?" pressed the captain. "Because we'll have enough on our hands with Transport. I don't have time to babysit you, too."

Hatch narrowed his eyes at Mary. There it was again, that uncaring, aloof attitude he both admired and loathed in her. Even Stug stopped what he was doing and watched the two women.

"No, ma'am," said Pusher, not the least bit put off by her captain's icy challenge. "But you might need an extra hand.

And I'm tired of sitting on my ass all day."

Stug's hooting drowned out the frogs.

Mary allowed herself a bleak smile. "Smoker, can I borrow your sergeant for a few hours?"

Lieutenant Gray made a *whatever* sign. "Not much going on around here, ma'am."

The QB said, "Trick, we'll be back by oh-four-hundred. If we're not, get the rest of B Company back to Little Gibraltar. And I expect that brevet rank might be made permanent."

"Don't say that, ma'am," admonished Trick.

"You're too superstitious," she teased, though secretly she was touched when her soldiers showed they genuinely cared for her. "We'll see you in a few hours. Come on, Pusher."

"Welcome to Alpha Squad," Stug said to Ellis. "Consider it a temporary promotion. Don't expect my position to open up anytime soon."

"Honestly, Stug," said Pusher, looking down in approving appraisal, "I could never fill your shoes."

The big man smiled and clapped her on the shoulder.

The soldiers got their river legs as Sticks made ready to cast off. Logan asked him, "How long till we reach the City?"

"Coupla hours," estimated the ferryman. "Should be full-on dark by then."

Logan nodded. "The darker, the better," he said.

As night came on, the *Pittsburgh*—a name Sticks insisted fit his workhorse vessel to a T—rolled up the Susquehanna, its single paddlewheel stroking against the current. The ferry's smokestack puffed black clouds that were almost invisible in the night, and the low rush of the river masked the slow churning of the ferry's small steam engine. To anyone on the riverbank, the *Pittsburgh*'s dark wood painted black with pitch would appear as only a specter gliding over the water.

Logan walked the small deck fitfully. B Company's soldiers lazed around, mostly because standing upright threatened to bring up the meal he'd fed them earlier. When Logan finally lit on the bow, staring forward toward the City, the QB joined him.

"I can have Hawkeye scan ahead more often, if you like," she said to break the ice.

The Wild Ones' leader gave a half smile, though she couldn't see from where she stood. "That's okay. I'm a deal-with-it-as-it-comes kinda guy."

"Comes in handy in the spy business, I guess," she said.

He looked at her, the low moonlight etching his face with frown lines. "I'm not a spy anymore. I told you that."

After a couple of breaths, Mary said, "I suspect that's a little like leaving the military. You can muster out, but you never stop sitting with your back to the wall."

Logan's voice sounded cheerless when he said, "Too true." He stood up and began pacing again. It was a short walk in the narrow bow.

"So, what's wrong?" she asked.

"Ah, there's that directness. Have I told you how much I like that quality about you?"

"I think you just did. For the second time."

A flit of moonlit gray at his temples showed her he was nodding. "I don't know you from Eve," he said suddenly.

"She's a lot older. Also, I've never trusted snakes."

Logan cracked a genuine smile at that. He settled again on the bow's gunwale.

"My people are caught between—not just a rock and a hard place—*everything*. They scrape for every scrap they can find. Unlike the Amish, they produce nothing, so Transport sees them as useless parasites on the system. At worst, we're a threat because, well, we must want what they have, right? That's the way the people in power always think. They fear covetousness because they got where they are by *being* covetous. The Amish don't trust us, but then the Amish don't trust anyone, really. 'Love everyone, trust no one.' And who can blame them? And TRACE…" He let it hang there, an invitation for her to say something and make him believe the resistance was different somehow, more noble perhaps in its motivations.

"Part of that is your reputation," she said, not taking the bait. She didn't like giving anyone exactly what they wanted. Doing so made her feel weak. "People think you're cannibals. That you ambush Plain People and steal their food and take them back to your cookfires and make Pacifist Pies for supper."

"Only two-thirds of that is true," said Logan sardonically. "And even that part—taking from others, just to be clear—is the exception, not the rule. But I take your point. We encourage the rumors, of course. About cannibalism."

Interesting, thought Mary. "Why?"

"It isn't obvious?" The *Pittsburgh* climbed over a

particularly foamy rush of river water before settling down again to the comforting chugga-chugga-chugga of its engine. "Ever wanted to be left alone? So much so that you snipe and snarl at anyone who comes around you?"

The QB turned her head away from him so he wouldn't see the bitter grin on her face. "Never. I'm not like that. I love all mankind all the time."

"Yeah, well, good for you," Logan replied bitterly, missing her sarcasm. "We don't have that luxury. We've cultivated what others think of us very carefully. If people think you'll eat them if they bother you, they tend to leave you alone. Honestly, our reputation as savages is all we've got."

Mary thought about that. Transport had weapons, personnel, technology, and a dogged desire for control. TRACE would have fallen before the Authority long ago but for luck and the SOMA's technowizardry. She tried to weigh what it must be like to be a Wild One in that reality. Skins on your back, Stone Age weapons to hunt with, and no place to call home but whatever nature provided. She recalled the Wild Ones' simple, stone apartments and the wild deer roasting on the fires. And how enthralled the children had been to see the soldiers in their midst. Enthralled, or simply terrified? She recalled her mirror image out of time, the girl with the defiant stare, daring the armed stranger to raise her laser rifle against them. If the captain had, what could the little warrior have done about it? Stabbed her with daggers from her young eyes? And that girl and all she knew of her family and community, every bit of it, was protected only by an illusion. A myth.

"I see now why the guns are so important to you," she said

quietly.

"Without them, we'll die," Logan said with grave surety. "Transport is eliminating anyone it perceives as a threat to its ultimate power. The Wild Ones are just rats in their grand scheme of things, but they've already begun moving against us, with one goal: extermination. You saw the field where Eeguls found you. And if they've gotten so aggressive as to come after the rats ... well, I wouldn't be surprised to see the City go eventually."

"Go?"

Logan sighed, the sound lost as the water shushed against the ferry. "When you have a cancer, you cut it out to save the body."

"Destroy the City?" Mary asked, as if saying the words could make them somehow more believable. "That's crazy." The sudden realization that murdering an entire city full of people wasn't beyond Transport after all sent a shiver up the back of her neck. "Do you know this for a fact? Is Transport planning it?"

"I used to be a spy, remember? I hear things when we scavenge. It's not a plan, as far as I know—yet. But whispers of a Final Solution to the TRACE problem are out there. Take that intel back to your superiors, Captain. Nothing is beyond the Authority. *Nothing.*"

She had always thought the same. But to destroy the City? Could even Transport be that desperate? That evil?

The deck thumped. Mary turned her shocked face toward Hatch as he approached. She quickly put her QB mask in place. She didn't think he'd seen.

"Sticks says to be quiet. We're getting close to ears friendly to Transport."

Logan gave him a sad smile. "Time to be a mouse, not a rat, Lieutenant?"

"What?"

"Never mind," the captain told him. "Private joke."

"Ah. Well. Mouse or cockroach, take your pick. But shut up. Ma'am." He wandered away again to leave them to their privacy and its jokes.

"You let all your soldiers talk to you like that?" asked Logan.

She sighed, grateful for the distraction from her own thoughts. "No. Just him."

"Ah…" In that one syllable, all understanding.

"It's not like that," she said defensively.

"Not anymore, I take it," he answered with half a laugh. The water soon swallowed the sound and they were silent again for a moment.

"We'll get you your guns," she whispered.

Logan nodded but said nothing.

Warpath

Sticks cut the engine for their approach to the dock. Momentum carried the *Pittsburgh* forward, and its captain swung wide to starboard to avoid a collision. The ferry barely nudged the pier before the old man hopped across and began to tie her off.

The lights of the City glinted off the Susquehanna a quarter mile upstream. The old dock Sticks had tied them to looked to have been abandoned for years. No homes, no farms, no lights. Just the sounds of the natural world settling down for the night.

"The target is half a klick inside the City," the QB reminded them as they hopped across to the pier. Stug and Bracer needed a moment to get their land legs back.

"Are you sure this man of yours inside is reliable?" asked Hatch.

"The distractions he has planned will pull the patrols away from the river entrance," said Logan, as if that answered the question. "Once they're preoccupied, we'll go in through the sewer, like I said before."

"And like *I* said before, that still sounds—" began Stug.

"Don't say it again!" ordered Hatch.

"—like a crappy plan to me." Whatever seasickness he'd suffered onboard the *Pittsburgh* had evidently passed.

As usual, the QB was short on patience and ready to move. "Let's go."

Logan and B Company followed her along the river's edge. They made sure to keep to the shadows until they reached a copse of trees from which they could observe the sewer entrance. Four large steel gates attached to chains protected the City from entrance via the river, while allowing the water and the refuse it carried to flow out.

They waited. There was the sound of an explosion from the City's interior. Then a second. And a third. Three different locations, each deep inside the heart of Columbia.

Alarms wailed. Lights came up, stretching out across the river and its surrounding banks. From their current position, they could hear the bustle of Transport troops stationed along the wall moving to high tactical alert.

"We move," said Logan. "*Now.*"

He led them out of cover, shuffling low and hugging the river's edge. Hatch glanced at the QB. "I guess there's no turning back now," he said, then ran after their ally. The infiltrators soon formed a line under the City's wall where it met the riverbank. Searchlights passed over them as a fourth explosion erupted inside Columbia. This one sounded closer, no more than a few blocks from their current position.

"And now..." Logan sounded like a magician willing his assistant to reappear inside an empty box.

A screech of metal on metal made them all cringe. One of the steel gates began to ascend to their right as they stood, backs flat against Columbia's wall. Two feet above the river's surface, it stopped.

"It's not going to get any higher," said Logan, starting to move.

"*Wait*." Hatch put a hand on Logan's arm, forced him back against the wall. "Bracer, count it."

"One-Mississippi. Two-Mississippi. Three-Mississippi."

"Hawkeye."

The unit's spotter directed his omni-lens up and along the length of the wall above them. No heat sigs. No movement of any kind.

"Nada."

"Can we go now?" asked Logan. "Or would you rather stay here till the guards return and actually start observing the river again?"

"Hawkeye, take point," ordered Stug.

The spotter moved slowly into the chilly river. The smell was horrendous this close to the City, and the water saturated their uniforms. Bracer and Pusher went next. Holding their laser rifles above their heads, the three slipped one at a time behind the steel gate and under the City wall. Hatch and the QB brought up the rear.

"Couldn't you have stolen our food in August?" Bracer's teeth chattered around the question.

"We'll be out soon enough," answered Logan.

Behind the gate, the sewer passage was lined only with dim lights. They were grateful for that. Smelling the sludge they pushed their way through was bad enough. Seeing it any better would only add to the fun.

Logan found a ladder ascending to a gantry, and liquid filth drained off him as he hauled himself up.

"Hurry up, Sergeant," he said, reaching down for Stug. "We need to close it again before someone notices it's open."

One by one they gained the catwalk as Logan found the manual override controls for the sewer gate. Thirty seconds later, the screeching metal was lowered back into place.

The QB noticed her soldiers had begun wagging their heads; she felt it too. Transport jamming apparently covered the length and breadth of the City, even beneath it. "BICEs off," she said. "Visual communication only."

"I sure hope the rest of your plan is sound," said Hatch to Logan, clicking off his device. "'Cause it's all on you now."

"I used to do this all the time," said Logan. "Trust me."

Logan led them out of the sewer through a manhole and into a dim alley. Damp stone walls reached two stories high on either side of them. One building, the ex-TRACE spy told them, was Transport's armory. The other was a flophouse for migrant workers from the cities of the Great Shelf, employed in Transport's factories not far from here.

The fall air drew a shroud of coldness around them as it funneled down the alley. "Fifteen minutes since the last explosion," said Logan. "They're as out of position as they're gonna get." They spotted no porters around the building or in the area; they must have been drawn away to deal with the bombs. Logan's plan was working.

The lieutenant positioned Hawkeye and Bracer on the roof of the flophouse opposite the armory's back door, its most vulnerable spot. Without his heavy machine gun, Bracer held position with only his laser rifle and sidearm, aided by his spotter. They stood above, watching the locked back door, which was painted red as a clear message to the locals to stay away. Hawkeye tracked his omni-lens constantly left and right, up and down. When he gave the signal, Logan and the QB joined them on the roof.

Hatch was careful to stay in the shadows, away from Transport's security cameras. Those all-seeing eyes monitored most of the City's roads and alleys, one more way the Authority controlled movement. He searched quietly through a trash container for camouflage, coming up with a huge cotton blanket. He cut a head-sized hole out of it, then draped it over Stug. With his broad shoulders beneath the makeshift poncho, he looked like a circus tent with a head attached. But at least the blanket masked his weapons.

"Is this really necessary?" whined the sergeant.

"Nope. Well, unless you want to survive the first ten seconds of this little play. Then yep."

Stug wrinkled his nose. "It smells awful."

"That's okay, so do you. Think of it as an opportunity to practice your method acting."

"Hey, look on the bright side, Sarge," said Pusher. "You get to punch people in the first act."

The sergeant smiled. "Glass is half full, then."

Mindful of the security camera scanning the back entrance, Hatch and Pusher quickly crossed the alleyway, setting themselves up opposite Stug some thirty feet from the red door. They would cover the back entrance while Stug did his bit.

Once in position, the lieutenant assessed the flophouse roof. The QB and Logan would be hunched down along the wall by now, preparing to leap across to the armory. Hawkeye's omni-lens dipped once, twice, the moonlight twinkling briefly off its glass.

All clear.

"You're on, Falstaff," Hatch whispered.

Stug splayed himself against the building in his circus poncho. Still hidden in a slice of shadow cut by the moon across the stone behind him, he waited patiently as the security camera panned across the alley. When it pointed directly away from him, Stug staggered forward.

The camera whirred, its motion sensor tracking the monotony of the empty alley on its return arc. A jerky shadow made it stop. Stug's irregular mass slowly took shape as he moved into the light.

"Citizen," came the computerized voice, impossibly huge, from the small speaker below the camera eye. "You have entered a restricted area. By order of the Transport Authority, you will leave immediately or face prosecution by a duly appointed magistrate."

Stug continued his jaunty progress. He took note of the order, jerked to the left, and fell into a mass of refuse bins. He lifted himself unsteadily to his feet and, mouthing gibberish, resumed his progress down the alley.

"Citizen, this facility is off-limits," said the voice. "Once before a magistrate, representation for your defense will not be provided. You will be tried for sedition for failing to leave a restricted area. This is your final warning."

Stug reached the door. He struck the reinforced metal with his fists.

Pound. Pound. Pound.

Then he began to cry-sing in the slurring voice of desperate loneliness only a drunken male can muster. "I shee a red door … and I hwant to pain'it black."

Pound. Pound. Pound.

"Lemme in, mothuh!" he shouted. "Pleashhhhhh!"

Pound. Pound. Pound.

"I wanna see Jonah! Mothuhhhhhh!" His baritone voice reverberated against the surrounding stone, a church bell's echo in an expansive belfry.

Tumblers turned. Stug staggered back six inches so he was no longer leaning on the red metal. With a creak of its heavy hinges, the armory door swung open. Two Transport soldiers stood ready, laser rifles trained on the intruder.

"Wha? You're hnot my mothuh." He looked beyond them. "Where'sh Jonah? Where'sh my dog?"

"I don't know where you think you are, fat man, but this isn't your home," barked one of the soldiers.

With a flit of his eyes, Stug noted the lieutenant's insignia across the pocket of the man's uniform. *You're the one I need to worry about, then*, he thought.

"But I guess you could say we're your keepers now,"

sneered the lieutenant. "Down on the ground, lard ass."

Stug affected a delayed reaction of hurt, affront, and detached ignorance, all at the same time. "That wasshn't very nishe."

"Christ, he *stinks*, Lieutenant." The other soldier was younger, likely not long out of Transport's boot camp for porters.

"Vermin like this always do," replied the officer. Returning his attention to the swaying circus freak in front of him, the officer shouted, "Ground! Now!"

The drunk trespasser suddenly slipped and fell, crying out as his right knee cracked on the cement. The younger soldier instinctively moved forward, putting out an arm to try and steady the smelly bastard who'd interrupted an otherwise quiet watch.

"No, wait!" the lieutenant warned.

Stug threw back the poncho, easily grabbing the inexperienced soldier and pulling him off balance. As he moved, the sergeant heard Bracer take out the security camera over his head with a single laser blast, right on cue. The big man's calves flexed as he stood, hauling the soldier in front of him off the ground, a human shield. The lieutenant's blast took the young porter square in the back. Grunting with effort, Stug shoved the soldier's body straight at the lieutenant, who pulled his trigger again wildly, blasting the floor.

Stug roared like a giant chasing would-be thieves from his treasure room. He fell upon the enemy officer, who was struggling to aim at the drunken vagrant who'd become a whooping demon and charged him from the doorway. The sergeant ripped the laser rifle out of the officer's hands and threw it behind him through the door. Terror blazed in the lieutenant's eyes as two huge meat hooks reached down for him. Stug grabbed him by the front of his uniform, hauled him from beneath the dead trooper, then set him down on his feet, light as a kitten.

Both men paused. The unarmed porter officer seemed confused by his sudden good fortune. Stug centered himself. It then dawned on the lieutenant what was coming, but he could only stand there, paralyzed with fascination and fear. Stug swung a haymaker that knocked his foe the length of the corridor. The fact that he'd been an officer, and a Transport officer at that, made the sergeant's face nearly break in half with a smile.

Stug stepped forward as the floor's friction brought the lieutenant to a squeaking stop. The man groaned and tried to get his hands under him. Stug aimed and fired. He hated dispatching even an enemy soldier so dispassionately, but the plan needed both the guards dead. Turning toward the door, he said, "You can come in now. The heavy lifting's done."

Pusher came through first, while Hatch paused briefly to give a hand signal to the others on the flophouse roof. Three seconds later, the QB and Logan were leaping across to the armory while Bracer and Hawkeye maintained their overwatch position, protecting the red door and their means of escape.

"Nice acting job," said Hatch. "You were certainly convincing as a stinking, loveless drunk with no hope for your future."

"Real life is the crucible for good acting," replied Stug.

"Which way from here, sir?" Pusher asked impatiently. She wasn't used to mid-crisis bantering.

"Guns in the basement," answered Hatch. "Logan says we should have ten minutes before Transport reinforcements arrive back here from the bomb sites."

From above, they heard a small, muffled explosion. That would be the QB, blowing the door on the roof in full view of Transport's cameras. With two points of ingress now on the enemy's collective mind, they'd theoretically be confused in their response—and since the camera observing the alleyway was destroyed, Transport would have no way of knowing how many of the enemy they faced from the ground. Hopefully, they'd focus on the two infiltrators they could see via their roof cameras, and the diversion would provide Hatch and his crew the time they needed to secure the weapons from the basement vault. According to Logan's timetable, they now had nine minutes to get it done.

Motioning Pusher to take point, Stug shed his poncho. Beyond a short entry corridor, branches went right and left. Logan's intel had indicated the secured basement with Authority weapons would be to the right. The left would be the way the enemy would come at them.

"Make sandbags," Hatch ordered Pusher, indicating the two deceased porters. Stug had already begun dragging the young trooper's corpse to lay across the left hallway. Pusher grabbed the dead lieutenant, and Stug helped her haul him on top of the other dead man. She went prone behind their stacked protection, watching the approach from the left.

"Let's go," Hatch said to Stug, heading to the right.

The QB and Logan got twenty feet inside the building, to the top of the stairwell, before the first laser fire shot toward them. Transport's response had been nearly instantaneous. As soon as they'd blown the door, klaxons had blared around them, drowning out all other sound but weapons fire.

They sheltered against the wall, both breathing hard. The captain quickly scouted the stairs leading down, saw at least one shadow also holding position from cover. But she and Logan couldn't afford to hold here. They had to move into a better position to lock down more of Transport's response teams and keep the heat off the others below.

She glanced below again, saw the shadow-soldier start to move, and popped her rifle around the corner without aiming. With the alarms blaring against the walls of the stairwell, she had no idea if she'd gotten lucky and hit anything.

Only one way to find out, her inner self said in a voice that sounded like Hatch's. And that annoyed her enough to fire her up.

She swept her rifle around the corner again, *crack-crack-cracked* the area below with laser fire, then thrust herself out of cover and knelt at the top of the stairs. She was exposed but able to see the entire stairwell below. Black marks from her blind fire pocked the wall as if Picasso had shot them. Her heart beat like a hammer in her chest, her blood pounding loud enough in her ears to drown out the klaxons momentarily.

The slow motion of battle kicked in as she saw the tip of the porter's rifle turn the corner. Though her profile presented the smallest target to the enemy, Mary felt like a wooden doppelgänger on the firing range just waiting to be split in two.

Arms came into view, bringing the laser rifle to bear.

The QB took careful aim.

She could see the enemy's upper torso now, his eye sighting along his rifle. She could feel his finger tensing on the trigger.

She exhaled.

Both fired, but the QB had been a hair's breadth faster. The porter's shot went wild as he jerked backward against the wall, already dead but still in motion. The QB took half a breath to realize she was unhurt, then grabbed one of three sonic grenades she carried, popped its clip, and tossed it at the body.

"Cover your ears!" she shouted at Logan above the sirens.

There was no sound as the grenade went off, since the explosion was at a frequency beyond human hearing. But it attacked the inner ear of anyone in range, causing acute vertigo and excruciating pain. The QB counted it out, then launched herself to her feet, pulled Logan to his, and swung down the stairs, her rifle targeted at center-mass height. As they rounded the corner, they encountered two Authority soldiers lying in the stairwell, hands covering their ears, faces contorted. Two quick pulls of Mary's trigger dispatched them both.

"You've done this before," said Logan.

The klaxons still sounded, but their ears had begun to adjust to the constant noise.

"A few times," she replied, "but it's been a while."

"Couldn't tell."

He bent down to the dead soldiers and rifled through their equipment. Handing one of their laser rifles over for her to sling on her back, Logan stashed the other two inside a netting bag. Three more prizes from their raid, assuming they made it out again.

Waste not, want not, said Hatch in her head. Having Hatch on BICE was bad enough sometimes. For her inner self to adopt his voice for its own made her more uncomfortable than staring down the sights of a Transport laser rifle ever could.

The QB noticed that the weapon Logan chose to wield was a .45-caliber automatic pistol he'd taken off one of the dead soldiers. He stuck a second one in his belt. Then she remembered how long ago it was that he'd done covert ops for TRACE ... long before even Transport had commonly carried laser weapons.

Kickin' it old school, her inner voice said in Hatch's I know-something-you-don't, sexy tone.

Okay, stop that, Mary pleaded.

They took up opposite positions on either side of the closed door leading onto the second floor. The QB stared at Logan, then flicked her eyes meaningfully at the nearest soldier's dead body.

"Oh," said the ex-spy, snapping to her unspoken command. "Been a while for me, too."

He knelt, grabbed the corpse under the armpits, and leaned the soldier against the wall next to the door. In one hand, Logan held his .45-caliber. In the other, he held the dead man's hand poised over the door's swipe pad. The captain nodded, knelt, and pulled the pin on a second sonic grenade.

Logan passed the still-useful palm over the pad, and they heard the snick of the door's release. He grabbed its handle and pulled it three inches open. The QB tossed the grenade in, and Logan slammed the door shut, nearly taking her fingers off.

"Sorry. Rusty."

"Uh-huh."

She counted it off, then nodded, and he swiped the corpse's hand over the pad again. The QB quickly pushed the corpse out of their way as Logan opened the door.

Laser fire blasted from their right. The sonic grenade must've missed at least one of its targets. Any movement into the corridor would face heavy, unceasing fire from the right. There was more than one porter pinning them down.

The captain assessed their situation. Theirs was a tactical diversion, not the primary mission. As long as they kept Transport tied up on the upper floor, they'd achieved that objective. But two people stuck in one doorway halved their ability to do that.

She flitted her eyes across the hallway. That door was closed and locked by a swipe pad, exactly like the one they'd just come through. But they needed to establish a second firing arc if they had any chance of holding Transport's attention here.

"Do we need to go any further?" asked Logan, knowing their tactical situation as well as she did. "Haven't we done our job?"

"Almost. You still got that Bowie knife?"

"We should've brought more grunts," said Stug, loading an okcillium battery into a twelfth laser rifle. "More grunts, more boxes."

"More grunts, more casualties. In small, out fast."

Stug paused.

"Don't *even* go there," said Hatch.

"Bah, you're no fun," said the sergeant, putting another rifle, battery installed, into the autonomous airbox.

The AAB was a supply drone with the capacity to carry a score of laser rifles. It operated much like an airbus, only on a much smaller scale. By programming the AABs with specific GIS coordinates, Authority Command could quick-flight supplies of weapons, munitions, or whatever else its soldiers needed in the field, even while combat raged around them. That capability provided a huge tactical advantage over TRACE. But in this situation, that kind of programming was less than helpful. If Alpha Squad input coordinates into the AAB, it would carry its payload along the most direct route to reach its objective. Great for getting supplies to soldiers as soon as possible with friendly combat drones clearing a flight path; terrible for keeping covert operations like this one under the radar.

"I still hate the idea of having this damned thing follow me like a puppy," said Stug, his signature nasality creeping into his voice. "I don't trust technology to know what it's doing."

"Quit complaining and get those batteries installed."

Pusher was upstairs, Hatch knew, buying them time. They'd heard intermittent fire from the first floor, but the fact that it continued told them she was still in action. Small consolation when your escape route depended on one trained sergeant keeping her head down at the right time.

There it was again, the sound of friendly fire quickly answered by the enemy. The age-old dance of opposing soldiers, mere feet apart, engaging in corridor warfare: a look around a corner, quick snap fire, and ducking back into cover. Each hoping for the other to poke their head up at precisely the wrong moment. Pusher was good and she was brave, but the law of averages wasn't in her favor. Eventually she'd make a mistake.

"I'm going up there," Hatch said. "Get the batteries installed and tote the AAB upstairs. Whistle to let me know when you're ready to move."

"We promised two crates, forty laser rifles," said Stug.

"They'll have to settle for half," breathed Hatch. "It's too hot in here. Double-time it."

Stug nodded. If Hatch was feeling the itch to bug out, the time for joking was over. Now the mathematics of battle became a simple matter of subtraction on both sides of the equation—of killing the other guy before he killed you. Honor and medals and tales for grandchildren came later. If you lived.

Hatch mounted the stairs from the basement and knelt at the doorway to the first floor. He quick-glanced, saw Pusher still prostrate, her laser rifle wedged between the bodies of the Transport soldiers. Even from behind the door, he could see that the blasted, charred bodies she used for sandbags were riddled with holes from heavy enemy fire. After five agonizingly slow minutes of combat, Pusher was much more exposed than she'd been when he'd first left her to defend their escape route.

"Sergeant!" he demanded over the mayhem. "Report!"

"Two porters down," she said, half turning her mouth to aim her words his way. "Two more still wanting to play."

Hatch smiled at her poise. Ellis's coolness was the product of a soldier's training, an expectation of performance under fire. He had no doubt she was actually scared to death.

"Pusher! Ears!"

Hatch spat the warning at her as a sonic grenade thrown by a porter landed behind her, bumping to a stop against the corridor's wall halfway between them. He threw himself toward the basement and clamped his hands hard over his ears. Hatch counted the grenade's timer, then gave it five extra seconds.

Up top he could hear the chaos of stomping boots, shouting, and blasting lasers. He pulled himself back up the stairs, threw himself prone, and laid his rifle horizontal over the lip of the landing. He almost fired without thinking. The corpses of the Transport soldiers had come back to life and were standing over Pusher, their weapons aimed at her head.

No, wait. The corpses were still on the floor. These were fresh Authority troops poised to execute Pusher. Her position had been overrun.

"Our orders are to stay here," insisted Bracer. "We're the gatekeepers."

"I know that," Hawkeye said, eyes glued to his omni-lens. Unlike his partner, he could see the heat sigs inside the building: their positions, their movements, and when they fired their okcillium-powered weapons. "But I think they're in big trouble on the first floor."

He shifted his gaze up by thirty degrees. The building was old and its walls hadn't been reinforced with glass. Glass in the walls would've bent the infrared spectrum just enough to prevent him from seeing the heat-producing sources inside. With nothing but simple stone and concrete between Hawkeye and his targets, finding heat signatures was easy enough. But his device couldn't differentiate between Transport and TRACE soldiers. Perhaps he should rename it.

Higher up, he thought he saw the QB and Logan holed up on the second floor, occupying an increasing number of Authority troopers. But just as many were on the ground floor, and that threatened their main mission. He stared intently at Pusher's position, then saw what must've been Transport soldiers charging it.

"Damn it! I think they just overran Pusher!"

Bracer considered moving down to flank the porters. Technically, he and Hawkeye both held the rank of corporal, but he'd been promoted before the spotter, and that meant the onus of making a command decision was his. It was at times like this that he wished for Stug's quick-sure field experience … or the QB's calm resolve.

"Maybe we should—"

"Wait!" Hawkeye motioned him to silence. A few moments passed.

"Well?"

The spotter turned to him and smiled. Then his face went white.

Bracer grew eyes in the back of his head. He knew without seeing exactly what Hawkeye was staring at. His ears had picked up the low, metallic buzzing a moment before his brain recognized the sound. The hum of a hovering Transport drone.

"Can I lend you a hand?"

Lasers plastered the corridor wall, forcing them back into the alcove.

"Funny," said the QB, wrinkling her upper lip. "Stug's been a bad influence, I see." She took the corpse's severed forearm from Logan. She wasn't squeamish by nature, but handling the dead weight of another man's limb made her queasier than humping it through the stink of the City's sewers had. Her ally carefully wiped his knife on his trousers and stuck it back in his belt.

"Cover me," she said, gathering her legs beneath her.

This was easier ten years ago, her inner self warned. Mercifully, not in Hatch's voice.

Shut up.

The porters fired on their position again. Logan went flat on the ground, aiming around the door and whipping out a brace of bullets inches from the corridor floor. He snapped off three rounds, then waited without returning to cover for his dance partner on the other end of the hallway to pop up. Up he popped. Logan squeezed his trigger repeatedly, taking the porter in the chest.

"Go *now*."

Knees popping, forehead furrowed, the QB launched herself across the corridor. Logan unloaded three more rounds down the hall to discourage enemy initiative. She slapped the dead soldier's still-warm palm against the swipe pad and the door whooshed open. The captain reconnoitered the dim room, clearing it for enemy presence, then spun around and took up a standing position. Her body blocked the door, holding it open.

"Hey, boys!" she shouted down the corridor. "Bury this, would you?" Winding up her underhanded pitch once, twice, she lobbed the forearm at them. It smacked the floor halfway between them, leaving a bloody trail in its wake as it rolled to a stop. The hand opened upward as if begging its living comrades for help.

Logan pulled back under cover as the captain watched for a reaction. She thought she saw half a face gape in shock at the mutilated flesh. She unloaded three blasts in its direction, and the half face withdrew.

"Now what?" hissed Logan.

Her BICE offline, Mary accessed her inner clock, the one that woke her in the morning for reveille thirty seconds before her implant's alarm sounded.

"Three more minutes. Then up and out."

Shouts and screams down the hall. She couldn't tell if the enemy was enraged by the sight of their butchered comrade's arm or if someone was having a disciplinary problem with his troops. Then the QB heard the heavy *thunk* of a metal ball hitting the floor, followed by the eerie echo of a loud, hollow roll in a suddenly silent hallway.

It was the first one, then, noted her inner voice, unflappable as always.

"Grenade!" shouted Logan.

Hatch ducked hard away from the doorway. It was all he could do to get out of the way in time to avoid being flattened himself. He felt the speed of the AAB as it blurred past, shooting like a rocket at Pusher's position. One porter barely had time to turn before it took him airborne and dragged him past the dead sandbags.

Pusher fell backward as the AAB passed overhead, then swung her leg out and around. Her second would-be executioner lost his balance as she swept his legs out from under him. She was up and straddling him before he even realized he'd dropped his weapon. He had time for one fleeting look of knowing awareness before her rifle butt stove in his nose.

"I hate when I can't do that myself!" shouted Stug, racing into the doorway next to Hatch, who lay stunned on his side. "We rely on technology too much," he groused. Then he winked at Hatch and whistled. "I'm ready to move."

As the reality of what had just happened dawned on him, Hatch gawked up at the sergeant. "You're not as dumb as you look," he said.

"I keep telling you that," said Stug, his voice burdened with the weight of the unappreciated.

The buzz of the AAB's engine competed with the soldier's gasping as it pinned him to the wall. Pusher lay across the corpses, took aim, and fired. Only the sound of the purring engine remained.

"We better get that box and get out of here," said Hatch, "before more bad guys show up."

Outside, they heard shouts and the rapid fire of a Transport drone's Gatling laser.

Stug's shoulders sagged. *Just once*, he thought. "Too late."

Bracer fell flat on his face. He felt more than saw Hawkeye go for his weapon, but the spotter first had to let go of his omnilens, then kneel and draw. The drone shot him in the chest before his knee even hit the roof.

Bringing his rifle to bear, Bracer rolled left. The drone redirected its targeting sensors, tracing its fire across the gritty roof, ranging in on him. Bracer stopped, breathed, and sighted. One long, straight beam of laser fire hit the drone's camera eye.

The blast overloaded its circuitry and the resulting explosion showered the roof with white-hot metal. Bracer hissed in pain as a chunk of shrapnel took him in the upper thigh. Metal, wiring, and one heavy Gatling laser rained down on the alleyway below.

"Hawkeye!"

Bracer crawled across the rooftop to reach his friend, pain arcing like lightning in his left leg. The spotter's eagle eyes had saved the members of Alpha Squad and others in B Company more times than they could count. His squadmates often joked over drinks after an engagement about how Ole One Eye had kept them from being overrun or flanked. Hawkeye hated the moniker and its double entendre, but that just made his fellow soldiers, especially the women, laugh all the harder. His usual response was, "Well, maybe when I'm dead, you'll stop calling me that goddamned awful name."

As he pulled himself up next to his friend, Bracer feared Hawkeye would get his wish. The spotter lay motionless, his omni-lens shattered and hanging uselessly around his neck.

The explosion knocked both of them back into their respective doorways. Transport had thrown a frag grenade, an almost passé weapon in an era of sonic grenades and laser rifles. Neither Logan nor the QB had expected it. The blast had taken out half the wall on either side of the corridor, its radius rocking everything for fifty feet in all directions.

The captain's inner ear hummed with the heavy concussive shock. She moved slowly, randomly, like each of her limbs had a mind of its own. Slow and clumsy, she tried to focus her brain on reality and get her arms and legs to respond. Her ears felt thick, like her head did on the morning after a bout of heavy drinking. Her brain seemed to be floating inside her skull. She knew she needed to move, to grab her rifle and prepare. Transport had thrown the frag grenade to put them on their asses. They were coming.

Weakly, her eyesight teary and unfocused, she saw that Logan had gotten it worse. He moved, but even more slowly than she did. Mary knew she had to get to him, to defend him. He was the only real leader the Wild Ones had. And if they were to be allies to TRACE, that made him more valuable in the struggle against Transport than she was. She had to protect him.

She could hear the grinding stomp of boots on the ground, stepping through debris. They echoed from what seemed like a hundred miles away. The QB's training took over. Muscle memory alone pulled the third and final sonic grenade from her belt.

Her numb fingers could barely hold on to its slick metal surface. She pulled the pin with her teeth. With a lethargic lob, she threw it at the star-like blast of black that scorched the walls. The enemy was almost on top of her.

The grenade landed behind their line of advance. Yelling. Scrambling. Boots moving quickly, crushing fallout from the earlier blast in their haste.

The QB covered her ears and turned her face away. It felt like an eternity to her: the covering, the turning, the waiting.

The grenade failed to go off. It was a dud.

She glanced back to find the enemy realizing the same thing at the same moment. Anger fired her limbs—anger at the tech's failure, at their desperate situation. Her ever-present, simmering hatred for Transport erupted, shooting adrenaline into her veins. She took a deep breath, her legendary calmness and hyper-awareness brought to bear on the task before her.

Mary screamed. But it was not the high-pitched cry of a woman forced into powerless paralysis by a fate beyond her control. Her Amazonian voice, strained and feral, carried a hate-filled promise of justice without mercy for her enemies.

That mortal wail filled the corridor as the QB leveled her laser rifle and fired, precise and deadly, at everything in front of her. Answering shots hit the walls and floor around her, but they were hurried and far less accurate. She ignored the death they carried. Her voice cut through the smoke and thorny burn of heavy laser fire in the air. Though her assault upon the enemy seemed to go on for hours, her shrill scream lasted less than thirty seconds. When there were no targets left, the captain's finger released the trigger by reflex. Her voice trailed away, its fury dying on the scorched walls.

The fog of smoking wounds choked the corridor. It was like the spirits of the dead hovered in the haze, releasing their mortal coils.

Mary crawled across the hall to Logan, heedless of the threat should more of the enemy come around the corner. But nothing living moved, save her.

"We're out of time!" said Hatch. "Get that goddamned box moving!"

Stug was at its controls, reprogramming it to auto-follow his biosign. Pusher guarded the hallway, allowing him to work.

Hatch moved back to the red door, sheltering behind it as pieces of a Transport drone hit the ground in front of him. He searched the roof across the alley but could see nothing of his squadmates. For all he knew, Transport had an entire squadron of drones inbound, and Alpha Squad had no cover on the roof.

Damn it, boys, where the hell are you?

He heard the thready vibration of the AAB as it followed Stug to his position. Pusher jogged backward behind it, guarding their rear. "I don't know what the hell's going on out there. We need to make a run for it. Get that damned box down into the sewer," he ordered.

"Yes, sir," Stug acknowledged, all business. "Pusher, with me."

Hatch became the rear guard, scanning the armory behind them. For now, Transport had run out of soldiers to feed TRACE's gristmill.

Stug scouted the alleyway. "Looks clear," he grumbled.

"Go!"

The big man sprinted, the AAB following close on his heels. Pusher resumed her rearguard duty, backstepping and scanning for enemy intervention from behind. Stug dropped feet-first through the manhole despite the distance to the sewer below. His thick legs absorbed the jump, and he looked up expectantly. The airbox hovered, appearing confused, until its tracking sensors and algorithms determined how to reach Stug. It turned ninety degrees, faced perpendicular to the ground, and glided straight through the hole. Pusher followed.

Hatch observed the roof of the flophouse again. He still couldn't find his team stationed there.

Now I'm officially worried.

Her head was finally starting to clear, and Logan was coming around. He struggled, tried to blink away the effects of the blast.

The QB reconnoitered around the corner. Hazy and filled with dead Transport soldiers, the corridor was still clear. But they were out of time. More porters would be arriving any minute, recalled from the explosions throughout the City to re-secure the armory.

She slapped Logan across the face. And again. When her arm swung at him a third time, he caught it by the wrist.

"The joke wasn't that bad," he mumbled.

"How many fingers am I holding up?"

He peered at her hand, then squinted to make sure. "One. And the same to you."

"On your feet, soldier."

"I'm a spy, remember?"

"Today, it's the same thing."

Logan stood up warily, as if trying out a new set of legs. She heard the crunching then. Boots again, pressing fragments of wall and bloody viscera into the floor.

"Crap."

"What?"

"*Go.*"

The QB unslung the laser rifle she'd taken off the dead porter and handed it to him. He took it without thinking and shoved it in his netting bag, then realized what she was doing.

"Now wait a minute—"

"No time! This is our mission!" she hissed. "Remember those children in Bedrock? Now go!" After a moment's hesitation, she handed him her own half-drained rifle as well. "Hurry!"

Reluctant but accepting, Logan backed away from her, moving as fast up the stairs as his unsteady legs, burdened by four laser rifles, would carry him. Mary watched him go, then grabbed at her uniform before she remembered she was out of grenades. Cursing silently, she pulled her .50-caliber sidearm.

This is it then, her inner voice said. Composed. Resolved. She settled into herself, felt the pit of her stomach harden. In that moment, she became the QB—mind, body, and soul.

She thumbed the pistol's safety off, kneeled, pointed her arm and one eye down the hallway. She didn't lack for targets. One enemy saw her weapon and shouted, raising his rifle.

Mary fired.

"Lieutenant!"

Bracer was limping from the doorway of the flophouse and into the alley. He had Hawkeye slung across his shoulder.

He must've carried him from the roof, Hatch thought. *Jesus, is he—*

"Wounded. Took a drone blast straight to the chest," reported Bracer. "Saved by his damned omni-lens, of all things."

Hatch allowed himself half a breath of thankful relief. Then he heard the Gatling lasers not far away. Transport was bringing its drones home to secure the armory, and they were cleaning up any problems along the way, it sounded like.

"Get below," he ordered Bracer, motioning to the sewer entrance.

"The others?"

"Stug and Pusher have the objective. Come on, I'll help you with Hawkeye."

Bracer nodded, moving toward the manhole. He leapt below, landing with a grunt of pain. Hatch fed the spotter's body through the hole until Bracer confirmed he could break Hawkeye's fall. Then they were gone into the sewer, and Hatch turned his attention back to the armory. Somewhere inside, his captain and their ally were still fighting. And that was the best-case scenario.

His quickest ingress to their position was the same way they'd gone in: leaping from the flophouse roof to the armory's, then down the stairs. But before he could move, he saw a drone fly past on the street at the other end of the alley. He sheltered in the back door to the flophouse and peered around the corner. Sure enough, the drone had stopped, reversed, and was now coming slowly up the alley toward his position.

Hatch felt movement behind him. He rounded quickly, bringing his rifle up.

"Lieutenant..." said the tired voice, out of breath. Logan stepped from the shadows of the flophouse kitchen and fell forward into Hatch's arms.

Hatch caught him, bore him up. "Where's the captain?" he asked immediately.

Logan couldn't speak. Weighed down by the laser rifles on his back, he was exhausted, disoriented.

"Logan!" Hatch shook him hard. He could hear a low hum thrumming off the sweating stone of the alley walls. "Where is she? Where's Mary?"

"Back there," he breathed, motioning upward.

"She's on the roof?"

Logan shook his head. He remembered where he was now. Where she was. "No. Armory, second floor."

"You *left* her there?"

Still shaking his head, the ex-spy said, "She insisted I go. For my people."

Hatch felt exasperation rising in him. Frustration. Anger. *Fear.*

Sounds like something she'd do, goddamnit.

The humming was closer. Hatch actually heard the drone's camera eye clicking its focal shutters as it read their heat sigs. He pushed Logan hard against the wall, turned, and swept a rapid burst from his laser rifle until it found its mark. The drone shook, sputtered, and exploded. Glancing down the alley, Hatch saw another coming to take its place. And another behind that. And they were coming faster. The first must have reported what it found before ceasing to function.

"Get down into the sewer, Logan, now!" Hatch took half of

Logan's load of rifles from him and pushed him toward the manhole. "Don't wait for me! Run!"

Propelled by Hatch, the salvager lurched toward the hole. The lead drone started to fire, but thanks to his uneven, staggering gait, Logan was lucky enough to evade it.

Hatch slung his new load over his head. Then he knelt, took careful aim, released a breath, and fired. He missed.

Logan bent over the hole, dropped his captured rifles below, and lowered himself down. It all moved too slowly for Hatch, but had Logan moved any faster, he'd likely have injured himself and become even more of a liability than he already was. At last Logan was through the hole and out of sight.

Hatch sighted in again. The drone was less than fifty feet away. It had the advantage of seeing his infrared signature inside the flophouse. He had no such advantage for seeing around corners with his human eyes.

Before he could fire, the drone's Gatling laser spat beams at the wall that hid him, spraying Hatch with stone and concrete. One small piece caught him mid-forehead. Another centimeter down, and he would've lost an eye. He retreated into the building, brushing brick and mortar from his face. The drone obliterated the doorway behind him, carving its own entryway into the flophouse.

Hatch paused behind the stoves. He wanted to go after Mary.

If she's even still alive, his training argued.

She's alive. His voice was savage and coarse in his own head. But if he were honest with himself, he only half believed she might still be living. She'd never surrender. And Transport wasn't known for taking prisoners.

The drone blasted the doorway to the kitchen, creating a flight path. Hatch ducked and scampered backward, using the cooking surfaces and cabinets for cover.

If you stay, you die, his training argued. *More are coming. Assuming she's still alive, you'll never have the chance to rescue her if you're dead.*

That was a simple truth. The TRACER drones would bring down the entire building, killing everyone in it, to achieve their rather simple objective: *Kill TRACE Operatives.* And Mary would never sanction that kind of sacrifice simply for a chance to save her life.

"Another day, then," Hatch whispered. He chanced a glance over the metal counter. The drone seemed distracted, perhaps honing in on another heat sig beyond the kitchen wall, an unknowing resident of the flophouse who'd done nothing more than be unlucky enough to be enslaved for next-to-nothing wages in the service of Transport.

He aimed his rifle, shouted, and fired. The drone jerked its red eye toward him, but his blast took it squarely in its gravimetric regulator. He ducked back into cover as the drone began an electronic coughing fit and dropped to the floor, unable to fly. Behind it, he saw its companion begin to enter the building. Then he heard the build-up in the first TRACER and hunkered down harder. An electronic scream, a flare of light, and the drone on the floor exploded, taking out the second machine hovering above.

Metal casing ricocheted off the kitchen's countertops,

clanging and ringing. The hiss of dying electronics whizzed and popped until it fizzled out. Hatch looked up from his hiding place. What remained of the two drones was scattered across the kitchen.

He paused at the obliterated doorway. From across the alley, he could hear Transport reinforcements landing on the roof of the armory. It would be secured now, and Mary either dead or in airtight custody. But his route to freedom was clear. One piece of good luck in an otherwise craptastic operation.

You should've listened to me, he thought petulantly, angry with her for being lost to him. Angry with Transport for existing. And feeling an impotent fury at himself for failing Mary now.

Hatch took a deep breath. Then another. He sprinted for the manhole, pausing only long enough to lower himself down without injury. Once below, he angled his gaze toward the facility where his former lover and commanding officer remained, dead or alive. Leaving her there was the single hardest decision he had ever made in his life.

Another day, he promised.

Guns and Butter and Bourbon

"You have to let us go back," Hatch insisted. It was barely dawn, and he'd rushed to Colonel Neville's office to make his report as soon as Alpha Squad, Pusher, and Logan had returned to Little Gibraltar.

After field dressing Bracer's wound and assessing Hawkeye's condition as superficial, they'd waited in the sewer till close to dawn, hiding with their prize of twenty-four fully powered laser rifles. Hatch had paced nervously, itching to effect an immediate rescue. Logan and Stug had restrained him with logic and muscle, respectively. The pre-dawn return on the *Pittsburgh* had been quiet and uncomfortable. They all hated leaving her behind.

Now Neville was attempting to restrain him with the military chain of command. "You seem to forget, Lieutenant. This isn't a democracy. And one officer is not worth risking TRACE resources and personnel to recover. No matter who she might be."

Colonel Neville's tone was serious, perhaps even sincere, if Hatch stretched his imagination. But to Hatch it sounded like he was reading from a field manual, specifically from the chapter titled "How to Console Troops When Their Commander Has Been Lost." *Just one more example of O-ba-di-ah's placing form over substance and calling it leadership.*

"In a way, she got what she deserved," the colonel muttered. "I've told her before about being impetuous. About not consulting with me before running off half-cocked. Had she done so, perhaps we could've had a more positive outcome."

It was all Hatch could do to stay on his side of Neville's desk. He wanted to rip the colonel's self-important head off his pompous shoulders.

This is not the time for an I-told-you-so lecture, you insensitive ass.

"Nevertheless, I must admit, her negotiations with Logan and his people achieved their primary goal. We have our food back, and a protected supply line besides. I can't say I trust those cannibals as far as I can throw them, but they do have a vested interest in maintaining our good will. For now, the situation is stable." His pronouncement sounded like he was already making his report to the SOMA. No doubt he was trying out the way the words sounded to determine how best to represent his own contribution to the victory.

"Glad to hear you agree with the captain's plan," said Hatch. The words were neutral enough, but his tone betrayed him. It was pregnant with words unspoken, most of them consisting of four letters.

Neville regarded him impassively. "I know you think I'm an idiot," he said, noting the amused, then quickly hidden expression on Hatch's face. "I am *not*, sir. And you'd best remember that. Without that Amish reject to insulate you, I suspect we'll be seeing more of each other in campaigns to come."

Maybe I could just strangle your chicken neck and save us both the trouble, spat Hatch in his head. Hearing Mary called a reject made his calf muscles twitch. His fingers longed to feel Neville's windpipe crushing beneath them. He was glad Stug wasn't here. They'd both be in front of a firing squad by daylight tomorrow if he were.

"You're dismissed," finished Neville. "And send in Lieutenant Mason."

"Trick?"

"Lieutenant *Mason*," growled Neville. "I hate those bloody nicknames you people use. So damned unprofessional. Yes, send him in here. When he walks out again, you will salute him as the new commanding officer of B Company."

Hatch was stunned, and Neville took some satisfaction in putting the cocky lieutenant back on his heels. Nodding, Hatch left the colonel's office on auto-pilot.

Shortly after oh-four-hundred, Trick and the rest of B Company had walked into Little Gibraltar with three wagonloads' worth of food supplies, to the cheers and accolades of everyone in camp. If the fort's soldiers weren't awake when the food arrived, they were soon after. The news, and the aromas, spread quickly.

Hatch considered recent events as he walked to the Rock Slide, his skin tingling with shock. Though Neville hadn't initially been happy with the arrangement the QB had made with the Wild Ones, he soon warmed to the idea of having guaranteed food shipments from the Zone guarded by allies armed with advanced weaponry. And since Bravo Squad had led the escort that had brought the missing foodstuffs home, its lieutenant was to receive Caesar's head wreath from Neville as a reward. Hatch had no doubt Trick hadn't sought that reward for himself, and Hatch had no ambition to command Bestimmung Company either; seeing anyone other than Mary in that role had never occurred to him. To any of them. The very thought of it made his stomach twist. Then he recalled Mary's crack to Trick before they'd left on their mission.

I expect that brevet rank might be made permanent.

If only her skills at predicting the future could've helped her see a way out of that armory, could've brought her home again. The ache in his stomach moved into his chest.

As expected, he found Trick in the Slide, having drinks with his squad. As if from a distance, Hatch watched himself tell Trick that Neville wanted to see him. Mason's face became concerned. He asked why, but Hatch just shrugged.

Trick excused himself, downed the shot in front of him, and shuffled off with a worried look on his face.

Hatch spied an empty corner table. Driven by a box fan, a hanging bulb, burned out and neglected, squeaked overhead like a pendulum.

Perfect.

His feet took him there and he ordered two fingers of bourbon from the private serving as a waitress. It was still early in the morning, but the Slide stayed open twenty-four hours a day. And whatever the time on the clock, it wasn't too early for a drink or six. Especially on this day. Before the private turned away, Hatch ordered a second shot to go with the first. She gave him a look but moved away to bring him his drinks.

After he'd drunk himself eight fingers deep, she brought him the bottle. Not long after, he felt a presence standing over him.

"Anyone drinking that?"

Hatch pulled his eyes up slowly to find Logan. The salvager motioned again at the still-full second shot sitting across the table from Hatch.

"I could use a drink," Logan hinted.

"Then pour yourself one. But leave that one alone."

Motioning to the private to bring him a shot glass, Logan sat on Hatch's right. The unclaimed shot occupied a third spot all its own.

"How are you doing?"

"Better by the minute!" said Hatch, downing two more fingers.

The waitress quickly dropped off a glass and retreated. Logan was quiet as he poured himself a drink.

"I see you're feeling better." Hatch's voice was bitter.

The ex-spy chose to ignore the tone. "Yes, thanks. Mostly concussive damage. The ride back on the *Pittsburgh* did me some good, I think."

"Well, bully for you."

Logan was not a man to take crap from anyone. But he figured Hatch had some cause to be angry with him. *Toward* him, anyway. In the lieutenant's eyes, the mission to secure the guns had cost Hatch his captain. *And something more,* acknowledged Logan, recalling the non-conversation he'd had with the QB as they churned their way up the Susquehanna. He downed his own shot of bourbon.

"Well, I just wanted to say how much I appreciate … how much her sacrifice will mean—"

"Sacrifice?"

Damn it, thought Logan. Hatch wasn't slurring yet, but the bourbon was definitely working in him. *Got here too late.*

"You say that like she's dead," Hatch said.

"That's not what I meant."

"It's what you impl—impl—it's the way it sounded!"

Logan backed off. Now wasn't the time. "I chose my words poorly."

"You goddamned sure did."

Pouring another drink, the salvager downed it quickly before rising. "I appreciate the drink," he said.

"Take your guns and piss off."

Logan walked away. Hatch resumed his descent into a hole, clawing his way there two fingers at a time.

"He's been like that for nearly an hour, Sergeant," said the private-waitress. Hatch lay sprawled across the table, snoring. The empty bourbon bottle lay on its side. The shot for their absent comrade sat undisturbed. "The brunchers will be coming in soon…" Her need to be rid of a drunken officer was clear and immediate.

"I'll take it from here, Private. Do me a favor and don't add this to your list of bar stories."

"No problem, Sarge. There's hardly been anyone in here all morning anyway," she said. "I'll clean up. What do I do with that shot? It's been sitting there for hours. I'm afraid to touch it, frankly."

Stug grunted. "Drink it. No sense letting it go to waste."

"No, I don't think so," she replied, gathering up the bottle and empty shot glasses. "That wouldn't be right. I'll just throw it out."

"Suit yourself."

He shot a questioning look at Bracer. The machine gunner had come into the barracks after checking on Hawkeye, when word had arrived they were needed at the Slide. He'd had to roust Stug from slumber, always a dangerous mission.

"Best to let him sleep it off," said Bracer. "Want me to help you carry him?"

"Naw. You've got a bum leg. Get the door, though. Don't want to chance waking him up by bumping his noggin."

Stug moved around behind Hatch and lifted him out of the chair. He thought about slinging him over his shoulder, combat-rescue style, but figured he'd just end up with Hatch's vomit down the back of his fatigues. So instead he cradled the lieutenant and carried him in his massive arms.

After the dim, artificial light of the bar, Stug had to squint against the late morning sun. He moved across the assembly ground, tired but strong. Bracer walked with a half-limp next to him. The camp was fully awake now, bustling as usual, but with renewed energy now that the food supply had once more been secured. Crowds of two and three stopped what they were doing and watched as Stug walked past, lugging his lieutenant.

"Hey, Sarge! Hatch have too much to drink? Must run in the squad!"

Stug had the absurd thought that even insults sounded nicer with a Spanish accent.

"Not today, Garza," he said under his breath. The rest of the company hadn't yet been briefed about the QB, though the rumor mill was grinding at high speed. Stug had other things on his mind, so he let Garza be a horse's ass. Just this once.

Bracer peeled off, but Stug brought him back with a quick, "Let it go." The last thing they needed was Bracer court-martialed for striking his superior. They'd need every man they could get. And so with some effort, they ignored the laughter behind them.

Once inside the barracks, the handful of soldiers still there at this time of the morning made way. Bracer helped Stug lay out Hatch on his bunk, pull off his boots, and cover him up.

"Draw those shades," ordered Stug. "Everybody else, out."

"Right." The room cleared as Bracer made the rounds, pulling the shades down on the half a dozen windows they usually kept open this time of year. Barracks get rank with sweat, and fast. In the fall, at least, the wind swept the air clean and kept the interior cool at the same time. This morning, though, the breeze coming off the Susquehanna was downright nippy. Stug pulled an extra blanket off the shelf.

"What now, Sarge?"

"Now? Now we go get her. How long will Hawkeye be down?"

"A day, max. Mostly bruising from the omni-lens. The doc's insisting he stay in the infirmary for at least twenty-four hours." Bracer hesitated, but felt like it needed to be said. Just so they were clear. "I heard that Neville put the kibosh on a rescue attempt," he said quietly.

"I won't ask him to go, then."

"What about the rest of B Company?"

The sergeant thought about it. "Trick's in command now. Can't ask him or Bravo Squad. I'll have to think on the others."

"I'd like to go."

They turned toward the doorway where Pusher stood, leaning casually.

"Well, now I guess you kinda have to," said Stug. A knowing smile stretched across her face. It reminded him of the QB's rare, cynical grin. *Why do all women know just how to look at you like they know something you don't want them to know?* he mused.

Stug returned his gaze to Hatch and saw that he was shivering. The October air and bourbon were double-teaming him. The big man carefully laid the second blanket over his lieutenant, pulling it up to his chin and around his shoulders.

Rest well, my friend. We've got work to do.

Historical Note: *Susquehanna*

Unlike *Gettysburg*, *Susquehanna* wasn't inspired by a single battle from the American Civil War. I did, however, weave various elements from that conflict together into the story, so if you're interested in that kind of thing, here you go.

In October 1859, John Brown—a firebrand abolitionist who advocated open slave revolt in the United States—conducted a raid on the federal arsenal at Harper's Ferry, West Virginia. His goal was to secure weapons to facilitate said revolt by arming the slaves themselves. Some historians even view that raid, rather than the firing on Fort Sumter two years later, as the actual beginning of the Civil War. From a contemporary perspective—when everyone should agree that slavery of *any* kind is not a good thing—Brown might be seen as a freedom fighter. At the time, though, he wasn't just seen as radical; many considered him unhinged. And the way he conducted his raid—not with the most realistic expectations or best tactical sense—only added to that impression.

After two days, Brown and his raiders were captured when U.S. Marines, led by Col. Robert E. Lee, stormed the armory.

(Yes, that's the same Robert E. Lee who was offered command of the Union army when hostilities first broke out with the South, and whose strategic brilliance, until the debacle at Gettysburg, would nearly lead the Confederacy to victory. History loves irony.) Brown was hanged for sedition a couple of months later. Irony followed him beyond the grave. The music for "John Brown's Body," a popular marching tune in the Union army during the war, was repurposed during that conflict. You might recognize its refrain, "John Brown's body lies a'mouldering in the grave," by the more popular lyric, "Mine eyes have seen the glory of the coming of the Lord." That's right—though hanged for treason against the United States, John Brown inspired the Union's Civil War fight song "The Battle Hymn of the Republic." You can't make this stuff up, folks.

In my story, Logan sets his sights on the Transport armory in Columbia (a.k.a. the City) to arm his people, the Wild Ones, for their imminent struggle against the Authority. The idea of raiding the armory of the controlling power is pretty much all I lifted from Brown's story. Obviously, Logan's motivation is, from our perspective, a pure and justified one. But I wonder: if anyone were to ever interpret Michael Bunker's world from the point of view of the Transport Authority, might Logan be seen as a bit lacking in the noggin, as Brown was perceived? Understanding is really all about perspective, isn't it?

Logan gets his name from a famous Native American of the Old Planet's Pennsylvanian history. Logan Elrod, who in turn was named after a friend of his father, lived in the middle of the eighteenth century and had a love-hate relationship—or so it would seem; the history is obscure—with whites. He was involved in several campaigns against the white settlers, theoretically launched in response to their having killed members of his family. Part of Lord Dunmore's War, these reprisals eventually led to "Logan's Lament," a speech so well regarded by Thomas Jefferson that he reprinted it in *Notes on the State of Virginia*. I took the historical Logan's apparent gift for oratory and handed it to my character (he *is* a smooth talker), as well as made Logan the de facto champion of the closest thing New Pennsylvania has to an indigenous population.

Speaking of Native Americans, tribes fought on both sides in the Civil War, choosing to ally themselves, like everyone else, with whoever best served their interests. As I've intimated, the Wild Ones represent the Native Americans in the land of New Pennsylvania, and they join forces with TRACE for one simple reason: both have a common enemy in the Transport Authority, which is trying to stamp them out. The enemy of my enemy is my friend, and all that. Hatch raises a good point, though: is arming the Wild Ones a good idea over the long term? The QB's response is all too common throughout history and often the default position today: "We'll worry about that tomorrow."

Even using the Susquehanna River for moving supplies recalls aspects of the Civil War. In that conflict, the ability to move goods by water was vital. A primary Union strategy, known as the Anaconda Plan, was to strangle the Confederate economy by blockading key Confederate ports and cutting off its supply of European capital to fund the Southern war effort. The Mississippi River was another necessary artery for the Confederacy to move goods, men, and materiel, and the Union extended its strangulation strategy by capturing large river port cities, the most famous of which was Vicksburg.

So, there is historical precedent in Transport's obsession with controlling the movement of its citizens. If you think about it, every aspect of our lives relies on transportation—it provides access to work, play, education, goods, and services; even the Internet (remember when we used to call it the "Information Super*highway*"?) is a transportation system of sorts, albeit for information exchange. When you lose that freedom, your world suddenly becomes much smaller, your options much more limited. Hence the strategic significance of controlling how and where people moved along rivers like the Mississippi during the Civil War, and Transport's own obsession with regulating how everyone and everything moves in New Pennsylvania.

Chris Pourteau

October 2014

COLUMBIA

A Little Night Work

The waitress left the bourbon on the table and waited. Sean Hatch extended his uni bracelet and tapped it against the exchange scanner she held.

"Wasn't sure you'd have one of those," he said.

"Most people pay by BICE," she said. "But I know you TRACE types prefer staying off the grid, especially in the City."

When the waitress didn't move, Hatch looked up from beneath his fedora and found himself facing a raised eyebrow, expectant and impatient. He sighed, tapped her tip into the reader and received a bored, half-satisfied smile in return.

The bourbon better be good at least, Hatch thought, pulling his long coat closer around him. It was chilly in here. *Probably used to having more body heat in the place.*

He picked up the glass and swirled the bourbon. The dark-brown liquid reflected the low light of the bar as it moved. Hatch pretended to appreciate the contents of his glass, though in reality his eyes peered over its rim, surveying the establishment for threats.

Nearly deserted this close to midnight, the place was furnished with traditional tables and chairs of real wood, something you didn't see much anymore. For atmosphere, no doubt. Part of its appeal to the locals. Initials engraved on tabletops proved that. In the Age of Okcillium, people still liked carving wood, even in bars—perhaps especially in bars. When a person wanted a drink, they sought out old-fashioned intimacy: the scrape of a chair's legs on a hardwood floor; the low murmur of half-hidden conversations in a corner unmolested by synthetic light. But this late at night, that particular aspect of atmosphere was missing from this bar, one of the TRACE network's best-kept secrets.

Intermittent light from a flickering streetlamp beyond the window made the shadows dance. The bar's sign out front swayed in the breeze. If you watched long enough, you could piece together the name of the place: "Ye Olde World English Tavern."

Sitting at a table across the bar and facing the door, the other half of Hatch's team caught his eye for a moment. To anyone looking on, it would appear as though the second man was merely coveting Hatch's amber elixir. Not that there were many other patrons in the bar to be looking on. And if there had been, it wasn't likely anyone would challenge the second man. He looked too much like someone had thrown a trench coat and fedora over a small mountain.

All clear then, thought Hatch as he assessed Stug's impassive gaze and downed his drink. Sitting near the window in his camel-colored coat, Stug returned his watchful eyes to the street outside.

Hatch motioned first to the bartender, then to the empty glass in front of him. The man set down the mug he was drying, picked up a glass and a bottle of bourbon, and made his way to the table.

"You're hot," the bartender said.

"I'm not your type."

Stug snickered from his window seat.

Clucking his tongue, the bartender sat down and poured himself a drink. Remembering the waitress's quiet efficiency earlier, Hatch raised his own expectant, impatient eyebrow. So the bartender poured him one too.

"I mean, *everyone's* looking for you, Hatch. Transport, TRACE ... if it's wearing a uniform, it's after you. Even your friends are your enemies."

Hatch aired out his new drink with one hand and pulled his fedora down a bit tighter with the other. From under the brim, he said, "Well, it's a good thing I'm here then, since the place is practically deserted. You seem to be doing crap for business, Wainwright." He gestured to the vacant chairs around them with the bourbon in his hand, then emptied his glass again.

"It's after curfew. And ever since Transport started pulling out of the City, business has been crap all right," acknowledged the tavern's owner. Wainwright downed his own drink and made a disgusted sound before pouring himself another. "That's what happens when you lose paying customers."

"Ha!" The commentary sounded from behind the bar. The waitress with the entitled eyebrow. Hatch felt her barb aimed right at him.

Even her voice is annoying, he thought, though Hatch didn't look in her direction; he didn't want to give her the satisfaction. "Try keeping your voice down," he said to Wainwright. "It's the latest thing when you're trying not to be noticed."

"Miranda? Oh, she's all right." The tavern's owner grunted. "We had a bunch of TRACE VIPs through here recently. Brought a lot of heat with them, too, after the fact. We weathered it, but … yeah, let's conclude our business, and you and your friend find another place to hole up in."

Hatch held out his glass. "Well now, Jeff," he said. "I thought we were friends."

"*Were* is right. Now TRACE wants you in custody. Anyone finds out you're here—good guys or bad guys—and I didn't tell 'em? Jams me up. So chop-chop."

Hatch wiggled his glass. Wainwright was slow to pour him another, obviously begrudging both the liquor and what little time Hatch would take to drink it.

"All we need is confirmation of where they took her. It's been a week. I don't even know if she's still in the City."

"Oh, she's still—"

A chair scraped across the floor in the rear of the bar. Its former occupant stepped unsteadily toward the exit, feeling his way along the backs of chairs. Apparently he'd reached his limit. He passed their table, then Stug's lookout position in front of the window, and stumbled into the dark, slick street outside.

"As I was saying, she's still here. Still at the Central

Detention Center. Scarface Gutierrez arrived from the Great Shelf today, in fact. So, if you want her in one piece ..."

Tap-tap.

Hatch looked up. Stug had turned the empty shot glass over on the table and kicked his hat to the top of his forehead. Seeing the sergeant's face always reassured Hatch. Unless the big man was drunk. But that wasn't in the cards for tonight. Stug was their designated hitter. And he'd just given the signal that someone was angling toward the tavern's front door.

Hatch asked quietly, "This your man?"

Wainwright looked sideways without turning. In walked a short, thick man with lines on his face that spoke of a lifetime of anger barely subdued.

"Yeah, that's him. Name's Ducky. He's Pook Rayburn's second-in-command in the City."

As the man entered the tavern, Hatch removed his hat and wiped the top of his head once. Stug pulled his own fedora back down over his eyes and returned his shadowy gaze to the street beyond the window.

"Ducky, this is Hatch," said Wainwright as the man approached their table.

"The guy who's hot?"

"Ha!" The waitress again from behind the bar.

"Are you sure she can be trusted?" asked Hatch, jerking his thumb in her direction. "She has the ears of a Vulcan."

"A what?" asked Wainwright.

"Ancient pop culture reference. Answer my question."

"Yeah. I told you, she's solid."

Ducky took a seat at the table. Glancing at the woman

behind the bar, he said gruffly, "Hey, luv, bring me a glass, would you?" Back to his tablemates, Ducky said, "A night like this, a hard drink goes down smooth, I can tell ya that."

Even when ordering a drink this Ducky seems irritated, Hatch thought, sizing him up. "Do you have what I asked for?"

"Sure," said Ducky, watching the waitress walk around the bar. "Do you have the unis?" His wandering gaze landed squarely on Hatch.

In response, the lieutenant brandished his bracelet.

"How many extra unis do I get for not turning you in to TRACE?" asked Ducky, his eyes level.

Wainwright visibly stiffened. "No, Duck—"

"Just sayin'. This guy's wanted, and TRACE needs all the unis it can get. We're *this close* to driving Transport out of the City for good. *This close.*"

The waitress approached, and the men at the table fell silent. She placed the empty glass on the wooden surface— warily. She'd heard the challenge in Ducky's voice too.

Hatch regarded Wainwright's man coolly as the waitress turned and walked away, this time without waiting around for a tip. "Well, how about this instead of extra unis," Hatch said. "How about I don't turn my partner over there loose on you?" Hatch grinned from beneath the shadow over his eyes. His expression invited Ducky to believe every single word he said.

Ducky looked over to the window. Stug kicked back his hat again and winked at the smaller, boar-like entrepreneur, who sneered in response.

"Because I have a feeling that whatever I pay you,"

continued Hatch, "would be exactly how much it'd cost to set your bones and bind up your bleeders."

Ducky turned a death's-head stare to Hatch and began to rise. Wainwright grabbed the bottle of bourbon quickly and poured two fingers for the short man.

"Duck, maybe you weren't listening," offered the tavern's owner. "This is *Sean* Hatch. He and his crew took the okcillium at Gettysburg. They pulled the guns out of Columbia—right out from under the noses of Transport—for Logan and his people. The Wild Ones that shepherd food for TRACE from the Amish Zone to Little Gibraltar?" The man's voice was knowing and suggestive in a way Hatch didn't understand.

Ducky looked at Wainwright. "That's this guy?"

Wainwright held the bottle in the air expectantly. Ducky grabbed the shot, downed it, and sat back down. Wainwright poured him four more fingers.

"Yeah, I'm that guy," said Hatch. "So how about we avoid paying Jeff here for his broken furniture and get down to the business we came here to do."

"Sure." Ducky laughed; it wasn't a pleasant sound. But the air seemed to be cleared. "Sure, no problem. It's just that Transport's getting desperate. And we need all the help we can get. There's just a lot of our people dying out there, ya know? But yeah, I guess you do know. So, BICE ID?"

Hatch blew out a breath. "You kidding? You think I'm gonna give you direct access to my BICE? I wouldn't do that if you had the backdoor codes for Transport's foreclosure collections server."

Ducky spread his hands. "Hey now, given what Jeff just said, I thought we were on the same side."

"No one's on my side but him," said Hatch, nodding at Stug. "And usually, that's all I need." If Ducky was still thinking of selling him out, Hatch's tone suggested he rethink it.

"Fine." Ducky pulled a slip of paper out of his pocket. "Log in to this channel. Once you do, the information will be live for five seconds. Then it burns off the drive forever. Backups too."

Hatch took the paper. "Old school. I like it. These are the schematics for the Columbia Detention Center?"

Ducky nodded. "The Dungeon below, too. And that's where you're gonna find her. Not up top in the luxury suites. Now, transfer the unis." He held up his bracelet.

"After I get the info." Hatch glanced away as he accessed the Internet with his BICE. The dampening field the Authority maintained in the City, geared to interfere with TRACE's ability to access and communicate through the Internet, made him wince as always.

Ducky looked at Wainwright. "That's not what we agreed to," he said, his tone considerably more irritated than before. "War hero or no, that wasn't the deal."

"Maybe not, but that's how it's gonna be," said a gruff voice behind him.

Startled, Ducky began to rise from his chair again. Bear paws landed on his shoulders.

"Not to worry, friend," said Stug. "We're all on the same side, remember?"

Ducky returned to his seat. "Tell you one thing, you're quiet for a big guy."

"I'm sober tonight," Stug said simply.

Hatch cleared his throat. "Got it." He tossed the paper in the candle burning in the middle of the table and extended his hand. Ducky touched his bracelet to Hatch's, then weathered Transport's interference long enough to check his account balance.

Nodding, Ducky said, "Our business is concluded, gentlemen," and rose.

"Good," breathed Wainwright. "You know the way out."

Stug stood back and gave Ducky room, then extended a hand. "No hard feelings. We really are on the same side."

Ducky took it. "Yeah, no hard feelings. In fact, I can hardly feel that grip at all," he said wryly.

Stug smirked.

Ducky nodded to Wainwright, then headed toward the back of the bar. "Best of luck, gentlemen," he called, disappearing into the men's room.

"Where's he going?" wondered Stug.

"Back door," said Wainwright. "Now, everyone out before all this Internet activity trips someone's—"

Stug held up his hand.

The waitress continued noisily cleaning glasses. "Quiet," hissed her boss.

Then they heard it. The quiet thrum of a Transport drone on the street outside.

"You left your post," said Hatch, glaring at his sergeant.

"Still an officer I see, even without rank," breathed Stug,

moving quietly toward the window.

"Quiet, both of you," said Wainwright.

Keeping to the shadows, Stug glanced at the street. "TAC team with a drone escort. They'll hit the door in twenty, nineteen—"

"This way!" barked Wainwright, hopping up and following Ducky's exit strategy.

"We can stay and fight," offered Hatch, following.

"No fighting, just running. Done it before. Do what I tell you."

Wainwright propped the men's room door open and ushered them through.

"I don't much like being trapped like a rat," growled Stug.

"Flush the toilet on the left."

"The one marked 'out of order'?" asked Hatch.

"Do it!"

Wainwright moved back into the bar. An old spring *thronged* the door closed behind him.

Stug stared at Hatch, concern manifesting on his face. "You look a little flushed."

"Shut up."

Hatch entered the stall and pressed the lever on the commode. No water moved through the pipes, but a thin wall panel opened next to the seat.

Hatch stared into the darkness beyond, dubious. "You're not gonna fit," he said, angling himself to slip through the small space.

"Aw, come on—"

"Don't say it!"

"I can bear down and squeeze."

Through the men's room door came the sounds of Transport entering the tavern. Wainwright was welcoming them in his best salesman's voice.

Hatch pushed through and found himself in a lightless, claustrophobic passageway lined with sweaty stonework. He offered Stug a hand, but the big man batted it away, then angled himself to move through the hole in the wall. Halfway through, he found himself wedged in tight.

Voices outside. Officer-speak. Wainwright placating, offering free drinks.

The indifferent hum of the escort drone, getting louder.

"Suck in your gut."

"Then my chest expands."

Hatch rolled his eyes and held out a hand.

"Don't tell Bracer and Hawkeye," said Stug, wrapping his palm around Hatch's forearm.

Hatch braced one foot against the wall. "I won't have to if we're dead." He grabbed Stug's arm with both hands, pressed with his foot, and hauled backward. The mountain finally came through with a ripping sound.

Hatch found the old-fashioned pull chain on this side of the wall and yanked it. The panel closed, leaving them in darkness.

"I think I ripped my coat," groused Stug. "At least I hope it was my coat."

"Shhhh!"

They both froze as the men's room door squeaked on its hinges. The hum of a drone echoed around the porcelain fixtures.

"We're dead," whispered Stug.

Hatch had a split second to make a decision. Dash down the dark corridor, making all kinds of noise, or pull their weapons and blast through the wall, hoping to hit the drone while drawing Transport's human soldiers in on them like sharks to blood. There was a third option, but it was a death sentence: do nothing until the drone registered their heat signatures through the wall and opened up with its Gatling laser.

Stug reached inside his coat, but Hatch felt the movement and stopped him. Even in the blackness, Hatch imagined the incredulous, "Are you crazy?" look in his sergeant's eyes. But Stug stayed his hand.

The drone purred as its sensors surveyed the men's room, taking measurements, searching for heat sigs. They could hear it, right outside the stall they were hiding behind. It seemed to sit and hum and whir forever, as if contemplating whether or not to bother killing them.

Then they heard footsteps.

"Lieutenant! Drone's cleared the men's room. Looks like the owner was telling the truth."

Someone in command said something unintelligible in the main bar.

"Yes, sir," said the trooper. "Come on, you."

The drone's servos spun up and it moved away. Hatch heard the sound of the men's room door opening wide on its loud spring and then banging shut. Muffled voices sounded beyond the door again, and Hatch could tell from the tenor that Transport was wrapping up and moving on.

"Huh," said Stug. "Wainwright must've lined his walls with glass to reflect infrared scans back to the scanner."

Hatch clicked on a flashlight. "No shit."

Stug cocked an eye at him to let him know he got the joke, then asked, "How'd you know?"

Hatch scouted the close corridor with the light. Nothing but weeping stone, angling sharply down.

"The tavern is a TRACE hidey-hole from way back," the lieutenant said, starting down the passageway. "Makes sense he'd take precautions."

Stug followed, stooping to keep from bumping his bald head. He slipped once, but righted himself quickly. "We're going down."

"Beats dying."

"We're going into the sewer, aren't we?" whined Stug in his little boy's baritone. "Again."

"Looks that way."

"I bet we find plenty of shit there."

"Keep walking, hero."

"Could you squat downwind?"

"Quiet," said Hatch.

From their position across the street, Transport's Detention Center appeared almost as deserted as the tavern in the calm of after-midnight. A drone passed quietly back and forth along the sidewalk fronting the street. A single electric light shone on two steel-reinforced doors providing entry to the facility. A few pieces of paper, stirred by the wind, flitted around the otherwise empty street.

The quiet didn't surprise Hatch. Of course the streets were deserted. Transport had long ago imposed martial law as part of their doomed attempt to restore order in the City. Since the Authority had begun evacuating essential personnel to its cities beyond the Great Shelf, no one would be caught dead near the Detention Center at this time of night. Or rather, dead was the only way they *would* be caught there.

Glancing at Stug, Hatch said, "I have no idea how we're gonna get in there."

Braving the static humming in his head from Transport's dampening field, Stug connected his BICE to the Internet. He accessed the building's layout using the files they'd secured from Ducky. There were three levels up top, including the roof, and two under the street. Multiple security checkpoints and low-level administrative offices made up the first floor. The second floor contained larger, better-furnished offices for high-level Authority types.

Transport designed its buildings hierarchically. The higher up you went, the more ornate the offices. Going down wasn't nearly as pleasant. In Ducky's files, the first level below ground was labeled as "interrogation rooms and reeducation chambers"—both of them soundproofed, for obvious reasons. There were also a few common rooms for holding large groups in one space. Below that level was "The Dungeon," as TRACE called it, where Transport housed its most dangerous political prisoners.

Not exactly the New Hilton.

"I'm more worried about getting back out," said Stug, scanning the plans with his mind's eye. He disconnected his BICE from the Internet, and the static stopped immediately.

Hatch kept silent.

"Why don't we just find a couple of Transport mooks, clobber 'em and take their uniforms, and file in when the shift changes?"

Hatch shook his head. "They BICE-scan when you walk in the door. You know that. The only people who get in without scanning are prisoners with their BICEs already removed. And it's not like we're on a sanctioned mission for Covert Ops, with idents programmed in. We'd have fifty rifles pointed at us before we made it to the front security desk."

Stug grunted. "Well, how about until we figure out a better plan, we just find a couple of Transport mooks and clobber 'em anyway? You know. For fun."

"Quiet, Neanderthal. I'm trying to think."

In the distance to the north, the vibrating hum of anti-gravs caught Hatch's attention. The wind blew it in over the top of Transport's Justice Building, which connected to the Detention Center on one end, forming an L. Lady Justice, her traditional blindfold removed by the Transport Authority decades ago, stood atop the Justice Building, her arm holding the scales of justice stretched out toward detention, as if pointing the way.

An airbus appeared over the statue. Hatch and Stug watched it make its way to the center of the street between them and the Detention Center. Dust kicked up as the ship's airjets cushioned the bus's descent.

"A little late for a delivery, isn't it?"

"Transport likes to bring in political prisoners after midnight," Hatch said. "Less chance for a public spectacle that way."

The airbus settled, its hydraulic legs locking. A door opened and a ramp extended, and two fully armored Transport soldiers marched out and took up positions at the bottom of the ramp. Running lights popped on in succession along the walkway as the first of the passengers stepped out.

A woman, her hair tangled and her clothing stained and hanging like rags, walked forward unsteadily. She was followed by another, then a man, then three children. All had their hands bound in front of them. Most stumbled with fatigue. Hatch saw that some of the prisoners were walking wounded, their injuries apparently field treated with hastily wrapped bandages. A few had to be helped down the ramp by others. One soul was carried on a litter by two other prisoners, their hands bound despite their burden.

Hatch caught a gleam of starlight moving to the north. Though he couldn't hear it yet, he could see the running lights announcing the inbound flight of a second airbus. He arced his head northward, and Stug followed his gaze.

"Five minutes?"

"Sounds about right," said Hatch. He glanced back at the offloading prisoners. The drone by the street was monitoring their transfer with its one red eye. Looking down at the crumpled state of his clothes, Hatch said, "I have an idea."

"Great. I get to hit someone, right?"

"Eventually, I have no doubt."

"Then I'm in."

Hatch took out his knife and extended the blade.

"You're taking a knife to a gun fight?"

Instead of responding, Hatch handed Stug the knife. "Say goodbye to your BICE."

Stug stared. "Wait, what?"

"Not a lot of time to discuss. You cut mine out, then I'll do yours."

Still the sergeant hesitated. "You really have no intention of going back to B-Company, do you?"

Hatch turned his head to offer Stug a better angle. "Likely more a matter of them not wanting me back. And me not wanting to spend the rest of my life in prison."

"Yeah, I guess that ship has sailed."

"Four minutes, thirty seconds. And we have two surgeries to perform."

Nodding, Stug reached over and rubbed his thumb along the skin below Hatch's right ear. "Kinda dark," he said. "And I usually only do this to dead guys."

"Make do."

There it was. The telltale bump of the BICE implant below the skin. Stug spit on his friend's neck, then wiped the skin as clean as he could with one thick thumb. He placed the tip of the knife a quarter inch above the bump.

"This is gonna hurt."

"Four minutes."

The big man cut a vertical line across the bump. "You gonna remember the schematics?" he asked as he cut. Blood welled from the wound, and Stug wiped it away. He could feel Hatch trying to keep his neck muscles from jerking beneath the blade.

"I hope so." Hatch winced. "For her sake."

Stug cut a second, transverse line across the bump. Though he largely ignored the blood, which was flowing freely now, he had to constantly clean the wound to see what he was doing. Slowly, delicately, he worked Hatch's flesh back to expose the implant.

"Remind me not to let you carve the turkey at Thanksgiving."

"Never had any complaints before."

"Right!" Hatch clipped the word off, squeezing his eyes shut as Stug dug into his neck.

The big man carefully dug the knife through the slit he'd just made. Then, placing its tip below what he thought was the center of the implant, he said, "This is gonna hurt."

"You said that al—ow!"

Stug's meaty hand came into view. Resting on the tip of a bloodied index finger was Hatch's BICE. "Want to say a heartfelt goodbye?"

"Crush it. Two minutes till that second ship lands."

Stug handed the knife to Hatch and turned around. "Be gentle with me. It's my first time on the receiving end."

"Uh-*huh*," said Hatch.

The airbus on the ground was spinning up its engines, so Hatch was forced to work faster than Stug had. A minute later—counted in the number of new curses the big man coined for the occasion—both men were BICE-free.

"Feels a little like being naked, doesn't it?"

"More like unchained," said Hatch. But Stug was right. Being without the Internet for support and communication made him feel a bit like his left arm had been cut off. "Stow your pistol up that drainpipe. And throw the Raymond Chandler duds in the trash can there."

"The what duds?"

"The coat and hat," said Hatch, exasperated. "Leave 'em." He wrapped a strip of cloth around his neck to stanch the bleeding and shook his head. "No one has any appreciation for classic pop culture anymore."

"Hell, I don't appreciate *today's* pop culture. Not that there is any."

Both men stood silently in the shadows of the alleyway, away from the constant surveillance of Transport's security cameras. The first airbus lifted off, heading for its landing bay on the roof of the Detention Center. In the rumbling wake of its engines, they could hear the second one coming in; the ships were like two runners passing off a baton.

The second bus's landing ritual mimicked the first's. While the anti-gravs swirled dust noisily around on the road, Hatch and Stug stole away from their hiding place and slid around to the left side of the landing zone.

Crouched and careful, they made their way from trash can to apartment stoop to a second statue of Lady Justice, this one on the ground. She stood as the centerpiece of a stone fountain in the middle of the square and pointed toward the Justice Building, a sister to the statue on its roof. The fountain's display was turned off for the night, so no water pumped to afford them cover. But the moon had slipped behind the clouds, and their silhouettes blended with the night well enough as they knelt near the stonework. From this position, the second airbus, its jets settling its legs into position, was no more than twenty feet away.

The door slid open and the ramp extended. Once again, two soldiers descended, taking up positions to either side of the sloping metal walkway. Another crowd of men, women, and children began to file out slowly.

"Hey, some of those people look familiar," said Stug.

"Yeah, me too—but I don't know where from. We'll figure that out later. Focus on the timing."

Hiding behind the fountain, the two men were outside the guards' direct line of sight. Hatch estimated it should be easy enough to blend in with the offloading prisoners while avoiding detection by the guards. It was the prowling drone on the sidewalk, its heat sensors ever watchful, that worried him.

"You watch the guards. I'm pacing the drone. When you and I both agree on the timing, we go."

Stug nodded, though his eyes were elsewhere. How many times had they been in a similar situation together? the big man wondered. When the quips ceased and the focus sharpened. When they thought and moved and fought together like two halves of the same killing machine. Or in this case, the same covert mechanism, gliding quietly along its course.

Twenty prisoners, nearly half the airbus's complement, had unloaded when Hatch said, "The drone follows every fourth person into the facility with its sensors. That gives us a pretty big window to join the line."

"As long as it's not counting how many come off and how many go in," said Stug. "And doesn't notice we've added ourselves to the herd."

"Yeah, that."

They waited a moment longer.

"Drone's tracking," said Hatch. He watched it follow the progress of a large woman with a child attached to her hip. The child clung to her tattered skirts, terrified.

"Guards are talking about something. Not looking this way."

"Now," said Hatch, rising and leading the way.

They approached from behind and to the right of the guards, who stood talking to one another in their boredom. As he moved, Hatch glanced at the drone to make sure its sensor eye was still aimed at the woman and child.

Two prisoners stepped off the platform together. Holding his wrists together, Hatch slipped in behind them. Stug knelt below the ramp a moment longer, then joined the line when another hole appeared.

The guards kept jabbering. The drone kept humming.

Slowly, Stug moved up nearer to Hatch, but he remained three feet behind him as the line made its way from the airbus to the facility.

"I know where I've seen these people before," he whispered.

"Me too," said Hatch over his shoulder. "But shut it for now."

The two men walked freely into Columbia's Detention Center, now political prisoners destined for The Dungeon.

Obadiah's Orders

"Do you understand, Sergeant?"

Emma Ellis stood straight as a new recruit in front of Obadiah Neville's desk. Pusher was dressed in civilian attire, per her orders to report. It'd been less than twenty-four hours since Hatch and Stug had gone absent without leave. *Right on time*, she'd thought when the summons to the colonel's office came.

"Yes, sir," Pusher said, eyes forward. She stared at the portrait on the wall behind Neville's head. It was a photograph of Neville receiving a commendation from Amos Troyer, much earlier in the war. Not looking Neville directly in the eye helped Pusher concentrate.

"As Sergeant Miller's replacement, you might get some guff from the rest of the company," said Neville, standing up. "But you're tough. Until he gets settled into his new position, Lieutenant—Captain—Mason is going to need some back channel support when the officers aren't around. That's your job."

Still staring forward, Pusher blinked. "Sir, yes sir."

"I have no doubt of Captain Mason's loyalty. Some of the others, I'm not so sure of." Neville glanced out the window—a momentary lapse of discipline for him. "I know some of you loyal to Hatch think I'm an idiot. That being an officer of higher rank, I don't know how things really work around here."

"No, sir, not at all sir," replied Pusher, her voice flat as iron. "I'd never make the mistake of equating rank and intelligence." Her eyes darted from the photo to the colonel as she heard the words that had just come out of her mouth. "Sir."

"Yes, well," said Neville, his attention back as he tried to parse her statement. "Yes, well, intelligence is a demonstrated thing, Sergeant. Like any characteristic you can trust. True ability is shown—that's my point. Avoiding assumptions is always best." Neville's inflection was staged, as usual, for impact. Like he was dry-running quotations for a future edition of *Obadiah Neville's Guide to Leadership During a Time of War*. "Especially when it comes to another man's—or woman's—intelligence."

"Couldn't agree more, sir."

"Right." Neville's tone seemed to close the book on that discussion. "Now, I briefed Captain Mason earlier. But I wanted you here so we could have this little chat, out of his earshot. Are you clear on the rest?"

"Sir, yes sir. Trick..." She saw Neville flinch. "Sorry, sir. Captain Mason and I are to go with two others into the City to locate and retrieve Lieutenant Hatch and Sergeant, uh, Miller. Two teams of two, civilian attire. We have thirty-six hours. We're to be out by dusk tomorrow, well before curfew. We're to make use of various TRACE assets and contacts in the City as necessary."

Neville nodded curtly. "And if you fail to retrieve the two traitors?"

Now it was Pusher's cheek that twitched. Her eyes refocused on Amos Troyer's image on the wall, and that steadied her.

"Then, sir, we're to consider Lieutenant Hatch and Sergeant Miller lost as prisoners of war."

Neville put his hands behind his back. He even managed to make parade rest a stiff show of projected pomp. As if listening to a movie director, he paused to let the gravity of those orders stake its claim on the room.

Pusher heard Stug's voice in her head. "*I didn't know being a bad actor was a qualification for being an officer now.*"

Actually, that was a lot of words for Stug.

"*Pansy-ass.*"

Yeah, that was more like it.

"And if any of *you* are captured, Sergeant?"

The cold of the grave weighed on his words.

"*Okay, not bad,*" allowed Stug's gruff voice in her head. "*For a pansy-ass.*"

"Then, sir, we too are to be considered lost."

Neville nodded again.

"Sergeant, you and the others are performing a great service. A great ... sacrifice ... if necessary."

He was pausing in all the right places again, she noticed. Maybe he was editing his future tome on the fly. *Chapter*

Three: Acknowledging the Noble but Necessary Sacrifice of Cannon Fodder.

"Uh, yes sir. Thank you ... sir."

"Dismissed." Neville waved her away and returned his butt to the creaking wooden chair.

Pusher saluted, received the colonel's acknowledgment, and turned to leave.

Before she made it halfway to the door, Neville slapped his desk. "Sergeant!"

She stopped immediately. She'd almost made it. Now she wondered if the whole briefing had been an act, not just practice for the good colonel's memoirs. What if Neville had actually known everything all along?

"*Nothing for it now but to let it ride.*" This time it was Hatch's pragmatism voicing her thoughts. She turned around slowly to face the colonel.

"One more thing," Neville said. His eyes were intense, piercing.

Pusher half-thought the slap on the desk had been a signal for members of A or C Company to come charging through the door and arrest her.

"Hatch and Miller are no longer to be addressed with rank. They're deserters. I'd give you orders to shoot them on sight, but it'd likely draw Transport down on you like a bunch of hornets. They are no longer to be saluted, and they are *certainly* no longer to be obeyed should they attempt to issue orders. Am I clear, Sergeant Ellis?"

Pusher stiffened her back, legs, and shoulders to attention. She hoped it looked to Neville like she was acknowledging his authority in the matter—a little stagecraft of her own. But she knew it was really to keep herself from charging the overstuffed uniform in front of her.

"Sir! Yes sir!"

"Very well," he said, stabbing his fingers toward the compound. "Uh, you're still dismissed. Again."

Pusher turned on her heel and exited the office, releasing her frustration with a silent sigh. It was going to be a long day.

"Bet you never thought you'd see me again," said the ferryman. He flashed his near-toothless smile.

"We'd hoped," said Bracer under his breath without looking at the man. Instead he stared across the Susquehanna at Little Gibraltar. He wondered if it was the last time he'd ever see the TRACE stronghold. Whichever way this thing went—right or wrong, success or failure—he knew that was likely the case.

"Oh, sure! Be like that," said Sticks. "I'm your ticket into the City. Just like last time."

"About that," said Trick, squinting one eye against the rising sun. "I thought you could only move safely after dark."

"That was last week," answered Sticks, untying the first of two ropes securing the *Pittsburgh* to Shenks Landing. "And you're just citizens looking to do some business in the City, not decked-out commandos like last time." He didn't offer further explanation.

But Pusher wanted more. "Transport's still there. And

they've been cracking down on everyone—TRACE, the Amish … everyone." Her voice grew quiet.

"Oh, sure," said the ferryman, pulling the second rope from its wooden post, freeing the *Pittsburgh* of all moorings. "Now that they've gotten their assets in gear and headed to the Shelf, Transport has bigger fish to fry. They're mopping up behind themselves, a last gasp in the region, so to speak. Still, it's like they *want* folks to move into the City. All I know is, I got this."

He held up what looked like a broach. It was really a metal badge shaped in the symbol of the Transport Authority. Called a SLACK—a Shipper Locator and Consignment Key—it tracked inventory data and the GPS location of its bearer. The Authority sometimes granted free, though monitored, movement to shippers who carried food, goods, and, in some cases, people. But Transport usually reserved the keys for a select group of Authority-approved collaborators, and even then only those rich enough to own their own air transport.

"How'd *you* get a SLACK?" asked Trick. For Sticks to have such a treasured item—essentially permission to move freely, if anyone could be said to move freely in New Pennsylvania— struck him as mighty suspicious. His confidence in Sticks's loyalty was still as shaky as it had been when the ferryman had delivered them right into the hands of the Wild Ones. And that had been barely a week ago.

The ferryman waved his way past Hawkeye and into the *Pittsburgh*'s pilothouse. Firing up the boiler, he cracked the pilot's window and raised his voice. "I applied!"

"You what?" asked Pusher, cocking her head to hear over

the din.

"I applied! A long time ago. And then, three days ago, Transport started granting these little beauties left and right," called Sticks, revving the engines. "Probably to encourage private shippers to help move their own people out. All I know is, I was top of the list!"

Water began to slowly *sloosh … sloosh … sloosh* over the paddleboat's big portside wheel.

"Like I said, Transport's loosening up!" Sticks turned his attention to piloting his beloved riverboat safely away from Shenks Landing.

"Maybe they think it's easier to control all the rats in one cage," said Hawkeye, rubbing his chest. The impact wound he'd taken when they'd raided Transport's armory still ached seven days later. "But like the sergeant said, that doesn't make any sense." His eyes flitted from Trick to Bracer, then back to their newly minted captain. "Sir, like Pusher said, Transport's been cracking down. Martial law in the City. Increased military activity between Columbia and New Detroit. The attack on Bedrock."

Pusher clenched her jaw. She was staring hard at Little Gibraltar as they crawled upriver, perhaps assigning blame with her eyes. "We should never have let those people go back there. Not without support."

"Don't go there, Sergeant," said Trick. "That was the colonel's decision. And we can't do anything about it now."

The deck jerked below them as the *Pittsburgh* found her river legs again. In a few moments, she arrowed smoothly over the dark water, white cream foaming at her bow.

"We've got a difficult task ahead of us," Trick said solemnly. "It's a shame Colonel Neville wouldn't let more than four of us go on this mission. But I appreciate that the three of you—those closest to Hatch and Stug—agreed to take the duty with me."

Hawkeye's gaze flitted briefly to Pusher, but she steadfastly refused to meet it. Instead she watched Little Gibraltar fade slowly behind them as Sticks fed coal to the boiler.

"Well, sir," said Bracer, "it wasn't up to anyone else to do it."

"No one else *should* do it," added Pusher, at last prying her eyes away from the hidden fortress in the middle of the river. "And we don't *need* anyone else. It's up to us to help them."

"Help them?" Trick's tone sounded confused.

"Help them see the error of their ways is what she means," supplied Bracer. "They can't expect to run off when TRACE needs them the most, when we've almost won. We've got Transport on the run. We need every soldier more than ever now."

Trick nodded. "That's why the colonel kept it to four, in case you're wondering. He thinks it's important to show the troops you can't just walk out of camp against orders and get away with it. But any more than four is a waste of vital resources. That's how he explained it to me, anyway."

"Any more than four would just piss Stug off," said Bracer. "And no one wants that."

Smiling at a memory, Trick steadied himself on the gunwale and watched the water pass up and over the paddlewheel. Like their captain, the other members of B-

Company stood quietly, recalling their own private run-ins with the big man and his temper.

The *Pittsburgh* found her groove soon enough, and the power of the river thrummed up through the deck and into their feet. It was a thrilling feeling, thought Pusher, staring at the clear blue sky, crisp with the chill of late October. And such a different experience from traveling beneath the stars on a covert mission that seemed so long ago.

"What about the QB?" asked Hawkeye. "That's why they went."

"The QB isn't our mission," answered Trick sadly. He tried to imbue his words with the power of command, but he wasn't very good at that. He really wasn't sure why Neville had even given him command of Bestimmung Company, other than because of the credit he'd received for having reopened the line of supply from the AZ. When he'd tried to share that credit with Hatch and the others, the colonel had waved off his protests as modesty. "A good quality in a good commander," Neville had said at the time, before adding the warning: "in moderation."

Shortly after the colonel had appointed him to temporary command, Trick had approached Hatch apologetically, but he'd found that the heir apparent to Mary Brenneman harbored no desire to replace her. "Take it," Hatch had said despondently, his mind clearly elsewhere. "Better the devil we know."

At least he was sober when he said it, reflected Trick. Otherwise Trick would never have felt comfortable assuming command. Besides, without Hatch's support, he suspected that all of B-Company would have worked against him. Not overtly, of course, but in subtle ways that would have made his assumption of command much more difficult in the wake of losing the QB.

A long silence followed Trick's declaration that freeing Mary Brenneman—adored by her troops or not—was not their objective.

"I still can't believe she's dead." Her comrades scarcely heard Pusher over the sloshing water and pumping engine.

"Apparently neither could they," said Bracer. "And I hate the idea of punishing them for their belief that she's still alive."

Trick cleared his throat. Even green in the role of CO, he knew this was a moment when he needed to keep them focused. "Yeah, but no one knows what her status is," he said, trying to sound dispassionate. That didn't come easy when they spoke of the QB. "And we're not 'punishing' anyone. We're enforcing the Military Code of Conduct. We're maintaining a tradition of discipline that goes back to George Washington and beyond. Our mission is to retrieve our friends, because if anyone else had volunteered for this job, they might not care so much about bringing Hatch and Stug back alive."

Bracer approached the side of the *Pittsburgh* and leaned on the rail next to Trick. He could hear Hawkeye walking away, then climbing the ladder to stand on top of the pilothouse.

No doubt so he can see better as we approach the City, thought Bracer. *Or maybe just to get away from this conversation.*

He pulled out a cigar and lit it. "Stug gave me this after the raid on the armory," he said to Trick, who nodded politely. "For bringing Hawkeye home." Bracer took a long drag, then watched as the wind puffed the sweet-smelling smoke downriver. "I always do right by my friends, Captain." The heavy-weapons man locked eyes with his commander. "You can count on that."

Glancing away from his subordinate and across the water, Trick missed seeing Pusher's lips curling upward in an involuntary smile.

Stepping off the *Pittsburgh* and into the City under the bright light of day was a strange thing, Pusher reflected. It made her uncomfortable. Her comrades' body language showed they weren't sure how to act either. Especially Trick, who was nervous by nature. They were commandos, not spies. They were used to night raids and skulking in the shadows, not role-playing and covert missions executed in the open.

"Try to act natural," said Trick, as much for himself as the others. "You're all too stiff."

"Perhaps if you led by example," grumbled Bracer. "Sir."

Trick glared in Bracer's direction, then realized the man was goading him. The same way he would have goaded Hatch. So, Trick thought, they were beginning to accept him in his new role as commanding officer. He tried to think of something Hatchian to say in return.

"If you insist." Lame but acceptable, he thought.

As soon as they stepped off the riverboat, they were

scanned, of course. Authority officials first checked the ferryman's SLACK, confirmed that four citizens were transferring to the City to take factory jobs, then scanned each of the passengers in turn to confirm their identities. The undercover soldiers held their breaths during the process, but there was no need: TRACE had programmed their BICEs with fake IDs and simple status updates, all backed with four canned personal histories that included no major run-ins with the Authority. They appeared to be four loyal Transport citizens, with no criminal records, taking advantage of an opportunity for employment left behind after four other loyal Transport citizens had been ordered by the Authority to move to the Great Shelf. Trick nodded at the customs officer as she waved them through with a lazy hand.

Sticks made a show of checking his engines before casting off—stalling to ensure his passengers were processed safely. After he saw them appear dockside, he headed back downriver, careful not to acknowledge them with a wave or other farewell gesture. As far as Transport was concerned, these people were merely cargo to him.

Trick stood silently, watching the *Pittsburgh* steam away. Hawkeye was turned in the other direction, already reconnoitering the City from the docks. Minus his precious omni-lens, of course. No private citizen would own such a sophisticated and expensive piece of military equipment.

"I feel naked," said Bracer. He shifted his shoulder, like he felt the ghost of his hundred-pound field gun resting on his back. Or maybe its absence.

"You and me both," said Hawkeye, squinting inland. "My

eyes aren't what they used to be."

"We'll pick up basic hand weapons from Wainwright," Trick reminded them. "Thanks to the 3-D printing, the plastic will be undetectable. Best we can do under the circumstances."

When the captain didn't move, Pusher got antsy again. "Any reason we're standing here, sir? A bit conspicuous, don't you think?"

Trick blinked. This was his first mission as captain of Bestimmung Company. And he was a fish out of water—on land, in daylight, and a bit jumpy to say the least. Then he remembered why they were here, and it steeled his resolve.

"You're right, Sergeant. Let's get moving."

After leaving the docks and breaking into their assigned pairs, they walked on opposite sides of the street; crowds tended to attract Transport's attention. Pusher and Hawkeye went first, with the spotter doing his old job using only his eyes. Trick and Bracer brought up the rear, half a block behind. They stayed on foot rather than taking public transportation, to avoid interacting with the Authority. The stories told by their BICE ident packages were, in theory, airtight—but you never knew when some Transport true believer might notice something about them that smelled funny.

They reached Ye Olde World English Tavern in a couple of hours. The walk had done them good. Even Trick was considerably less nervous when the proprietor finally approached their table during the mid-morning lull.

"I hear you're looking for work," said Wainwright, placing a pitcher of water and four glasses on the table. "Lots of opportunity here in the City these days."

Trick nodded. "Times are tough down south. We'll be glad to find work."

With the countersign given, Wainwright bobbed his head and began slowly pouring the first glass of water. "Your men were here," he said, his voice low. "Last night. They bought some intel and moved on."

"Moved on where?" Trick took the glass and swigged half its contents.

"Detention Center is where they were headed. Looking for someone."

"Mary Brenneman?" asked Pusher. Her tone was hopeful. Even she noticed it. She'd have to rein that in.

"That's her," Wainwright said, pouring water into the second glass.

"They got out clean?" asked Bracer, smiling like he'd just complimented the establishment to its owner.

"Barely. TAC team came in. I brushed 'em off."

"You mean they plan to infiltrate the Detention Center? By themselves?" asked Hawkeye. His tone was unbelieving. Not even Hatch and Stug were that stupid.

"Keep your voice down," warned Wainwright, smiling for the handful of other patrons in the bar. After last night, one of them was likely a Transport follow-up. A year ago, he'd never have agreed to meet TRACE operatives two days in a row like this. His bar was too hot now, too bright on the radar. But times were tough. Business was way down. And TRACE had paid in cold, hard unis.

Pouring the last of the pitcher's water into the fourth glass, he said, "They seemed hell-bent. And one other thing ... something's going down. Something big."

"Something like what?" asked Pusher, leaning forward.

Wainwright set the empty pitcher on the table, took out the rag from behind his belt, and began wiping the tabletop. "No idea. But this exodus by Transport is unprecedented. My theory: they're gonna turn this place into a maximum security dumping ground for all their political prisoners. The whole damned City is gonna be a Detention Center. Maybe build another Wall around it, like with the Amish." He made a show of studying a spot on the table, then scrubbed at it for a moment. Looking satisfied, he tucked the towel back in his belt. "But I have no idea, really."

Trick held his glass up again. "Any chance we can get a copy of those plans too?" he whispered.

Shaking his head, Wainwright picked up the pitcher and said in his best stage voice, "Sorry, sir. That's all I've got free for you today. Best of luck with those jobs."

The owner walked away to greet a new customer coming in the door. A Transport officer. Trick glanced at the newcomer, then quickly away. All of them fingered their water glasses while Bracer made polite conversation about how long it'd take them to get to the employment bureau.

Wainwright ushered the Authority officer to a table nearer the bar and pulled out a chair for him. The officer sat down, his back to Trick and the others.

"Assuming they did what we think they did," said Hawkeye in a low voice, "are we really going to try and ... *extract* them ... from the Detention Center?"

All eyes turned to Trick. He was looking at his empty glass like maybe the first free serving of water had been a tease. "We're going to pursue our mission to the best of our ability," he said, quoting the manual. "And do what we came here to do."

"And do right by our friends," said Pusher.

Trick looked over to her. "Yeah, and that."

The Tick-Tock of the Okcillium Clock

"Oh, I don't do this because it's my job," said Gutierrez. He turned around to face her directly. "I do this because I enjoy the work."

Mary Brenneman sat strapped in a converted dentist's chair in the middle of a cold room. The tile on the floor was chipped. The walls were concrete blocks pitted with what could've been bullet holes. A lone bulb hung overhead, surrounded by a wire cage.

"That much is clear," she said weakly. "That's why I like killing porters, too."

Gutierrez smiled wolfishly. The scar running along the left side of his face stretched at an odd angle. "It's important to find satisfaction in what you do," he said. "Would you like some water? I know it's easy to get dehydrated in our facility."

Mary thought she felt the saliva in her mouth actually dry up at the suggestion—a strange reaction. It was as if her body feared Gutierrez so much that even his thinking about her need for hydration made her want to curl around what little fluid she currently retained.

"Oh, wait," said Gutierrez. "You haven't answered my question. So, no water for you then."

She hated how her body still reacted to him—exactly as he wanted it to, even after all these years. Her mind knew the game he was playing, knew that *he* knew exactly what he was doing by suggesting the water. He knew how she'd respond, even involuntarily, and that she was powerless to stop her own reaction. She hated that he was so damned good at the job he loved so much. And she hated Gutierrez, as she had for a long time now.

"You've come a long way from that scared little murderess I met, what, a quarter century ago now? My how time flies," he said wistfully, pouring himself a glass of water.

Mary watched the liquid fill the glass. Listened to the delicious sound it made.

"A long way." Gutierrez took a long, leisurely drink from the glass. "What were you … twelve? We were all a lot younger then, of course. Less efficient at our jobs." He shrugged. "Gotta learn someway, right?"

Mary found the strength to smile at him pleasantly. The skin of her dry lips stretched thin. The cotton in her mouth … maybe she couldn't control that. But what she showed him outwardly—that was entirely within her power.

Even that appearance was hard for her to maintain though, and she knew, from long acquaintance, that he knew it was hard. When they'd first met, she'd been a terrified but defiant young girl, ripped from her family. Gutierrez had been young and zealous and, yes, less efficient at his job.

Her defiant side had come to dominate as she'd grown older. It had taken over her inner voice from that frightened little girl the young Lieutenant Gutierrez had questioned so rigorously. Sometimes the little girl—alone, cold, unsure if her entire family had been killed by Transport—still held up the mirror of Mary's fears inside her mind. But for now, Captain Mary Brenneman, the QB to her soldiers, the woman who bucked authority and often placed courage before prudence, soothed the little girl and said with her adult's inner voice, *Let me handle this.*

"How'd you get that scar?" she asked around a thick tongue. "Displease the wife again? Or is it that you can't please her at all?"

Gutierrez set the glass down on the table and sighed his satisfaction. Apparently he'd been thirsty.

"On the other hand," he said, gathering up his coat, "some things never change. Your humorous attempts to incite me to anger are as sad as always. The desperate braying of a frightened farm girl who needs to see herself as stronger than she really is. A bark that sounds so fierce to her scared ears. Pathetic to mine."

"Shove it up your scar, you sadistic bastard."

His smile widened. "Truth is, Captain, I'm going to miss you. I'm leaving the City. For good, I guess you could say. And you and all your friends from ..." He paused a moment to appreciate a private joke. "From Bedrock—what a name, I love it!—well, you all won't be leaving this fair city. Ever again."

Gutierrez stood, waiting expectantly. "Oh, I didn't really need you to answer my question about your scavenger collaborator friends at all. I just enjoyed your thinking I did."

The confusion showed on Mary's face. It sat, shaky and uncertain, atop the frightened expectations of a little girl who'd learned over time just how vast the human capacity for personal cruelty could be.

"Yes, we scoured Bedrock last night. Killed everyone there." Gutierrez was pleased by the reaction that formed on Mary's face. He let his news sink in as he approached the door of the interrogation room. "It's amazing the kind of surgical precision trained military personnel armed with heat-sensing equipment, night vision, and drones with Gatling lasers can accomplish. Especially when facing an enemy dressed in rags and living in caves. Even if they do have a few laser rifles stolen for them by TRACE to fight back with. A waste of good equipment, if you ask me."

Mary's tongue wouldn't move. But her eyes screamed bloody murder.

Gutierrez smiled at what he saw on her face. "No sharp quips now? How disappointing. Well, goodbye, Mary Brenneman. We won't be seeing one another again." The man TRACE had nicknamed "The Inquisitor" touched his hand to the door's bio-trigger. It popped open with a hiss of air. "I'll send someone to take you back to your cell. You can die in this facility knowing that everything you've ever done in your life—poisoning Yoder, all the battles you fought, helping those useless scavengers ... all of it—was for nothing." He winked at her like he'd just shared a private joke between two old friends.

"Your father says hello, by the way."

Mary stared, disbelieving, at the door as it snicked shut behind him. For the last twenty-four hours, he'd merely been playing with her. He hadn't needed the location of Bedrock at all. If she could believe Gutierrez, it had already been destroyed. The little girl inside her began to weep, and the QB allowed a single tear to escape her liquid eyes.

Hatch and Stug were thrown into a large common room with the rest of the prisoners from the airbuses. They kept to themselves in a corner, waiting for the Transport personnel to process them. Several soldiers were walking around, cutting the ropes used to bind the prisoners for transfer to the center. When one approached them, the two commandos made a good show of it, wincing and rubbing their wrists like one of his comrades had already removed theirs. He moved on.

"I don't see Logan," said Stug, looking at the floor. He was careful to keep his voice down.

Hatch leaned against the wall, scanning the large, gray room. "Me either. But I recognize some of the other council members. Don't see the old tobacco addict, though."

Half a dozen Transport personnel worked the room, attending to the nearly one hundred Wild Ones packing it wall to wall. At least two of the Authority types were medical personnel. They wore the emblem of Transport overlaid with the caduceus—the traditional symbol of the medical profession, the staff of Hermes wrapped round by two serpents—on their uniforms. One was an older male doctor who took the lead in performing the examinations; the other was a female nurse.

"You two wounded?" the doctor asked when he got to them. Stug rubbed his wrists again for show but said nothing.

"We're fine," said Hatch. "Are these all that are left?"

"I'm not here to answer your questions, scavenger. If you're not hurt, I've got others to see and patch up." The doctor moved on to an elderly woman sitting on the floor along the wall. The nurse lingered.

"Those that weren't killed in the attack are here," she confirmed. "I'm sorry for your loss." The woman seemed genuine in her condolences, if brief. She moved on to assist the physician.

When she was out of earshot, Stug said, "This must've happened in the last day, after we went AWOL. I wonder if Neville sent any—"

"What do you think?" scoffed Hatch. He noted his own reaction to the colonel's name and calmed himself. "It probably happened so fast that there was no opportunity to help. You know Transport. Shock and aw-shit."

Stug blew out a breath. "Not for much longer. They're on the retreat."

Hatch levered himself from the wall. "Does this look like a retreat to you?" He flicked his hand toward the wounded in the room. The former residents of Bedrock sat glassy-eyed, some trying to console others. Most seemed unsure where they were. Groans of pain had become the almost-forgotten white noise in the background of their communal jail cell.

"Actually, knowing Transport, it kinda does," said Stug. "It looks to me like a five-year-old just had his toys taken away and he's throwing a fit. Destroying everything—and everyone—because if he can't have what he wants, no one else can have it either."

Hatch nodded. "Maybe." Stug's description of Transport as a spoiled child rang true for him. But the scene before him seemed like more the spiteful work of a petulant child with massive weaponry at his disposal.

"Hey," said Stug, motioning. "I recognize her. I know that little girl."

Hatch followed his gaze. In the center of the room, a young girl, not yet a teenager, stood staring. But she wasn't in shock—she was glaring intently. She didn't look injured, and she seemed to be following the doctor with her eyes as he made his rounds, as if she was making sure the physician attended properly to his patients, her people. She stood straight-legged, her arms at her sides, her fists clenched. Her face showed a kind of flat anger, hard and focused.

Stug got up.

"What are you doing?" Hatch's tone carried a warning. He knew exactly what Stug was doing. "We're trying to fly under the radar here."

The big man began to slide slowly toward the middle of the room. "I'm just gonna see if she's okay. I like her grit."

"Stug, she's not our mission—"

"Sure she is." The sergeant turned his head back and smiled, bumping lightly into someone. "Pardon, ma'am."

"Stug—"

"Unwad your panties. I'll be right back." The sergeant winked and turned away.

Hatch let him go. Pursuing him, making a bigger scene than Stug was already making, would only compound the problem. He sat down on the floor to make himself less conspicuous again. *Someone has to*, he grumbled in his head. Once in a while, he flitted a glance their way to see how the girl was doing.

Still following the doctor on his rounds, the girl had her back to Stug as he approached.

"Hey," he said lightly. "Hey, girl from Bedrock."

She spun around, her fists jerking up to her chest. Her eyes tracked up, then up some more, and her mouth opened slightly. Then her teeth clicked as she clenched it shut again, and her eyes hardened to stones.

"Get away from me," she hissed. "I don't know you. You'd better leave me alone."

Stug smiled. "I don't want to hurt you, little girl. I want to help. What's your name?"

She took a half step backward. "I don't need your help. And none of your business. I don't know you."

"My name's ... Joseph. But most people call me Stug." The big man bent down and held out a massive hand. It hung in the air, unshaken.

"That's a stupid name," she said defiantly. "Sounds like a burp."

The sergeant stood up and chuckled so loudly, the girl took another step back. As his laughter tapered off, he realized he wasn't sure how to proceed with her. He was more comfortable punching Transport officers than talking to children, and her reaction made him hesitate. Then Stug noticed how hard she had to crane her neck to see him, how high she held her fists in front of her face. She was a cute kid, maybe even pretty in a few years, if she washed the grime of Bedrock off. And, most of all, he admired her willingness to fight to protect herself.

Stug knelt down on one knee so they were almost eye level.

"Hey, I do know you," she said over her fists. "You're one of the soldiers that came through our village last week. You're the Man Mountain."

Stug chuckled. "Yeah. Yeah, that's right. That's what the old man, the scout, called me. You remember me, huh?"

"Yeah, I remember. And his name is Eeguls."

"What? Who?"

"The scout. He's like my grandfather."

"He's your grandfather?"

"No, he's *like* my grandfather."

"Ah, I see. Where's your family then?"

"Dead."

She said it short and staccato and without flinching. Then her eyes softened, as if hearing it out loud in her own voice had made it finally, irrevocably true. Seeing his reaction, the girl flattened her gaze again.

"I'm sorry," said Stug.

"Anne."

"What?"

"My name's Anne," she said, lowering her arms. Her eyes tried very hard to stay angry, but the emotion stirring in them made that difficult.

"I'm sorry, Anne."

"You should be."

Stug hesitated again and rested his hands on his knee. He wanted to present the least threat possible to this little girl. She'd had enough of feeling threatened already.

"I don't know what you mean, Anne."

"You should've come back," the little girl said. Her tone was challenging. "We helped you. We helped you get food from the Amish. You should've helped us *back*." The steel in her voice began to weaken. "You should've come back and stopped them. So my mother ..."

The stones in her eyes submerged.

Stug didn't know what to say—because he knew she was right. "I'm sorry," was the only thing that would come out.

"I don't need your *sorry*!" she said, walking forward. "It's too late now! I don't need you! You're too late!"

Stug gathered the girl into the soft cradle of his iron arms. She struggled at first, the venom in her voice fueling her anger as she pounded his chest. Then she surrendered to her sorrow. She wrapped her own thin arms as far around his chest as they'd go and yelled into his shirt, "You're too late! You're too late! I hate all soldiers! I hate you!"

The sergeant stood, lifting Anne, and held her tight while she sobbed.

"What's going on here?"

A Transport soldier approached them, gun held across his chest at the ready, barrel pointed down.

Stug turned away and ignored him.

"Hey, scavenger, I asked you a question." The sound of a weapon being dragged away from a uniform.

A second voice. "This is none of your concern. Walk away."

Stug turned his head so his ear was cocked behind him, but he kept Anne protected behind his massive frame, away from the meddling guard.

The soldier turned to the voice. "Who the hell do you think you are? If you hadn't noticed, I've got a Transport symbol on this uniform."

"Oh, I noticed," said Hatch, moving between the guard and Stug. "But unless you want to find out what it feels like to have a rifle barrel tickling your throat by way of your ass, you'll move along."

The trooper chambered a round.

"Hey!" called an officer from across the room. "Stand down, soldier."

"Better listen to your commanding officer," said Hatch. "You might shoot me, but I'm guessing a hundred prisoners with free hands might decide a little revenge is worth dying for."

The man held Hatch's gaze a moment longer.

"Private! Now!"

Slinging his weapon, the soldier walked away.

Stug turned back around and met Hatch's gaze. "Thanks."

"Sure. It's not like we're trying to keep a low profile or anything."

With Anne's face still buried in his shoulder, the sergeant noted Hatch's sarcasm and glanced around. All the Wild Ones in the room that could were looking in their direction. Ironically, only the Transport personnel seemed occupied with something else.

"Hey," said Stug, shifting the girl in his arms, "they're bringing in the guy on the litter."

Two medical personnel carried a converted cot into the room with an older man lying on it. His right arm was missing; his shoulder ended in a massive bandage with a dark, round bloodstain.

The room was stirring.

"Someone important," said Stug.

Anne sniffled against his chest. She brought her head up and looked where everyone else was looking.

"It's Logan," she said.

Hatch peered harder across the room. Several of the prisoners were making their way toward the cot. They were careful to give the medical team space until the two Transport personnel moved off, leaving the injured man alone.

"Are you sure?"

Anne sniffed and wiped her eyes. "Of course I'm sure. He's been like a father to me."

Glancing first at her, then at Stug, Hatch said, "Stay here. This one's mine." He carefully made his way through the growing throng surrounding Logan.

The murmur was a strange mixture of voices both concerned about their leader's condition and angry over their own incarceration. Hatch heard one man already agitating for an immediate escape attempt. He was fooling himself, Hatch knew. Even armed, they'd already come to this end. How much more useless, then, would an unarmed prison revolt prove?

Patiently, graciously, Hatch pushed himself to the front of the crowd and knelt beside Logan. One eye was hidden behind a white half-mask of bandages, his gray locks splaying out from underneath. Hatch glanced at the stump where Logan's right shoulder ended. The blood seeping through seemed to be clotting. That, at least, was good news.

The clamoring voices around Hatch were getting on his nerves. He turned and said, "Give him some air. Let the man recover a bit before you start looking to him again for answers."

The voices died down.

"Who the hell are you?" someone asked. The woman was older—*probably a member of the council with Logan*, Hatch thought. "This man was our leader," she said. "We have a right—no, an obligation—to stand here with him."

Hatch addressed her without standing. "I absolutely agree with you. But at this moment, I need to talk to him."

"And who the hell are you again?" asked a man. It sounded like the agitator, the one who had wanted to lead an escape attempt, whatever its odds of success.

Hatch wasn't sure how to answer. Should he tell him—which meant telling them all—that he was an AWOL member of TRACE? Would one of them recognize him, any moment now, from their visit to the camp, as Anne had done with Stug? And either way, if they knew who he was, might one of them sell him out at the first opportunity to escape Transport's wrath?

None of his options were good ones.

Then, for once, Transport's interference worked in Hatch's favor.

"You there! Break that crowd up!" It was the Authority officer who'd dressed down the bully private. "Move away from the man on the cot. Now!"

Grudgingly, the circle of Wild Ones began to disperse around the room, crowded as it was. Even the grouser moved away. The councilwoman left Hatch with a nasty stare that promised their conversation wasn't finished.

Left alone with Logan, Hatch knew he didn't have much time.

"Hey," he said, touching the former TRACE agent's good arm. "Hey, Logan. You need to wake up."

Logan was unresponsive. Hatch shook him harder, but nothing. Transport no doubt had him sedated—maybe with morphine for the pain or Q to keep him docile, unable to whip up his followers into another frenzy of rebellion. Looking at the wounded man, Hatch doubted Logan would be whipping anyone up into anything anytime soon. Maybe ever again.

But he needed the man awake.

He looked around and saw Stug and Anne watching him. Despite the close quarters, everyone else seemed to have claimed a little corner of the big room, per the officer's orders. Hatch shook his head furtively at Stug. The sergeant nodded and turned Anne away so she was facing another direction, then began talking to her to keep her distracted.

Hatch braced himself and, with a final glance around,

placed his palm on the shoulder wound and squeezed.

Logan moaned.

"Wake up, damn it!"

He placed his other hand over Logan's mouth and squeezed the man's wound harder. Logan's eyes flew open, watering at the edges. His eyes darted left and right for the source of the pain, finally lighting on his tormentor.

Hatch released his shoulder and met Logan's gaze. The gray man focused as the pain subsided.

"Hatch?" Logan's voice seemed to wonder if he was real. "Sean Hatch?"

Placing a finger to his lips, Hatch nodded.

"Where the hell am I? What happened? Transport attacked, and then … everything … I can't remember anything after that."

"You and the survivors are in the City's Detention Center. Looks to be about a hundred of you left."

Logan's eyes widened, and his head came up. He winced with the effort. "The City? They brought us to Columbia?"

"Yes. Now listen to me, we don't have much time—"

"No. Damn it, no." The Wild One leader dropped his head to the floor.

Hatch was confused. "Where else did you think you'd be interred? Now listen to me—"

"You don't understand," said Logan. "There's a bomb. There's a goddamned bomb."

The lieutenant's mouth opened and closed again. "A bomb? What kind of bomb?"

"An okcillium bomb. The rumors were true." Logan's voice

sounded desperate and defeated. That worried Hatch even more than what the man was telling him. Logan had been a stalwart believer in the Wild Ones' ability to fight back when they'd stolen those guns from the armory. Now he gave the appearance of a man ready to grab the nearest handgun and blow his own head off.

"What are you talking about?"

"Transport is defeated here. They know it. Hell, everyone knows it. The evacuations, the clean-up operations. And now, a Final Solution."

Hatch sat down against the wall. He could see Stug's expression from across the room. The big man didn't appear to like what he was seeing in Hatch's face.

"How do you know this? How could you possibly know this?"

"I've heard rumors for weeks. Through old contacts. Fifth columnists that work with us. I should've listened more closely. I thought they were just rumors. I thought, not even Transport would murder an entire city of innocents. Then my contact was killed, and they tracked his information trail to Bedrock. It's why they attacked. I should have evacuated sooner." Logan closed his eyes, turned his head away from the crowded wounded in the room. "I should have evacuated sooner."

"A cruel, petulant child with massive weaponry," breathed Hatch.

"What? What did you say?"

"When is this thing set to go off? And you're absolutely sure?"

"As sure as anyone can be. The intel was solid. But when? Now? Five minutes from now? A week—wait, you didn't know about the bomb?" Logan was focusing again, his old operative's training kicking in. "What are you doing here? Why are TRACE commandos in the City then?"

Hatch closed his eyes. "TRACE isn't. Stug and I are ... we're ... pursuing a mission of our own."

Though he had only one good eye, Logan recognized the expression on Hatch's face. He knew exactly what their mission was. The lieutenant had been something of a rival in the short time they'd spent together. During a conversation with Mary Brenneman on the *Pittsburgh*, Logan had guessed the nature of Hatch's past relationship with her. He'd even harbored some passing, juvenile fantasy of pursuing her himself. He liked her—her fire, her humor, her unbending spirit. So seeing Hatch's face now was like seeing his own reflection in a pool. No words were needed to explain.

"You're here to rescue her." Logan said it as a statement of fact, not a question. "I wish I could help you. I wish I could help anyone." Again his tone became despondent. He looked down at the stump of his right shoulder, and his head dropped back to the cot.

"You really have no idea when this thing is set to go off? Or where it is? Maybe we can stop it."

Logan shook his head. "I have no intel as to its location. It could be anywhere. Hell, they could phase it in from the Old World, for that matter. Trying to find it is pointless. Where would you look for a bomb that can destroy an entire city?"

Hatch gritted his teeth. He watched Stug set Anne on the

ground. The sergeant bent down, probably making sure she'd be all right, and handed her something. It was his fedora from Wainwright's. *Damn it, I told him to get rid of that.* Then Stug sidled his way toward them through the crowd.

"Then we have no more time to waste," said Hatch, making to rise.

Logan reached out and grabbed his arm. "Take my people with you, Lieutenant. Get them out of here!"

Hatch stared at him. "If you haven't noticed, we're all in the same boat with a hole in it."

"Please! You've got to get them out! Out of here, out of the City!"

"Keep your voice down," Hatch hissed. "Or none of us will get out of here."

"What's all the hubbub about?" whispered Stug, nodding a greeting to Logan and leaning against the wall next to Hatch.

"There's been a complication," breathed Hatch. He stared at Logan, whose eyes pled silently to do as he'd asked.

"Eh, there always is," said Stug with a wry smile. "Never stopped us before."

The sergeant's confidence heartened him, but Hatch felt himself slipping downward to join Logan at the bottom of a well called despair.

"There's always a first time," he said.

Up, Up, Up!

"How the hell are we supposed to get them out?" asked Bracer. "And are we even sure they're in there?"

The noise and activity of the day criss-crossed the square in front of them. The two pairs of commandos sat at separate but adjacent tables outside a small café, positioned so they could see one another and hold a covert conversation but not appear to be together. Under the Authority's martial law, four or more people congregating was considered a crowd, and every crowd was assumed to be fomenting rebellion. Once, that might have seemed paranoid. These days, as Transport evacuated the City, it was more than a reasonable assumption.

The fountain in the middle of the square, its unmasked Lady Justice pointing toward the courthouse, arced water in a pattern that, seen from above, formed the emblem of the Transport Authority. From their tables in front of the café, the TRACE team watched the comings and goings of the square framed by the Detention Center and the Justice Building. The sound of the spraying jets helped to mask their conversation.

"Roof looks accessible," Hawkeye said, like he was

commenting on the weather. He had one eye closed, drawing lines and judging distances in his head. He'd tried accessing public records on the area, but the constant static on his BICE had given him a headache, so he'd turned it off. Besides, whatever he could find on the Internet about the Detention Center in the public record was likely to be disinformation anyway. Transport was neither stupid nor hubristic enough to publish its prison schematics online.

"They're there," insisted Pusher. "Wainwright said they had the plans. When have you ever known Hatch or Stug to sit idly by?"

Bracer gave her a look, conceding the point.

"If they're in there…" began Trick. The others turned their eyes on him expectantly, and he stopped speaking. The captain seemed to be mustering his next words like troops before a charge uphill. "If the Authority has them, Colonel Neville's orders are to consider them lost as prisoners of war. We're to return to Little Gibraltar immediately."

The fountain's pumping pulsed in their ears. The noises of daily life in the heart of the Authority's security sector occasionally broke up the serenade of its splashing water.

To his credit, Trick met each of their eyes in turn. He had to force himself to do it.

Bracer spoke first. "Our mission is to recover valuable assets that could, potentially, be very damaging to TRACE if interrogated successfully by Transport." He was paraphrasing their orders. Highlighting the parts that supported his argument, as it were.

"Unless that mission can't be fulfilled without undue risk

of providing the Authority with four more sources of information," parried Trick.

"Sir, we can't just leave them in there," said Pusher.

"That's exactly what our orders say we're to do, Sergeant," said Trick. "And if we disobey those orders, we become outlaws right alongside Hatch and Stug. Are you prepared to throw away your career, your part in an organization dedicated to the destruction of Transport and all it stands for?" This time, Trick had no problem holding their eyes. His own words had fired him up. "All to maybe—*maybe*—save two AWOL louts who let their emotions get the better of them? Who threw military discipline aside to pursue their own selfish goals?"

Bracer shifted uncomfortably. To Trick, it looked like he was trying to keep himself from punching his captain in the side of the head. Pusher's teeth were clenched. Her jaw muscles flexed. As always when he was under fire, Hawkeye simply sat and stared, gathering information to use against his enemy later.

Now was the time, Trick decided. "Two louts who pulled every one of you—and me—out of more scrapes than we ever would've lived through without them?"

"Sir, I know what our orders say, but we have do right by those men," Pusher said. Her words were calm, if bold. Her expression was determined, unyielding. Her ears, apparently, were closed.

"Yes we do, Sergeant," said Trick quietly.

Pusher made a gesture with her hand. "And if you don't want to be a part of that because it breaks orders, I under—

Sir?"

Reviewing the last few moments in his head, Bracer turned his eyes on Trick. He'd only been half listening, convinced the captain was Obadiah's man through and through.

"I'll wait for you three to catch up," said Trick, grinning. For the first time, he felt comfortable in his role as their captain. *And all it took was treason*, he thought.

"Sir, did you just agree to lead a prison break to recover Hatch and Stug?" asked Hawkeye.

"First to spot the obvious as always, Corporal."

Bracer sat back. "You sonofabitch. This whole time you were playing us."

"I wouldn't say that, Corporal. You had to believe it so Neville and the rest of B-Company would believe it. Or you might be here taking orders from someone else. Someone else less ... *flexible* in their interpretation of orders."

"You sonofabitch," said Bracer again.

"Why didn't you just tell us when we stepped off the boat?" asked Pusher. The expression on her face was somehow both incredulous and relieved at having been duped.

"Because I didn't want to suggest we break orders until it was absolutely necessary. That would've put *you* at risk as parties to mutiny. Hell, think about it. We might've found them face-down drunk in Wainwright's bar."

Hawkeye nodded knowingly. "To be fair, odds were pretty good for that."

"Sonofa—"

"*Bracer*," admonished Pusher. "We all know what you think of the captain's mother. So ... what now, sir?"

Trick stared across the combined length of both tables at Hawkeye. "Corporal?"

The spotter sighed. He missed his omni-lens. "They've got cameras everywhere. And drones at each of the facility's two entrances," he said, indicating the lone drone hovering on guard duty between the café and the building's main entrance.

"Don't give me problems, Corporal," Trick said, sounding for the first time like a commanding officer. "Your job is solutions."

Hawkeye stared for a moment, his brain working the angles he'd measured using his naked eye earlier. Then he shrugged. "I'll figure something out."

It had been a few hours since they'd brought her back to her cell following Gutierrez's mind games. She'd lain in her bunk wondering about what he'd said as he left. About her father, Abram. She wondered if—hope beyond hope—he was still alive. More than likely, that had been just another game, a seed planted by The Inquisitor to accomplish exactly what he'd wanted—to distract her with false hope of ever seeing her father again. Get inside her head and make her fixate upon old hurts by reopening them. Paralyze her with self-doubt. It was what Gutierrez was good at. It was why he took such pride in his work.

The electronic lock on her cell door hummed as it disengaged. Tumblers clicked and the latch released. When the door slid open, a guard moved into the space. "Stand away from the door," he said.

Wincing, Mary sat up on her elbows in her bunk.

"Oh, that's right, I forgot," said the guard, wagging his head like it was his way of laughing. "Here's your new roomie. We're wall-to-wall now. Hope you two ladies get along."

He stood aside, but no one entered.

"*Now*, savage. Get in the damned cell."

Mary wanted to get up and usher the newcomer in. Help her past Planck, the guard no one wanted to turn their backs on. Then a small shadow crossed into the cell, followed by the waif casting it. Her eyes darted left then right, as if already looking for a way out. She held something in her hands tightly: a piece of cloth. When she passed in front of Planck, he shoved her forward, and she sprawled to the floor.

"You take too long, savage," he said.

"Come a little closer," said Mary, grabbing Planck's attention. "And try that on me."

The guard smirked. "Don't tempt me, rebel. Kicking a cripple around might be fun." He backed out of the cell, and the door closed and latched with a vacuum-sealed *shunk*.

The girl lay on the floor. She'd raised herself up on her hands but rested on her right side, looking down. Her dirty hair covered her face like a veil.

Or an Amish kapp that's been dropped in the dirt, then stuck back on her head, Mary thought.

Where that image had come from, she had no idea. But as the girl rested there, seeming to recover her strength, it looked more to Mary like she was debating whether or not to get up ever again. Like maybe the girl thought standing up was just more trouble, would *cause* more trouble, than it was worth.

You can't think like that. Mary directed the thought silently through the air to her new cellmate. *You can't ever stay down. You always have to get up again. If you can.* Mary turned her eyes briefly to her legs, covered by a blanket.

The girl began to rise. When she got to her feet, she turned around and stared at the cell door. She clutched the cloth to her chest like a talisman—or maybe a shield.

"My name's Mary."

Her legs trembling, the girl simply stood and watched the door.

"Mary Brenneman." She shifted on the cot, trying to sit up. If the girl were closer, she'd reach out to her. But Mary thought how she might feel in the girl's place and reconsidered. Maybe space was best. "What's your name?"

Never turning, her eyes focused on the locked door of the cell, the girl whispered, "Anne." And then, after a moment, "I remember you."

Mary wasn't sure she'd heard right, so she moved in an attempt to better see the girl's face. But the angle between them was too great, and Mary could hardly get up and walk over to the girl. It felt like she had lead weights attached to her thighs. Lead weights with jolts of electricity that randomly arced pain to her brain.

"What? What did you say?"

"I said I remember you. You and the others. You came to my village."

"Please," Mary said, needing to know. "Please, turn around. Let me see you."

299

Anne obliged.

Recognizing her beneath the grime, the hurt, the mask of stone and steel the little girl wore, Mary smiled. "I remember you too. You're the little girl in Bedrock, aren't you. The one …" *The one who so reminded me of myself when I was your age.* "The one who watched us so carefully." *Unvanquished. Immovable. Immortal.*

"Watched you pass by."

"Yes."

"Watched you not come back."

Anne's eyes burned into Mary with dark anger—just as they had on that day, when her gaze had dared the QB and her men to make one wrong step, to threaten her people in any way.

"Anne was my mother's name," Mary said. "I've always thought it was very beautiful. I've never met another Anne before you." The girl's eyes didn't relent. Not sure she wanted to hear the answer, Mary asked, "What happened?"

"Transport killed most of us. And took the rest of us prisoner. That's what happened."

"And you're mad at me. At TRACE. Because we didn't come back and help you."

"You could've stopped them. You could've stopped *this*."

Mary closed her eyes, debating with herself. "Maybe," she said. She pulled the blanket off and opened her eyes so she would see what the girl was seeing.

Anne gasped.

"Maybe not," Mary said.

As Anne stared, aghast, Mary said, "I'm sorry for what

happened to your people, Anne. But we've fought hard, TRACE has. For you. For the Amish. For everyone. Even for Transport's own loyal citizens who don't know what they don't have. But we can't be everywhere at once."

"I won't! I won't!" shouted the girl. She kneaded the cloth in her hands furiously. "I won't cry again!"

Mary threw the blanket back over her legs.

After a few moments, Anne's anger subsided and she looked up at the woman on the cot. "Is that really true?"

"What?"

"That your mother's name was Anne?"

"Yes. Anne Brenneman. And I had a father and a brother. I—I'm not sure if they're still alive. I haven't seen them in forever. Since I was your age."

Anne began again to fold and squeeze the cloth she held so fiercely in her hands. "I lost my family too. My real family. When Transport attacked…" Her eyes threatened to overflow again.

"What's that in your hand?" Mary asked, wanting to distract her. "Something from home?"

Anne looked down as if she'd forgotten she had it. "No, it's a hat. The Man Mountain gave it to me before. He's my friend now," she said, not quite convinced of that herself.

Mary's heart skipped a beat.

"The—the Man Mountain?"

"Yes. We called him that when you visited, remember?" Anne grinned slightly through her anguish, thinking of her time with Stug in the common room. Then she noticed a peculiar look on Mary's face. "What's wrong?"

"The Man Mountain is here?"

"Yes, him and the other man. His friend."

Mary's heart skipped two beats.

"Which man? What did he look like?"

Anne blushed and looked down at the floor. "Um…"

"Never mind. You've answered my question."

"Are you okay?" asked Anne, moving toward the bed. "Did I say something wrong?"

Mary reached out, and Anne let her take her hand. The QB's fingers lightly brushed the rough wool of the fedora, as if she were afraid, just by touching it, she'd make it disappear.

"Want to hold it?" asked Anne.

Mary looked from the fedora up to the girl's eyes. Without waiting for Mary to answer, Anne offered it to her. Mary took Stug's hat in her hand and smoothed the creases made by the girl's kneading.

"Did I say something wrong?" repeated Anne.

"Oh, no, honey, not at all. Best stay here by me, though, away from the door. But keep your eye on it." Smiling, Mary handed the fedora back to Anne. "Our friends are coming."

"How long do we have to hang here?" whispered Bracer. "My arms hurt."

"Quiet," said Trick. "You complain worse than Stug ever did."

The last of the prisoners were pounding down the ramp of the airbus. Bracer and Trick held fast to the vehicle's undercarriage, waiting.

"I sure hope they follow protocol and stow this ship for the night. You don't think they have more prisoners to pick up, do you?"

"*Quiet.*"

Pusher and Hawkeye had gone ahead. In all, three airbuses had landed near the fountain and offloaded more prisoners, who were herded into the Detention Center. After lifting off, each of the three ships had landed on the building's roof to be refueled and readied for the next day. The sergeant and spotter had hitched a ride on the previous airbus; they should be waiting on the roof for Trick and Bracer to join them.

"It's gonna be really loud when those anti-gravs—"

Before Bracer could finish, the airbus fired up its booster engines. The doors closed. Air rushed around them. As the craft overcame planetary gravity, the main anti-grav engines kicked in and Bracer watched the ground fall away. He closed his eyes and turned his head to stare at the bottom of the vehicle. His knuckles were harder than the reinforced aluminum frame he held on to for dear life. He hated heights.

Less squeamish as the airbus lifted off, Trick watched the Transport soldiers that had guarded the ramp follow the last of the night's catch into the facility. Neither looked up to spot the infiltrators wedged beneath the airbus. Why would they? Their attention was focused straight ahead to ensure a prisoner didn't get desperate before being locked away.

Transport had ramped up its roundup of dissenters in the last week; half a dozen airbuses had been offloading prisoners every night after midnight. Why, Trick had no idea. The

Authority was abandoning the City to TRACE. So why go to all the trouble of gathering fugitives, Wild Ones, derelict TRACE operatives, and suspicious citizens? Why wasn't Transport focusing its resources on securing the cities beyond the Great Shelf? It made no sense that Trick could see, either strategically or tactically.

Bracer hardly had time to be terrified before the bus began its landing approach to the center's roof. A blast of the booster engines, and the craft descended. Though he was used to the rapid *thrrrit-thrrrit-thrrrit* of his 18-millimeter heavy machine gun, the screaming servos of the anti-gravs made him close his eyes in an irrational attempt to protect his ears.

Soon enough, both men felt the slight jolt of the hydraulic landing pads as the airbus settled onto its parking spot. A final blast of controlled air, and the engines themselves powered down.

"How long do we—"

"Quiet or you're a private again."

"How can you demote me?" Bracer whispered. "We're no longer officially in TRACE!"

The doors opened above their heads, and the ramp descended again. The heavy boots of the flight crew tromped down the metal gangway, the man and woman murmuring to each other after a long day. Once they stepped onto the roof, the ramp automatically retracted and the doors shut tight.

Trick listened to the tread of the flight crew crunching away across the roof. Bracer started to move, but Trick made a sound that stopped him.

Just then, the sound of a fist making contact with a jaw. A

startled half-cry. A grainy thud as one body fell to the roof, then another.

"Now," said Trick, detaching himself. Bracer winced as he pried his white-knuckled grip from the airbus's frame.

Crouching and keeping the row of airbuses between themselves and the roof's access door, the two men made their way to their companions. A quick glimpse showed them that the plan was working so far. Pusher and Hawkeye were hidden behind the first airbus, the one nearest the access door; they had ambushed the third bus's flight crew, stripped them of their uniforms, and were already almost fully dressed again.

Hawkeye motioned for Trick and Bracer to keep low, keep right, and advance. Trick went first, followed by Bracer.

"Hawkeye, report," said the captain as Pusher zipped up.

"There are four cameras on the roof, each facing a different direction from the point of entry there," Hawkeye said, pointing at the access door leading down into the facility. "But I found a blind spot. Once we slip under their eyes, we ease along the building and we're in. One AA Gatling laser, unmanned at the moment, protects the roof."

Bracer took note of the anti-aircraft gun positioned near the door. "No need to man a gun when you've got air superiority twenty-four seven," he said. "Guards?"

"None on the roof, just the cameras. Inside?" Hawkeye shrugged. "Unknown."

"Transport's bugging out," said Pusher. "All day we sat at that café and watched them. I only saw fifteen different faces, even with the guard shifts. They were rotating personnel in half shifts to make it look like they have more soldiers on duty than they really do. I think they're even sharing personnel between the prison and the military, two different branches of the service."

"Skeleton crew?" wondered Bracer.

Trick shrugged. "Like Pusher said, Transport's bugging out. Why not?"

"That's a big assumption to make, sir," said Hawkeye.

The captain nodded and paraphrased the manual: "Our plans are only as good as the intel we have."

"And no battle plan survives contact with the enemy," said Pusher, quoting battle wisdom much older than the TRACE *Manual for Engaging the Enemy in the Field.*

"So are we gonna try and impress each other by quoting Sun Tzu next, or are we gonna get them out?"

Trick granted Bracer's point. "Lead the way, Hawkeye."

"Only one direction sir," said the spotter. "And that's down."

When Transport began escorting the survivors of Bedrock in ones and two to more permanent accommodations in The Dungeon, they took the children first—including Anne. Stug almost started the party then, but Hatch restrained him. There were still half a dozen guards on hand to control the holding room, but they knew as the room became less dense with prisoners, Transport would likewise reduce its on-duty force. Executing their plan too soon would end their breakout before it ever started. And civilians could be injured.

After prioritizing the children, the Authority began remanding prisoners based solely on geographical convenience; each time the guards returned through the door that led to The Dungeon, they just rounded up whichever prisoners were nearest and took them away. So Hatch and Stug simply positioned themselves on the opposite side of the room. They sat on the floor next to Logan, who floated in a sleep-sea of morphine.

It didn't take long for most of the hundred prisoners to be removed. Soon, fewer than thirty remained. And only two guards monitored the room.

Hatch knew they needed to move quickly; he had no idea when Logan's bomb would go off. Actually, he wasn't even certain a bomb existed. Maybe it was a figment of Logan's imagination—stirred up by hatred for Transport, his injuries, and the morphine. Or maybe the rumor from his fifth-column source had been planted by Transport to flush Logan and his salvager rebels out.

But Hatch knew he couldn't take the chance that the bomb wasn't real. And in his gut he believed Logan. It sounded exactly like something a desperate Transport—that petulant child with massive weaponry—would do in the wake of TRACE's gains in the region. A way to demonstrate its power with a blatant disregard for life, all for the sake of maintaining a papier-mâché facade of absolute control.

It's true, Hatch assumed. *When will it go off? How can I possibly know that?*

He suspected that, as long as there were more prisoners to bottle up in the Detention Center, the Authority wouldn't set the bomb off. Perverse logic, that. It'd make a better public relations splash, a better object lesson, to have the highest death toll possible when the City was consumed. That might explain the constant influx of prisoners brought in by airbus every night. Transport was putting all the rats on the same ship before blowing a hole in its hull. The Authority prided itself on its efficiency.

"Notice how the same four or five guards are rotating back to pick up detainees and take them below?" asked Hatch. "And how they're only leaving two behind to guard the room?"

"Now, yeah. Less bodies to cause trouble, less guards needed. Short-staffed, are they?"

"Yeah, seems that way. Easier for us."

The room's two guards were coming their way, escorting the doctor and his nurse who'd examined Logan earlier. Those four were the only Authority personnel left in the common room.

Stug rapped Hatch on the shoulder. *Now's as good a time as any*, his look said.

Both men stood up.

"Any change?" asked the doctor.

"Still out," reported Hatch, sounding concerned. "I don't think he's gonna make it, Doc. He was breathing pretty heavily before. Now he's hardly breathing at all."

The physician took in the information, then knelt beside his patient. Hatch nodded to Stug.

The sergeant stepped forward quicker than anyone his size should have been able to move. He grabbed the barrel of the first guard's laser rifle and ripped it out of the man's hands.

Fatigued from long shifts, the second guard stood and gawped while Stug threw a haymaker with all the force his slightly off-balance body could muster. The man flew backward ten feet and landed heavily on the floor, his lungs whooshing out air.

Stug smiled. He recognized the man: the bully from earlier. *It truly is the little things*, he mused.

The doctor looked up. The nurse screamed.

Hatch dove on top of the first guard and delivered a right cross to the jaw. The soldier was out cold.

"Hey! I called dibs!" said Stug.

Hatch snatched up the unconscious man's sidearm and pointed it at the physician. "No personal alarms, please."

The doctor raised his eyebrows, like he knew something Hatch didn't, then slowly raised his hands over his head. The nurse shut her mouth.

When Stug had knocked him to the floor, the bully guard had lost his laser rifle. He fumbled with his sidearm now, crab-walking away from the mountain looming over him. Stug took two giant strides forward and pulled the man up by his uniform collar. Feet dangling in the air, tired eyes terrified, the man dropped his pistol.

"Wise," said Stug, grinning. He set the man lightly back on his feet. "Now see, wasn't that easier?"

The guard half-smiled his relief.

"Not so tough when it's not a little girl you're facing, huh?"

The bully's smile disappeared as Stug drew back his right arm. The blow shot out from the sergeant's shoulder like a cannonball, and the bully guard covered half the length of the room, unconscious before hitting the floor again. He was quickly surrounded by fascinated Wild Ones looking down at his still form.

"I must be getting old," said Stug. "That took two punches. Still … very satisfying." He bent over and picked up the man's rifle.

"Who *are* you people?" It was the older woman, the one who'd earlier protested Hatch's attention to Logan.

"You're too late," said the doctor. "I've already alerted the entire complex." As if on cue, the klaxons sounded around them. The ambient lighting snapped from standard to red.

Hatch stared at the doctor. The man had used his BICE, of course. Transport didn't suffer the same restrictions TRACE did in the City; there was no dampening field inserting an annoying buzz into their brains. Their IP addresses were shielded and their BICEs worked perfectly. The doctor had undoubtedly sent an alert over the Authority's security network the moment Stug had attacked the first guard.

A rifle butt found the back of the doctor's skull, and he crumpled into unconsciousness. Hatch gave Stug a look that was both amused and annoyed.

"He was a douche."

"Fair enough," replied Hatch. "But we don't have much time." He nodded at the floor. Stug turned his weapon on each of the unconscious Transport guards in turn. Two blasts later, they were both dead.

"Did you have to do that?" the nurse asked, her voice bordering on hysteria.

"Actually, yes," said Hatch. "And this, too." She watched, petrified, as he moved behind her and wrapped his left arm around her neck.

"Please ... please ..." Her voice was weepy and filled with paranoia bred of the disinformation about TRACE that Transport fed its loyal citizens.

Hatch put his right arm behind her neck and captured her throat in the crook of his left.

"This won't hurt."

The nurse started to scream again, maybe even pray to herself for the forgiveness of sins.

"*Please—*"

Hatch applied pressure. In seconds, she was out.

"Did you kill her?" the councilwoman asked, horrified. Maybe she believed the rumors about TRACE too, Hatch thought.

"Of course not," he said. "But she'll wake up with a headache."

"I like my way better," said Stug.

Hatch ignored him. "Listen to me, people. We're going to do our best to get you out of here, but you have to be patient. We all have people below we want rescued. That's gonna take time, and we don't have a lot of it. I need two volunteers— your best fighters."

The crowd looked around uncertainly at one another.

"*I don't have all day.*"

"Matthias," said a weak voice behind him. Hatch turned. Logan was pointing blearily. "The thin man over there. And Bridget. She's good too."

Hatch turned around and motioned to them. "Matthias, Bridget, front and center."

When no one moved, Stug barked, "*Now*, people!" in his best boot camp voice.

The two came forward.

"Take these rifles," Hatch said, handing them the recent acquisitions from the Authority's dead. "Guard the door at the east end of the room—the way we came in. Keep Transport out. We think they're working with a reduced force. If we're right, it'll be a while before they can bring enough troops down to try an assault. By the time they do, I plan to have us all on the roof."

"What about Logan?" asked the councilwoman. She was pointing at his cot. And his condition.

Hatch assessed Logan, knowing what the right answer to her question was. He gave her the fence-sitter answer instead. "Detail two of your people to carry him. When we come back up from below, he's your problem."

"I'll go last," said Logan, finding Hatch's eyes. To the older woman, he said, "So whoever volunteers needs to know, they're going last too."

Hatch nodded and turned away.

"Can we get on with it now?" Stug whined.

Hatch clapped him on the shoulder and led the way.

Going down was easy. The facility was virtually deserted. More evidence for their theory that Transport had, indeed, evacuated most of its troops already.

Hawkeye and Pusher descended the stairs from the roof,

cautious and covering one another like they were trained to do. Trick came next, and Bracer watched their backs.

When they made the second floor, the only way to get past the security lock on the door was to blast it. No one had the required palm print to fool the scanner. But they had to scout the floor, clear it if possible. As soon as they were through, the sergeant and spotter pushed into the hallway, pistols at the ready.

Empty.

They backed out again and continued down the stairwell to the first floor. Pusher flinched as she blasted the second palm reader granting them access to that level of the facility. They were trained to be quiet—and they were being anything but.

She cracked the door with her foot and swung her pistol down, ready to shoot anyone resisting their progress. But, as with the second floor, the first was empty.

"Maybe we can move a little faster," she said over her shoulder, descending the stairs.

"Don't get cocky," replied Trick. "When it seems easiest is the most dangerous time."

"Hey, Captain, you're really getting this command thing down," said Bracer.

"Move," ordered Trick.

Without warning, the lighting turned a harsh red and the facility alarm began pounding their ears.

"Shit," said Pusher, hunching down on instinct and sweeping the corridor with her pistol. No enemy were evident, but they soon would be. "What'd I do?"

"Maybe nothing," said Trick. "And there's no need to tread

lightly now, Sergeant."

"Sir, yes sir!" Pusher motioned to Hawkeye, and the two of them headed down to the common room level. The commandos switched from stealth mode to engage-and-destroy.

"Really think it was wise leaving the scavengers in charge of the rear guard?" asked Stug.

Hatch moved with his back against the wall. It made him a thinner target should an enemy soldier suddenly appear from below and start shooting while they made their way down the stairs to The Dungeon.

"Our other choice being?"

"Okay, there's that."

"You don't get paid to strategize."

"I don't get paid at all, now."

"Well, there you go. Stop trying to think."

Hatch threw up his hand, and Stug stopped short. Boots echoed from the other side of the door below—probably the escorts for the last bunch, responding to the alert.

Stug hopped to his left and kneeled, while Hatch dropped to one knee on the right. They were exposed on the stairs, no cover to protect them. But they had the element of surprise, as well as the high ground overlooking the open kill zone below.

The door below was flung open and a guard came through. Two more were right behind him. The first man had already taken two of the stairs before noticing the men blocking his way on the landing above. And then he was dead and falling back down.

His comrades stopped, surprised as he fell down the stairs in front of them, then took hasty aim. But all their recent overtime spent guarding prisoners had deadened their reaction time; they were slow. Hatch and Stug were not.

It was over quickly. Hatch and Stug stepped over three bodies at the bottom of the stairs.

They took up positions on either side of the door, now blocked open by the arm of one of the fallen Transport soldiers. Stug peeked through the crack.

"Looks clear," he said, one eyebrow raised.

"Don't you ever get tired of that joke?"

Stug popped his head through the open door. A laser blast shot past him, and he pulled back like a turtle on speed.

"Close?" asked Hatch.

"I'm bald now."

"You were bald before."

"Oh."

They were stuck. And running out of time, Hatch knew. How quickly was the question.

"We've got to clear those soldiers." Hatch could almost hear the tick-tock of the okcillium clock in his head.

"I have an idea," said Stug. "I'll go first."

"I like this idea already."

"When I say, open the door. You'll know what to do after that."

Hatch nodded. He had complete confidence in his old war companion.

Stug pulled the dead porter blocking the doorway into the stairwell. Hatch caught the door before it locked tight. The sergeant picked up the corpse and held it vertically in the air in front of him, the dead soldier's toes dangling over the floor.

"*Now.*"

Hatch yanked open the door and Stug barreled through the opening, the dead porter leading the way like a lifeless shadow cast in front of the sergeant. Stug hunkered down behind his corpse-shield, producing a long, ululating *yip-yip-yip woooooooooo* roar that heralded his charge up the long corridor.

Laser fire erupted from the far end of the hallway, slagging flesh and uniform together. Using Stug and his body-shield for cover, Hatch moved into the open and returned fire, slowly walking up the corridor behind Stug's steam train like an Old West gunfighter. He popped one of the soldiers with his first shot, but then Stug was too far away from him. Too close to the enemy for Hatch to shoot safely past the sergeant.

The other porter—there were only two—wised up and began firing at Stug's feet, clipping the sergeant in the ankle. But instead of stopping, Stug merely bellowed louder as he stumbled forward. When he neared the ankle-shooter, Stug launched the corpse, pockmarked with laser blasts and scorched beyond recognition, ahead of himself.

The porter fell backward beneath the weight of his dead comrade and shot wildly. Stug easily ripped the laser pistol from his hand and pummeled him with it till Hatch got to him and caught his hand in mid-air.

"I think he's done."

"I *hate* being shot," yelled Stug. A little boy with the lungs of a bear. "*Hate it!*"

Hatch bent over and searched the guard who no longer had a face. He found what he was looking for, a small box with two buttons on it. He took the man's laser pistol and stuck it in his belt, then handed the other porter's sidearm to Stug. He picked up a bandolier of frag grenades the dead man had been carrying and draped it over his back. "Can you walk on it?" he asked Stug.

"Yeah. Still don't want me to think?" Stug gestured at what remained of the corpse-shield and its former comrades.

"I rescind my order," said Hatch. He pushed the buttons on the device he'd found. First the left, then the right, then both at once.

"What are you doing?"

"This thing should open the cells down here. It's not working."

"Here, lemme," said Stug, holding open his palm.

"I just tried—"

"You remind me of my ex-wife," the sergeant griped. "Gimme."

Hatch handed it over. Stug smashed it against the wall.

There was a humming along the entire length of the corridor. Tumblers turned. Locks disengaged.

"See?"

"One of these days you're gonna do something like that and screw us worse than we already are."

"But not … today." Stug tried to pronounce the cliché triumphantly. But the searing pain in his ankle wrapped the words in a grimace.

Heads began peering out of cell doorways. Some of them were bleary-eyed. Some emaciated. All were terrified by the laser fire they'd heard, even through their sealed cell doors.

All but one.

"Man Mountain!"

Stug's injured scowl fled his face. "Anne!" This time when he ran up the hallway, his stride was limping, but his arms were empty and open.

"Put it down!" repeated Pusher. "We're on your side!"

"How do we know that?" asked a woman from behind a post. She'd already put three shots over the door—the same one Hatch and Stug had passed through on their way to The Dungeon, minutes before. Now it was full of armed soldiers.

"Bridget!" called Logan from his cot, weakly. "Stand down. Soldier! Identify yourself!"

"Sergeant Emma Ellis, Alpha Squad, Bestimmung Company, TRACE!"

"Logan, we don't know these people—"

"Logan? Logan is that you? It's Sergeant Ellis—Pusher. Remember me?"

Logan coughed, trying to form words. Bridget glanced around her post at the woman she'd been shooting at. Matthias stood up from his crouching position on the opposite side of the room.

"It's okay," wheezed Logan, trying to be heard over the facility-wide alert. "I know them. It's *okay.*"

Entering the room cautiously, Pusher kept her laser pistol in one hand but raised both as a gesture of peace. Hawkeye, Trick, and Bracer followed her through the door, weapons ready. Bridget and Matthias both mirrored Pusher's stance, weapons retained but pointed at the ceiling.

Trick rushed over to Logan as his soldiers took up guard positions at the door. The entire room stared open-mouthed at them. The red-alert lighting and screaming alarm only heightened the tension in the room.

"Logan, you've looked better," said the captain, kneeling beside him.

"Felt better too."

"Stug and Hatch. Seen them?"

Logan nodded. "The Dungeon. Looking for Mary."

Trick looked relieved, if annoyed. "Sounds about right."

"Listen to me," said Logan, grabbing Trick's left arm with his only remaining hand. "You need to get my people out of here."

The captain stared at him, then looked around the room. He catalogued what he was seeing in his head: more than two dozen civilians, many of them hardly able to move. And the enemy would likely attack them at any moment. *They aren't the mission*, his training said.

"Hatch promised," Logan lied.

Trick sighed. That sounded about right, too. "Sergeant!" he yelled over the klaxon. "Start ushering these people up the stairs. Get them to the roof."

Pusher hesitated, and Trick hardened his expression. She nodded and began giving orders to Bracer and Hawkeye.

Turning back to Logan, the captain of B-Company asked, "What about you?"

"I'll slow them down as best I can. Just get them out." The ex-TRACE spy dropped his head to the floor. "Wish I still had my Bowie knife—"

Behind Bridget, the door exploded inward. Caught in the back by the blast, she was killed instantly, pummeled by fragmented concrete and steel. Trick threw himself over the prostrate Logan, covering the wounded man's face against the raining debris. Screams erupted from the civilians in the room as they scrambled faster toward escape.

The shapes of Transport soldiers appeared through the smoke and rubble, firing wildly and randomly, assuming everything in the room was a target. Trick pushed himself to his knees and passed a last glance at Logan. The captain's expression carried with it a hard truth.

"Go!" Logan said. "I'll buy you what time I can!"

Bracer and Pusher had immediately dropped to defensive positions flanking the rear doorway. They returned Transport's fire as the civilians threaded between them, pushing one another forward in their haste to find freedom. Hawkeye had taken point and was leading the Wild Ones toward the roof. A few of the salvagers went down, shot in the back, as the porters established a defensive perimeter around the gaping hole they'd blasted in the far wall.

Transport troopers poured through that hole like cockroaches. A few surgical strikes by Pusher and Bracer took out enough porters to force their comrades to crawl over them, stemming the tide somewhat. But Trick knew his team would be overrun soon. In the end, warfare is always about the math.

Trick scrambled backward toward his soldiers, leaving Logan to his chosen fate. When Trick reached the firing line held by Pusher and Bracer, he turned and knelt, blasting laser fire as fast as his finger could pull the trigger. That gave Pusher and Bracer a chance to pass through the door behind them. They immediately took up positions in the hallway.

"Now, sir!" yelled Pusher. She and Bracer provided cover as Trick withdrew under heavy fire, lasers blasting chunks of concrete from the walls. The Transport soldiers were hunch-running to take up positions behind the load-bearing posts in the center of the room. Several were nearing Logan's cot. As Trick passed through the door, Bracer stood and pushed the last of the Wild Ones in front of him up the stairs.

Trick saw the final scene play out. Logan had played possum, but now he threw off the blanket covering his mortally wounded body, his one good hand gripping a laser pistol. Three skulking porters went down. The fire from the cot drew the attention of others, and numerous laser blasts zeroed in on the bedridden man who was shrieking, taunting death. An instant later, only a smoking ruin of bandages and pulp remained. It was the last image Trick saw before Pusher slammed the door shut.

The sounds of laser fire in the common room were muffled now. But closing the door had been a symbolic gesture at best. The porters were coming.

Pusher motioned for Trick to stand back, then turned her pistol on the locking mechanism and fired a long burst where the door and jamb met. The metal on both sides melted together. "It's not much, but it's better than nothing," she said.

"Nice job, Sergeant. Now get these people to the roof before the porters remember there are other doors they *don't* have to bang their heads against." Trick mentally tipped his hat to Logan as he spoke. Saving as many of the Wild Ones as he could was one promise he intended to keep. "I'll go after Stug and Hatch."

"But sir—"

"Go, Sergeant! That's an order! Up, up, up!"

Legacy

"Sean!"

Hatch moved quickly past Stug and Anne, who was back in the big man's arms, her own arms wrapped around his bull neck. Hatch stuck his pistol in his belt and knelt beside Mary's cot. He took in her face, the combination of sadness and joy and relief creating a new expression he'd never seen before. But that was Mary Brenneman. Just when you thought you had her figured out…

"I thought you were dead," he said, touching her cheek.

The old fire of the QB—her eternal will to resist a destiny beyond her control—replaced her initial relief at seeing him. Her eyes focused sharply, her jaw muscle clenched. Hatch was glad to see it. Her cold dedication to survival filled his heart with hope.

"No, not dead. Not yet," she said. Stug nodded a greeting to her and carried Anne into the corridor to give them a moment. "I see Stug's as subtle as ever."

"We have to get out of here," said Hatch, taking her hand. "No time to explain. Come on." He began to rise and draw her forward off the cot.

The sadness returned to her face.

"Sean, I—"

"Talk later, move now!"

Hatch pulled her arm with more urgency. He'd expected her to swing off the cot and bound into his arms. Instead, she half fell out of bed, releasing her hand from his in a desperate attempt to catch herself on the cold floor. She screamed in pain and Hatch backed up, unsure how he'd hurt her.

The blanket fell from across her legs.

Hatch looked down. At first his brain refused to process what his eyes saw. Though still wearing the tunic of her TRACE uniform, she wore only civilian shorts from the waist down. And her legs … they didn't look like legs at all.

Bloated with wounds, they resembled blackened alien appendages attached to a human torso. Her shins were dinted inward in multiple places. Cavities marked them with purple bruises like craters in the smooth surface of the moon. Like someone had scooped out bone and left bloodied skin resting in its place. Her knees, too, were swollen, the body's reaction when bones are crushed. The top of a shin bone shone white where it poked through the skin.

Hatch couldn't stop staring at Mary's legs. Or thinking, perversely, of how he hadn't been able to stop staring at them when they were together—what seemed like a lifetime ago. They were now a grotesquerie, a sideshow for carnivals, a tribute to human cruelty inflicted for pleasure.

Mary cried out again as she tried to raise herself back onto the cot. Her voice bound humiliation and fury in a ferocious shout of pain.

Hatch snapped out of it and hurried to help her. He heard her gasp, groaning, as she tried to minimize her movement.

"The day they took me at the armory," Mary said through gritted teeth. The throbbing pain subsided to its normal level of the past week: a constant, piercing ache. "They broke my legs, Sean."

Hatch found Mary's eyes. His own wavered beneath tears as the reality of her condition bloomed inside him like a black cancer. Fear, rage, grief, frustration—all fought with one another inside his gut.

"Gutierrez," she said, her own gut churning at the look on Hatch's face. His expression betrayed a feeling of abject defeat. "He learned his lesson when I was a kid, I guess. He wasn't going to let me escape again."

"We'll get you out," Hatch whispered. "Stug! Stug, get in here!"

"Sean—"

"Quiet, no time for debate. There's a bomb—"

"A bomb?"

"No time to explain! Just sit tight ... Stug, get your ass in here!"

"Sean!" she said, trying to make him stop, to get him to see reality.

"What the hell's taking so long?" asked Stug as he stuck his head back in from the hallway. Anne was still in his arms.

Hatch turned his eyes to the big man, and Stug stopped moving. If he'd been holding anything other than a twelve-year-old girl, he might have dropped it then and there. Stug had never seen the look on his friend's face he found there now. He wasn't even sure what it meant. But the hopelessness mixed with an unwillingness to accept the inevitable frightened the big man more than a firing squad of porters ever could.

Then his eyes found Mary's legs.

"Holy Christ."

"Put the girl down," said Hatch. "I need you to help me make a litter."

"Sean, there's no time for that, you said so your—"

"Shut up!" Hatch's voice was sharp and bitter. He looked at Mary, apology in his eyes. "Just—we can do this."

"Stug!" came the call from outside. The sergeant pried his eyes away from Mary's mangled legs to see Trick jogging up The Dungeon's main corridor. He was pushing his way through a sea of Wild Ones heading for the stairs and escape.

"Friend or foe?"

Stug said the words automatically. Some part of his brain knew Trick was probably here on orders from Neville to arrest two deserters, but he was still processing the sight of his maimed QB.

"Friend, you big lummox!" chided Trick as he reached the doorway and clasped Stug's hand in a loose greeting. "What's all the—"

Trick followed Stug's gaze. "Captain ..." was all that came out.

There wasn't time for more. Hatch was moving around to the head of the cot. "Stug, get in here and help me secure her. Get your belt off, you too Trick, and we can tie her down for evac."

Trick moved in to follow orders. Stug put Anne down and followed him in.

"Sean, you're not listening to me," said Mary.

"You're damned right I'm not."

"*Stop!*"

The old QB's voice of command. The Queen Bitch tone that had earned her that nickname from Neville.

"Sean … the move will kill me. My legs … my legs … they've treated them just enough to keep me from dying. They even drop in some morphine now and then. But it's not enough. You can see the gangrene starting. I won't survive if you pull me out of here like this."

"You don't know that," Stug said. His voice was quiet.

Mary blinked. "The pain when I move, Sean. It's horrible." She sounded embarrassed to admit it. To ask her subordinates, even those she considered her friends, for an ounce of consideration.

"Please," said Hatch, kneeling beside her again. "Let me try. All of Columbia is about to die, Mary. Please … at least let me try to save you."

"Let him try," said Anne. "You always have to try."

Mary sought the girl's eyes, so like her own, then dropped her head to the cot, moaning. "At least give me my blanket. Please. At least give me that."

Stug picked it up off the floor and draped it lightly over her shattered legs. As Hatch used his belt to secure Mary on the cot, the sergeant turned to Trick and asked, "Sitrep topside?"

"There's a shit-ton of porters in the common room. Pusher and Bracer are evacuating as many salvagers as possible. But we're gonna have to fight our way up."

Stug glanced down at Mary, then shared a knowing look with Trick. There was little chance they'd get out carrying her on a litter. Everyone in the room knew it but Hatch. Maybe he knew it too and simply refused to accept it. The odds were just too great.

Transport would kill them all.

Anne will die, Stug realized. It was like a physical blow to his heart to admit it.

"Sean," he said, not knowing how to speak the truth out loud. Hatch glanced at him, tying the buckle securely around Mary's chest. "Sean—"

"You gonna help me here or we just gonna wait for them to come to us?" Hatch was grinning like his old warrior self, his hope renewed by the insane idea that they could get Mary out and somehow all survive.

Stug felt a hand in his. A small hand.

"You always have to try," said Anne, looking up at him.

Aw, crap. Stug squeezed her hand and let it go, then started to remove his belt.

"Trick—Captain, *sir*—you're in charge of Anne here," said Stug. "If she dies, I'll kill *you* myself."

Trick reached down and took Anne's hand, pulling her deeper into the cell, away from the doorway. Establishing an overwatch position, he saw the last of the Wild Ones heading up and out of The Dungeon.

"Sergeant, if Anne dies, I'll already be dead."

Nodding, Stug began securing Mary's lower body with his belt. It was all he could do to stay on task and ignore her screams.

"That airbus!" said Pusher. The Wild One standing next to her seemed dazed, in shock. So she grabbed the woman and pointed at the nearest ship. "*That* one. Get over to it and huddle beneath the fuselage as best you can. Keep your people hunkered down, okay?"

She and Bracer, who held the landing one flight below, were acting as traffic cops. The limping, shambling band of salvagers filed up the stairs and onto the roof. Pusher motioned for Hawkeye to leave his position near the airbus and rejoin her at the access door.

"How do you expect to get that airbus off the ground?" shouted Bracer from below. "Only Transport personnel can open 'em up."

"Yeah, but once they're open, anyone can fly 'em."

"You didn't answer my question," said Bracer, his arm pinwheeling Wild Ones toward the roof.

"I've got a plan," she answered, almost to herself. As Hawkeye joined her, she assessed the small, confined accessway, her training noting it as a defensible chokepoint. If they could hold Transport here, the airbus might actually be able to get away. Until Transport dropships and attack craft showed up. Then they were screwed.

"I want you to go below and help the others get here," she said to Hawkeye. Twirling her index finger at the doorway around them, she said, "This is the hardpoint. We'll hold it as long as we can. Got it?"

"Yes, ma'am!"

Agony.

Every jolt, every bump, every step toward freedom.

Not freedom, Mary reminded herself. *Not that kind, anyway.*

Even if she got out of here, she knew they were merely taking her to another place to die. She wanted to tell Hatch, "I'm going to die anyway. Let me die, Sean. Let me at least make the pain less."

But leaving her here like this to merely waste away would kill *him*, too. Maybe not today; maybe not tomorrow. But he would always blame himself for leaving her here to die a meaningless death. This she knew.

And Anne wouldn't understand it. The girl was a fighter, like she was herself. And so Mary endured—for the sake of a man she'd once loved; maybe still loved. For the sake of the little girl she once was. And for the legacy she could leave Anne—an indomitable resolve to never surrender, however unavoidable the future seemed.

The crushing pain in her legs unexpectedly subsided, if only for a moment. She looked around, brought back to herself and the sterile hallway of The Dungeon. Stug was reconnoitering the stairs heading up.

Mary caught Hatch's eyes as they awaited Stug's signal. She'd moved beyond her embarrassment at crying out. It had become too common to worry about any longer. Command be damned. Some things surpassed the need to maintain protocol.

"I'm sorry," said Hatch from the head of the litter. He

stared down, upside down, into her eyes.

"A ... little ... late to admit ... you're wrong," she said. She was making a snarky attempt at their old banter. Mary's words were playful, but her tone betrayed the excruciating pain barely contained. Held in check by willpower alone.

Hatch was about to reply when Stug called, "Clear!" The sergeant was already on the move to the common-room level.

Trick mounted the stairs, and the QB's litter tilted. Hatch hadn't been ready to move; he was pulled off balance and stumbled. Mary grabbed the sides of the litter with both hands, knuckles white.

"Stop!" cried Hatch, adjusting his grip. "Okay, now, go."

Mary began to weep.

"So, what's your brilliant plan?" asked Bracer, staring at the Wild One huddled beneath the airbus. "Only a Transport pilot can open one of those tin cans without a blowtorch. And then only with their BICE."

Bracer was right. That didn't bother Pusher. It was true that after TRACE had made off with tons of okcillium by hijacking the airbus at Gettysburg, the Authority had re-keyed its aircraft to the biometric signatures of Transport personnel. No one could get into a Transport craft without the BICE code of one of the flight crew.

"Why do you think I left the flight crew alive?" asked Pusher.

A light dawned in Bracer's eyes. "That must be why you get

sergeant's pay."

Pusher smirked. "Get those gags off them." She nodded at the two pilots they'd knocked out when they first arrived. Both were awake now and, by the look in their eyes, frightened. Pusher was glad of that. Because if this went where it might have to, being scared would be the least of their worries. She was prepared to do what needed doing.

"Two choices," said Pusher. "I throw you off the roof or you open up that airbus." She moved to the edge of the roof and, for effect, craned her neck to the dark pavement below. The silhouettes of the Lady Justice twins, one high one low, pointed toward one another across the open square.

Bracer hauled both pilots over. He held the woman up next to Pusher so the pilot could get a good look down.

"Even though it's dark, you know what's down there," said Pusher. "A sudden stop to a short drop."

The female pilot was trembling. She just kept turning her head back and forth, as if by refusing to believe her present reality, she could make it be only a dream.

"Key the sequence to open the doors to the bus," ordered Pusher. "Last chance."

"I ... I can't," said the woman. "I'm sorry. I swore an oath to protect the Authority and all its citizens. I swore—"

"Throw her over," said Pusher, her tone already writing the woman off. She turned her attention to the male pilot. He was shaking too.

Bracer hesitated.

The woman looked from one to the other. "Please! I have a son!"

"Then for his sake, open the bloody bus!" insisted Pusher.

"I can't! For *his* sake! The Authority would—"

"Bracer ..."

"Sergeant, I—"

"Corporal, I'm giving you an order! Do it or I'll do it myself!"

Bracer moved the woman closer to the edge. She struggled against him. She began to scream, but the wind carried it away. Bracer lifted her over the concrete barrier, and the woman caught it with her foot, pushing frantically against him.

"I'll do it!" yelled the second pilot. "I'll open it!"

Turning to Pusher, Bracer's eyes showed his relief. Killing soldiers in a fair fight was one thing, but this… His sergeant nodded to him, and he pulled the woman away from the edge of the roof.

"I don't have any family," said the second pilot, exhaling his relief. "It's just me. I'll do it. Please don't kill her."

"Hold her right there," said Pusher. Bracer stopped backing away from the edge. His stomach began to twist.

"But you said—"

"As soon as you open it, I'll honor my word."

The second pilot stared in disbelief. "You people—it's just like the Authority says. You people are monsters."

Pusher leveled her laser pistol at the head of the woman in Bracer's grasp, who was mouthing silently. *Maybe praying*, thought Pusher. "We're made in the image of our creator," she said. "Now open the damned bus."

There was no obvious signal, of course. But from the

corner of her eye, Pusher could see the bus's doors part and the ramp begin to descend. She walked up to the man and clocked him across the jaw with the butt of her pistol. He faded once again into unconsciousness. She nodded at Bracer, who applied a quick sleeper hold to the female pilot. She, too, collapsed to the roof.

"Get those people on board," said Pusher. "And be quick about it."

"It's going to be mighty packed in one transport. A hundred Wild Ones? And us? Can we even lift off?"

"We've only got one certified pilot. Me. One ship'll have to do the job." She glanced back at the stairs leading into the Detention Center. "Hurry, Bracer. Our friends are down there."

Hawkeye was alone.

He stepped quickly down the stairs, pausing at each landing. He was one flight from the ground floor when he heard a noise below.

Hawkeye froze and aimed his pistol at the ground floor door.

The door cracked open. A barrel inched its way through the hole. Someone else was being cautious too.

The door opened wider. A young Transport soldier edged out—first his laser rifle, then his head. His entire attention was focused on the stairs leading down.

Hawkeye tightened his grip on the pistol with both hands

and sighted down the barrel. He held his breath and homed in on the details—like the old-world binocular symbol overlaying the Transport emblem on the soldier's right front pocket. His enemy was a scout too.

You should always remember one thing, son, Hawkeye thought as he waited patiently. The scout pushed through the door and held it open behind him. Hawkeye watched him stand quietly, assessing the stairs below him. Maybe the man was reporting back about his recon mission via BICE.

Then Hawkeye heard heavy, dragging boots on the stairs, like someone was climbing with a bum leg. And someone else was moaning. A woman, sounded like.

The porter moved into position to aim his rifle down.

Hawkeye squeezed off a single shot, taking the enemy scout in the head. The man collapsed to the floor, wedging open the door.

"As a spotter, you should always assess the high ground first," Hawkeye whispered, finishing his thought. But he held his position, keeping his laser pistol aimed at the half-opened door.

The dragging sounds stopped. Hawkeye slid on one knee a half foot to the left and twisted thirty degrees right, increasing his field of fire to cover the approach below. Now he could hit anything coming up the stairs or through the door before either threat would see him.

The heavy tread resumed, albeit slower now. Cautious. When Stug's bald head appeared, Hawkeye let himself breathe again.

"Watch the door, Sarge," Hawkeye said.

Stug rounded instantly and brought his pistol to bear on the landing above. "I nearly fried you, boy."

"The door," said Hawkeye, lowering his own weapon. "Might be more up the hall. Not sure—"

Three laser blasts streaked past Stug. He dropped back and down, using the half-open door as cover. Hawkeye descended the stairs quickly and took up position on the near side of the doorway.

"Well, *I'm* sure," grumbled Stug. He reached forward without rising and grabbed the dead scout by the shirt collar. Hawkeye wrapped his pistol around the doorjamb and fired four random shots down the corridor to cover Stug as he pulled the corpse into the stairwell. Before the door closed, Hawkeye chanced a glance after his salvo.

"I saw two."

"There'll be more," said Stug as he rifled through the corpse's clothes. He found three frag grenades and an extra okcillium battery for the dead scout's laser rifle. Grabbing up the rifle, he added, "Pusher sealed the door below."

"So a good news, bad news thing then."

"Stug, sound off!"

Hatch's voice from below.

Laser fire *pop-pop-popped* the other side of the door.

"Hurry up! We might still thread this needle!"

Stug regretted the words as soon as he said them. Their need to move carefully because of the QB's condition was not playing well with their need to move fast. He watched Hatch maneuver around the stairwell below. The QB was motionless. *Passed out from the pain*, Stug guessed.

Then he heard something metal hit the other side of the door, plink to the ground, and roll to a stop.

"Grenade!" shouted Stug, seizing the corpse as he fell backward and pulling it over him like a heavy blanket.

Hawkeye leapt up the stairs, ducked and covered. Hatch and Trick jostled Mary to the ground, and Hatch threw himself over her. Trick turned quickly, gathered Anne against his chest, and pressed them both against the wall.

The door blasted off its hinges, striking the wall of the stairwell and clattering to the concrete. It came to rest hard atop the corpse Stug was using for shelter. As the concrete from the walls and dust rained down around him, Stug raised himself—door, body, and all—and found Transport soldiers already moving in force up the corridor toward their position. He saw four pairs of partners jog-running in flanking formation along the corridor, plainly confident that the grenade had done their work for them.

But they pulled up short when they saw what looked like one of their own, with his back turned to them, coming through the hole where the door had been. He looked odd and his head drooped, and the two-man team in front dropped to one knee, quickly followed by the others taking up cover positions. The whole thing looked eerie in the hanging, gray haze following the blast.

"Soldier, identify your—"

A big hand tossed a frag grenade around the body like a bowling ball. It rattled metallically down the hallway, coming to rest in the middle of their squad. One of the porters shouted a warning, but too late. A second explosion rocked the narrow corridor, fragments of shrapnel erupting in all directions.

Stug felt pieces of metal thump into the body he held up in front of him. He was starting to like this tactic of recycling dead porters for body shields. With his ears clouding up from the two massive concussions, he could barely hear the muffled cries of the now-prostrate squad over the last of the blast—but the cries were there. That meant soldiers who could still fight, and maybe more coming in behind them.

The sergeant thumbed the trigger of a second grenade and overhanded it as far down the hallway as he could throw. He backed quickly into the stairwell and hunkered down behind his shield again. The second frag grenade went off, caving in the ceiling where the blast had been heaviest.

Stug dropped his deadman shield and unslung his rifle, training it on the smoking ruin of the corridor. The third explosion had effectively cut off access from the other end of the corridor. This route, at least, was secured. For the moment.

"Move!" Stug shouted. Hatch and Trick resumed their duty as litter bearers, advancing up the stairs. "Hawkeye, get up to the next landing! Reconnoiter that door! And here," he said, underhanding the last frag grenade he'd secured from the dead scout. "You might need this."

The spotter caught the pineapple Stug tossed, careful not to thumb the trigger. "Yes, Sergeant," he said, clipping the grenade to his belt. He shook his head to clear his ears and headed up.

Two more floors to go, then we're on the roof, thought Stug.

"I see you've been busy," Hatch said, maneuvering around the railing.

"I hate party crashers."

Stug stole his eyes from a final assessment of the corridor's security to observe the QB. She was still out, her head lolling back and forth on the litter as her bearers climbed.

Anne followed, lightly brushing Stug's arm with her fingertips as she passed by.

The big man's eyes touched hers in return.

We're not giving up, they promised one another.

Pusher and Bracer found Hawkeye on overwatch. He had the door to the second floor cracked an inch.

"Status?" asked the sergeant.

"Look down the stairs," said Hawkeye, annoyed at having his attention drawn away from the door. "Um, ma'am."

Pusher glanced over the railing and found Stug's eyes looking back over a rifle barrel. He lowered the gun. "About time," he said, glancing down. He jerked his head at someone she couldn't see and limped up the stairs.

"Movement," warned Hawkeye.

The door at the far end of the second-floor corridor opened. A single porter with a transparent body shield, the kind they used to mask heat sigs against infrared, walked through. Hawkeye sighted and fired, his laser ricocheting harmlessly off the shield. The soldier flinched but continued forward, and others followed.

"They've got shields," said the spotter. "Best hurry up."

Stug joined him on the landing. An explosion pounded the

roof above. "Bloody hell," he said. He looked up at the ceiling, which was shaking with the aftereffect of the blast. "How about a break?"

"Drones," explained Bracer.

"Those civilians are sitting ducks in that airbus," said Pusher.

"Go!" Hatch struggled with his footing, found it, and hauled Mary onto the landing. "You two get up there and protect those people."

"Sir, yes sir!"

Pusher led the way; Bracer followed. Hawkeye squeezed off round after round, but now there were four soldiers in the corridor: two with body shields and two behind them, firing laser rifles. All advancing with resolve.

"This hallway's getting shorter all the time," the spotter growled.

"I gave you that grenade for a reason," replied Stug as Trick and Hatch began their final ascent to the roof.

"Right," said Hawkeye. Enemy fire compelled him to shut the door. He holstered his pistol and pulled the frag grenade from his belt.

Stug picked up Anne and followed the litter up the stairs. "Don't take all day," he called down.

Hawkeye nodded, thumbed the grenade's trigger, cracked the door, and toss-rolled it down the corridor. An arc of light, a sear of heat, a gasp of pain. He slammed the door shut but not before his left arm went numb.

"Lucky bastard shot," Hawkeye gasped, bracing himself against the door.

The blast rocked the corridor beyond. Hatch and Trick staggered on the stairs, then found their balance again. Mary moaned, a breathy sound of waking awareness and intense pain. Stug passed them as fast as he could with his injured ankle.

Hawkeye opened the door an inch. The middle of the corridor was blackened with a star cluster of blast marks from floor to ceiling. The porters had hunkered down behind their shields, one of which was now cracked. Though shaken, most of the troopers seemed fine. They were assessing their situation, preparing to move forward again.

Hawkeye slammed the door and glanced up the stairs. His friends were almost at the top. But Transport was closing in from below, and those drones harassing the people on the roof would make escape damned near impossible.

Shit.

They were trapped.

"Stop! Stop, Sean!"

Mary's voice was haggard. Played out. Like a horse that's been run to death.

"We can't, Mary." Hatch tried to sound patient. Tried to sound sensitive to the misery she was suffering. But the explosions from the drones' Gatling lasers on the roof forced him to raise his voice. "We have to keep moving!"

"Please. Please, put me down," she whispered. Her head lifted off the litter, her eyes finding his, demanding he obey her. "For the love of God. Please, just for a minute."

Hatch nodded at Trick, and they set her down on the landing just inside the access doorway. Beyond, flashes of laser fire peppered the roof, throwing up concrete and gravel.

"Report, Pusher," said Trick.

"Amazingly, I only see two drones. So far. They're concentrating on the airbus, and the salvagers have closed the door and turtled up inside. The hull's thick enough for now, but if they take out an engine or—"

"How do we get that thing to lift off and take out both drones too?" asked Hawkeye, joining them. He kept one eye and his pistol on the door below.

"There's that anti-aircraft gun on the roof," said Bracer. "I can keep 'em occupied."

Trick nodded. "Pusher, get Bracer to that gun. Stug ..."

The big man turned and stared at him, Anne in his arms. Trick knew Stug didn't really trust him anymore, not since he'd stolen command of B-Company from Hatch. That's how it had happened in Stug's mind, at least. But they didn't have time for that personal drama now.

Trick infused his eyes with the power of command. "Sergeant, get that little girl on board the airbus. Then provide cover fire for the rest of us."

Stug glared a moment longer, then nodded.

Pusher and Bracer looked at one another for confirmation of the timing, then charged onto the roof.

Trick turned to Hawkeye. "Hold here while Hatch and I get the QB to the airbus. We'll move as soon as Bracer takes out one of the drones." As if to punctuate the captain's orders, explosions pounded the roof.

"Here," said Hatch, standing up. He took the bandolier of frag grenades off his back and handed it to Hawkeye. "You're gonna need these."

In the brief moment of quiet that followed, Mary spoke. "No."

It was the old, familiar voice of command. The voice of the QB. Its tone was that of a woman who expected to be obeyed.

The swoop of the drones repositioning for another pass at the airbus rode the wind into the accessway.

"What?" Hatch's voice was at once incredulous and relieved. Reluctant to allow a delay. Glad to hear the woman he respected more than anyone else in the world speak with authority again.

"Give the grenades to me," she ordered.

Hatch darted his eyes to Stug, who stared back over Anne's shoulder. The sergeant held the girl's small head to his chest, her hair stringy with sweat and concrete dust. Stug's eyes softened as he looked at his friend.

"Back up! They're coming!" yelled Hawkeye, kneeling and aiming his pistol.

"Sean—" Stug began, but Hatch cut him off.

"I'm not giving up!" he said. "We've come this far. The goddamned bus is right there!" His finger pointed outside. His eyes were wet.

"Sean." Mary's voice was quiet.

Outside, it sounded like Bracer had made it to the anti-aircraft gun. It's *thrrrit-thrrrit-thrrrit* sizzled the air.

"Sean, I'm not giving up. I'm winning," she smiled. An

odd expression through the wet grime on her face. A fresh tear trickled from her right eye, washing a small trail through the dust and pain. "Leave those grenades with me. The porters will never reach the roof."

"Mary—"

"Sean, we have to go," said Stug quietly. Anne was fidgeting on his shoulder. She was trying to turn her head to see Mary.

"You go!" said Hatch, his eyes blazing toward Stug.

The big man had never seen those eyes so full of fury. Not in the bar. Not on the battlefield. For the first time, he felt fear when he looked in his friend's eyes. As if Hatch was becoming unhinged. Unreliable. The death of them all, maybe.

"Get that girl out of here!"

"I'm not going without her," said Anne. Now she was crying too. Fidgeting against Stug's chest. Trying to get down. But the sergeant held her close.

"I'm not leaving without you, my friend," said Stug to Hatch. "And I'm not letting this little girl die."

"And *I'm* not letting *Mary* die!"

The door below blew off its hinges. Instinct kicked in, and everyone dropped to their knees on the landing, away from the blast.

"They'll be up these stairs any second!" said Hawkeye. His useless left arm hanging at his side, he took careful aim at the doorway. He began firing before targets even appeared.

"Sean, I'm already dead." Mary worked hard to make herself heard. Her throat was hoarse. Her words were sadness spoken aloud.

Hatch stared down at her, then moved to her side.

"Sean—" Stug's voice was impatient. Desperate to save Anne.

"I'm sorry, Mary." Tears were flowing freely down Hatch's face. He didn't care if Stug saw. He didn't care if anyone saw. "I love you. I'm sorry I didn't show that more. I'm sorry—"

Hawkeye ducked as laser fire lanced up from the doorway below. A porter with a body shield had wedged himself into the opening. Another was adding his own fire, shooting over his comrade's head.

"No more time!" yelled the spotter.

"Sean!" Stug again, insistent.

"Show me now, Sean," said Mary. "Give me those grenades. Save Stug. Save Anne. Save them all."

Hatch handed over the bandolier as if her gaze had cast a spell on him. Then he leaned over and kissed Mary on the lips. "I love you," he said, his mouth a rictus of regret.

"I know." She smiled up at him. "Now go."

An explosion outside, the crushing screech of metal hitting the roof. It sounded like Bracer had taken down the first drone.

"We have to go now!" shouted Stug. He wasn't waiting any longer. "Hawkeye, take point!"

The spotter pulled the trigger of his pistol three more times, but produced only two rounds of laser fire. One found the porter behind the shield-bearer. Hawkeye tossed the useless sidearm to the ground and leapt past Stug, who quick-passed him his own sidearm.

Hatch rose, his hand trailing along Mary's own.

"But you said to always try!" shouted Anne as Stug moved to the door. Her eyes found Mary's and focused there. "You said to never give up!"

Mary's smile remained. It held the confidence of someone who'd chosen her own path—who'd taken the best of what life had offered her. Never compromising. Never negotiating. Always insisting she'd live life on her own terms.

"Do I look like I'm giving up?" she asked Anne. "Now go and keep Joseph in line. He needs all the help he can get."

"No, wait!"

But as Anne kicked and fought against the sergeant, Stug followed Hawkeye out the door and headed for the airbus, bellowing at the salvagers inside, "Open the door! Open the damned door!" amid the chaos of laser fire.

"We'll never stop the fight," promised Hatch. He stared into Mary's eyes. *I want to brand my memory with your bravery and beauty*, he thought.

"I sure as hell hope not. Make this count for something," she said, reaching up to touch his cheek.

Heavy boots tromped up the stairs. Hatch heard the scrape of a body shield against a railing. He drew his pistol and fired randomly below, and the porters hesitated.

Hatch closed his eyes briefly, gathering his courage. Not the courage to face the Gatling lasers ripping the roof to shreds, but the courage to run. The courage to leave Mary—and his heart—behind.

And then he leapt from the doorway, screaming a war cry of pain and loss and sorrow unbound.

The porters ascended the stairs with cautious intent. They found a woman, dirty with dust and pale as death, strapped to a cot, her lower half covered by a blanket. *Maybe she's dead already*, mused the officer leading them. Then she moved her hands beneath the blanket, and it slipped off.

"Hold it!" said the officer, training his rifle on her. "Don't move another muscle!"

More Transport soldiers gained the landing. They could hear the Gatling fire of an Authority drone finding targets on the roof. Some of the men gasped when they saw the woman's legs.

"See, men?" said the officer. "TRACE left this rebel behind. They have no honor, no personal code of loyalty. No clarity of purpose like we do."

Mary turned her head toward the officer, raising an eyebrow. She held her hands palm down on her stomach. "I have something for you," she said. She made sure her voice sounded weak. Abandoned and angry. "Come closer. I can't move."

He didn't see her thumbs jab inward.

The officer motioned his men to surround her, then moved in closer, morbidly curious. "What could you possibly have for me before you die? Ready to sell out your rebel friends before shuffling off the coil of your wasted life?"

Mary turned her hands over to reveal two metal balls with blinking red lights.

"Muffin, anyone?"

The doorway to the roof burst apart with flame and metal just as Hatch reached the airbus. The shock made him duck, and Stug offered a hand to pull him inside. The second drone, which had managed to evade Bracer's deadly aim, tracked straight through the fireball of shrieking shrapnel. It choked on the debris sucked into its anti-gravs and began a fast descent to the hard ground of the square below.

Hatch watched the flame and smoke climb. Then it arced downward again as gravity claimed the wood and concrete and metal. And the atoms of his best friend, his former lover, Mary Brenneman.

Goodbye, Mary.

Such small words for so massive a hole, growing like a dark sun, burning inside him.

Through the gray haze, a body appeared. Pusher, limping stiffly, with Bracer's arm draped around her neck. He looked unconscious. Hatch ran down the ramp to meet them and take him off her hands. Pusher fell momentarily to the ground, then yanked herself to her feet and hobbled up the ramp after them.

"You hurt?" Hatch asked over his shoulder.

"Not as badly as Bracer," she grunted. "The explosion blew him off the gun."

Pusher made her way through the press of civilians crowded into the airbus. With everyone aboard, there were nearly a hundred souls packed into a space built for a quarter that number. She made her way to the pilot's seat and fired up the engines. Damaged by the drone attack, they were anemic, but they were functional.

Now if we can just get out of here without being shot down, she thought, flipping switches.

No drones, no attack craft, no dropships.

Transport seemed content to let them go. Or perhaps the Authority had simply run out of equipment and men to throw at them after stripping the City bare. Whatever the reason, the airbus was undisturbed as it hummed over the wide expanse of the Susquehanna below, and its occupants finally began to relax. The former homesteaders of Bedrock laughed nervously—the beginnings of a celebration. A celebration of life, if not victory.

Then Pusher called her fellow commandos forward with a trembling voice. Hawkeye demurred, having found a tiny square of sitting room where he nursed his arm. And Bracer was still out. So only Hatch, Trick, and Stug came into the cockpit.

They found Pusher weeping and staring forward, as if willing what she was seeing to change.

"Report, Sergeant," said Trick. Her demeanor unnerved him. He'd only ever seen her cry once, in the aftermath of Gettysburg. When only she, of her entire squad, had survived.

But then she heard him gasp and knew she didn't need to report anything. The reality was clear through the windshield of the airbus.

Little Gibraltar was a smoldering ruin. The morning sunlight, usually bent around the Umbrella and making the fortress invisible, showed the devastation in detail. Blackened trees. Gutted buildings. Smoke rising from everywhere, like a hundred tiny campfires set by ghost soldiers from a time long past.

"How the hell did they find it?" wondered Trick aloud. He thought of the rest of B-Company, of their two sister companies in Neville's command. Of the men and women stationed at Little Gibraltar who'd supported their missions.

"Neville probably left a comm channel open," said Stug, his own grief expressed in anger. "Incompetent peacock bastard." For some reason, the blowhard Garza, the sergeant he'd bumped heads with in the Slide, came to mind. And the considerate private, the bar's waitress, who'd called him in to help a blacked-out Hatch get home to his bed. Both gone.

Pusher wiped her eyes and glanced at the fuel gauge. The airbus had never been refueled after delivering its last payload of prisoners. They were running low.

"Sir, what do we do?" she asked, angling the bus around the fort's perimeter a second time. "There might be survivors down there." But as they scanned the gutted fortress below, nothing moved. Most of the 18-millimeter machine guns mounted on the walls were gone, blown out of their mounts. Bodies were evident everywhere. But only charred remains.

"Sergeant ..."

Hatch and Trick had spoken together.

The captain of B-Company looked to the AWOL

lieutenant of Alpha Squad. Hatch blinked once and nodded.

"Sergeant," Trick said, "let's get these people on the ground. But not here."

"Where, sir?" Pusher asked. She reached over and tapped the fuel gauge for emphasis. "It'll have to be somewhere close."

"Bedrock?" suggested Hatch. "What's left of it must be in better shape than this island."

"I don't know what kind of weapons Transport used in their assault," said Trick. "It could be irradiated, poisoned—"

"The Amish Zone," said Stug to Pusher, ignoring the debate of his superiors. "Get us to the AZ."

Pusher took one last look at the devastation below and pulled her eyes away, heading east.

They landed in a barnyard. The loud boosters and the anti-gravs, both working at less than peak efficiency, created chaos among the homestead's chickens and goats. Amish men and women stepped onto the porch of a modest house or stood up from the fields where they'd been working. They all stopped to watch the airbus. Pockmarked and streaked with carbon residue, it landed with a mechanical sigh.

As the doors opened and the landing ramp descended, one older man dressed in the familiar clothes of his people— broadfall pants, suspenders, a plain shirt, and a straw hat— approached.

Trick descended the ramp first, with Stug and Hatch flanking him. The old man recognized Trick and seemed to relax a little, though he maintained a wary expression.

"Elder Noffsinger," said Trick. "Good to see you again. I wish it weren't under these circumstances."

The old man walked closer, extending a hand of greeting. "And what circumstances would those be ... Lieutenant Mason, I believe?"

"Captain now," said Stug under his breath.

Paul Noffsinger regarded the big man briefly, then returned his attention to Trick. "Captain, then. What's the meaning of this? Why is this airbus in my barnyard?" His tone was cordial but firm with the history of his people. And despite his piety, it carried an impatience for the imposition of anyone carrying firearms on his land.

Before Trick could answer, a low thump and puff erupted to the northwest. Everyone turned to see, then immediately shaded their eyes and jerked them away, an instinct against tragedy.

The muted thump became a grumble of thunder, then a roar of wind. The chickens and goats and family dog began to yip and call and cackle their terror. Elder Noffsinger pulled his hat down over his forehead, a man who knows the weather readying himself for a stiff breeze.

Blackened air climbed into the sky with a dark growl. Highlights of blue and purple, the signature of an okcillium blast, swirled within the rising shadow. The initial blast now past, they watched the mushroom cloud blossom into the once-pristine October sky of New Pennsylvania like a fast-growing tree of death and destruction.

"Lord in Heaven," breathed Noffsinger. "What in the

world?"

Hatch stared hard at what they were all seeing. "Transport," he said, as if that one word explained the entirety of evil in the world. The destruction of Columbia. The senseless waste of life. Mary's death.

The petulance of a child with an okcillium bomb at his disposal.

"What?" Noffsinger was disbelieving. "Surely not. Surely not! Not even Transport—"

Anne appeared at the door of the airbus. The explosion had rocked the craft as well, but now the distant thunder of air and matter being disrupted and fused sounded like nothing more than an angry storm on the horizon. Noffsinger watched the little girl as she walked down the ramp. Behind her, another Wild One appeared at the door and began to descend. Then another. Tattered clothes. Bloody rags wrapped around weeping wounds. Shocked, overwhelmed expressions of hopelessness on face after face. Those already on the ground were gazing toward Columbia with disbelief. Like what their eyes were showing them simply shouldn't be seen.

"My Lord, what's happened to these people?" Noffsinger moved forward, ready to help Anne off the ramp.

Hatch didn't answer. He didn't need to. He'd already laid the name of the guilty at the elder's feet.

More of the Wild Ones came down the ramp, one after another, brought forth by the boom and lingering roil of shaking air. There were a dozen of them now, striding down toward the comfort of good soil and good people. Noffsinger helped each one off the ramp, clasping in his own the hand of each person in turn. Others of the Amish community were coming forward to help and offer solace as well. One woman rushed from the house dipping a white cloth into a bucket of water.

The mushroom cloud grew in the distance.

"An entire city," breathed Noffsinger. "My Lord. My Lord God."

Anne stood and stared at the black tree of death rising from the City. She fell to her knees and began to cry, as if this final act of cruelty and murder by Transport had broken her spirit. Stug moved forward to comfort her.

"What happened to her?" asked Noffsinger.

"These are her people," said Trick. "They were massacred by Transport. These are all that's left of their community."

Noffsinger's expression saddened, if that were possible. "I am truly sorry for this young girl," he said. "But I meant your captain. You said you're captain now." He turned to Hatch. "Where is Mary Brenneman?"

Hatch's eyes spoke for him.

"I am ..." Noffsinger faltered. Beneath the sound of his voice, the air around the dying city thrummed like the hoofbeats of a hundred horses. "I am overwhelmed."

"We won't stay long," said Trick reassuringly, mistaking the reason for the elder's words. There were a hundred people here now. A hundred refugees. A hundred hungry mouths to feed. "We just need to rest, recover. Then we'll be on our way. Our home was ... it was destroyed too. We need to find out what happened to it."

Noffsinger turned to him. "You may stay as long as you

need," he said, forthright and generous even as tears slipped unchecked down his cheeks. "Anyone who survived that ..." His voice trailed off, weighed down by the impact of the horses pounding the air of the distant, dead city.

"Are you okay?" asked Stug, kneeling beside Anne. His hands rested on her shoulders. "Anne, are you—"

She whispered something in response.

"What, sweetie?"

"I want to learn to fight," she said. Her voice was steel, cooling and fresh from the forge. It cut through the roiling air like a knife.

She stood up and turned to Stug. "I want to learn to fight, Joseph. I want to learn to fight just like her."

Stug looked up at her, meeting the cold black of her eyes with his own soft resolve. His reply stopped in his throat. He remembered when he'd come to this moment himself. When he'd turned his back on the pacifism of the Amish and taken up the gun on their behalf.

He turned to Hatch, who stared at the two of them, his gaze hard and unblinking. He'd heard Anne's words too—and in them, her decision to choose her own destiny. Hatch nodded to his friend.

"Then I'll teach you," said Stug, tenderly pushing the hair over one ear with his thick warrior's fingers. "And we'll kill all those Transport bastards together."

Anne nodded absently, her gaze looking through the big man, beyond him. Her face became flat, though tears coursed down her cheeks. As if they were supposed to be there. Expected.

Tears for Mary.

For the City.

Then the girl's eyes reabsorbed the last of their grief, like she'd made the conscious decision to simply stop crying. The corners of her lips swept upward into a feral smile of determination, an expression reflecting her iron desire to direct the course of her fate by strength of will alone.

"Yes. All of them," Anne said. "Every last one."

Historical Note: *Columbia*

So, here we are: the end of the line for the heroes of Bestimmung Company. At least for now.

Columbia completes a story arc that sort of generated itself, actually. Back in the spring of 2014, I approached Michael Bunker about an anthology of short stories set in his world of Pennsylvania. He was enthusiastic, and we recruited some top-flight writers, both established and new, from the independent fiction world. That anthology became *Tales from Pennsylvania*.

My contribution was a story called "Gelassenheit," a tale of one Amish family trying to work their land how they see fit, while dealing with the long shadow Transport casts over their lives. One unintended consequence of the story when I wrote it was that it became the origin story for one of our heroes—heroine, actually: Mary Brenneman. "Gelassenheit" was supposed to be a one-off short story for the collection. But Mary's twelve-year-old character kept demanding more stage time from me. So I decided to write about who she might have become twenty-five years later as a contemporary of Jed, Pook, and the rest of the characters in *Pennsylvania*: a true believer in

TRACE's cause. That story became *Gettysburg*, and here we are, three novellas later.

In each of the afterwords to the B-Company tales, I've talked a little about the historical inspiration for each story. Although there was no direct antecedent for *Columbia*—I was working with events established by Michael in *Pennsylvania*, which culminate in the destruction of the City—I did have history in the back of my mind while writing. The sieges of Petersburg and Vicksburg during the Civil War. The destruction of Nagasaki and Hiroshima in World War II. Present-day roadside bombs, 9/11, and public beheadings by terrorist groups across the globe. In short, the human toll of warfare exacted on civilians (who never signed up for a fight and are just trying to live through it) became a primary theme. In the fictional *Columbia*, as with its historical precedents, one side grows so desperate to win that it throws out the rules of warfare—if those even truly exist beyond our own need to embrace a somewhat naïve chivalric code—to achieve victory.

In the historical cases, one could argue that the ends justified the means. Take Grant's siege of Vicksburg, for example. Mississippians in the city were reduced to living in hillside caves and eating pets and draft animals during the constant bombardment of the city proper by federal troops. Many were killed by the forty-eight days of siege guns pounding the city, a strategy—like Sherman's in Georgia—specifically designed to break the civilian population's will to resist (and thereby apply pressure to the political arm of the Confederacy to capitulate). From the Union's perspective, such measures were necessary in the case of Vicksburg—both to make sure the British didn't intervene on behalf of the Confederacy and prolong the war, and to strangle the Confederacy's ability to move men and materiel up the Mississippi to prosecute the war.

A similar justification for dropping the A-bomb was apparently in President Truman's mind when he approved its use against Japan in World War II—not just once, but twice. When the first bomb dropped on Hiroshima didn't convince Emperor Hirohito of the hopelessness of Japan's position, a second was dropped three days later on Nagasaki. Within a week, the Japanese surrendered.

Is Transport's use of the O-bomb in *Columbia* and *Pennsylvania* any less justified? Most would answer yes, I think. Hatch and Stug would say that for sure, especially given their characterization of Transport as a "petulant child with massive weaponry at his disposal." But is it nothing more than our perception of "who's the good guy" and "who's the bad guy" that makes that rationalization hold water? It's perhaps easier to accept that Truman acted without malice when he made the decision to drop two A-bombs because, many believe, he was trying to avoid an even costlier means of ending the war; means that would've required invading Japan itself. The United States' experience with fighting Japanese forces entrenched in island strongholds in the Pacific certainly provided evidence that Truman's fears were well-founded. From his perspective, dropping the A-bombs really *was* the lesser of two evils. On the other hand, ask a Georgian or Mississippian today about the necessity of Union scorched-earth tactics during the Civil War and—even now, 150 years after that bitter conflict's end—you're likely to get a less than sympathetic response.

Since Transport is cast in the role of villain in the *Pennsylvania* universe, the wanton—and unnecessary, from our perspective—destruction of the City and its inhabitants is hard to see as anything short of evil. But I wonder how a historian writing Transport's side of the Second War for Pennsylvanian Independence might characterize the destruction of the City. Or, even, if that scribe would call it "the Second War for Pennsylvanian Independence"; perhaps their name for the war might reflect more sympathy for the Authority's cause such as "the War to Unify New Pennsylvania" or some such noble sentiment. While we don't have that moral quandary—Transport, as we know, is a totalitarian state, the epitome of evil in Michael Bunker's New Pennsylvania—it's interesting to ponder the perspective of the other side, isn't it?

Speaking in 1862 to his "Old War Horse," James Longstreet, Robert E. Lee is famously quoted as having said, "It is well that war is so terrible, or we should grow too fond of it." After the Battle of Waterloo, Arthur Wellesley, the Duke of Wellington—who managed to defeat Napoleon by the skin of his teeth—surveyed the blood-soaked cornfields of Belgium and wrote in a letter, "Nothing except a battle lost can be half as melancholy as a battle won." No one, it seems, appreciates/laments the cost of warfare more than the soldiers themselves. Sometimes, however, it's the civilians—without the choice to "muster out" of the fight—who pay the highest price. In *Columbia*, we see that encapsulated in Elder Noffsinger's reaction: "An entire city. My Lord. My Lord

God."

Yet the war with Transport isn't over, and its cost continues to grow. The QB, Mary Brenneman, is dead. Many of the inhabitants of Little Gibraltar have apparently been killed too. Yet some of our heroes remain, and new ones, like Anne, have joined the fight. The good guys live to fight another day.

I'll be honest: I don't have plans—at this moment—to write more B-Company tales. But I didn't plan *Gettysburg*, either. Young Mary in "Gelassenheit" demanded more life from me. Perhaps young Anne will start calling to me from the wings as well. We'll see.

Chris Pourteau

May 2015

Acknowledgments

My Alpha Reader Extraordinaire and the first set of eyes to ever see anything I write is my wife, Alison. I conceptualize stories and characters with her, and she always has a nuance or texture to add that I hadn't thought of. I hand her drafts tentatively, always anxiously awaiting her response—hoping it's positive but wanting it to be honest. And she never fails to deliver, usually with both praise and a suggestion for improvement at the same time. She's my biggest supporter, and I love her for it (one of many reasons). Thanks, my best friend in life, for your unwavering support of my writing.

Beta readers are a great asset to any author. They're a friendly "first audience" that helps you iron out the embarrassing moments in your story before the public points them out in reviews that make you cringe. My "official" beta readers for these stories were David Bruns, Michael Bunker, Ellen Campbell, Nick Cole, Harlow Fallon, Ed Gosney II, Samuel Peralta, Kim Wells, Catherine Violando, and Bridget Young. The B-Company tales wouldn't have been nearly as good without their sharp eyes and willingness to tell me when something sounded goofy or was just plain wrong. They gifted me their time in reading and responding to drafts, and for that I'm very grateful.

A special thank-you to my nephew, U.S. Marine Captain and Judge Advocate Alec Pourteau, who helped me fill in some practical gaps in my knowledge of squad tactics. Howard Hendrick and Bob Rink, my geek gaming buddies for decades—and two of the most intuitive, knowledgeable men I know when it comes to military history—helped me with some fact checking. Much appreciated, guys!

David Gatewood, perhaps the most widely respected editors in independent publishing, lent me his insights and corrections for all the stories. His suggestions—sometimes sharply, if winkingly, barbed—always smooth things out and help me see a scene or sentence from a perspective I hadn't considered before. In my opinion, he's the best at what he does; it's that simple. And Michelle Benoit, an old friend and the sharpest proofreader I know, helped me with some final line editing from time to time. Thank you, Michelle, for always being willing to look over my shoulder.

Dave Monk Fraser Adams designed the classic covers for this entire series. His style recalls the designs for the sci-fi novels I grew up with. His knack for modern "coolness" mixed with a bit of steampunk on the side really captures my own authorial intention in the stories. Dave is an awesome Aussie and never minds my asking for one more tweak. Thanks, Dave, for your flexibility, patience, and willingness to lend me your talent.

Ben Adams's fertile imagination provided the excellent

illustrations you see throughout this collection. They look like electronic woodcuts to me—the perfect mix of contemporary expression and traditional composition that appear both polished and raw at the same time. He really captures the adrenaline-pumping edginess of B-Company's battles without losing the emotional depth of its combatants. Thank you, Ben, for perfectly capturing these moments in time from my stories.

Thanks also to my authorial inspirations who, by example, have shown me what good writing really is and thrilled me with their stories at the same time. C.S. Forester's Horatio Hornblower series (begun in the 1930s and set during the Napoleonic Wars) created the modern standard for this kind of adventure fiction. Gene Roddenberry was so inspired by its derring-do that he based his own Captain Kirk on Forester's Royal Navy Captain Hornblower. Bernard Cornwell reinterpreted the military hero contemporary with Hornblower (but on land this time) in his Richard Sharpe series, which follows the adventures of a British rifleman battling the French across Europe. By the way, if you're a fan of Cornwell, you might have noticed a nod to one of his most loathsome characters, Obadiah Hakeswill, in my choice of first names for B-Company's colonel. So, a tip of the hat, Mr. Cornwell, via Obadiah Neville. Other inspirations for these stories include Joe Haldeman, John Scalzi, and a rather obscure Marvel comic from the 1960s called *Sgt. Fury and His Howling Commandos*, created by the legendary team of Stan Lee and Jack Kirby. If you want to find Stug's literary grandfather, look no further than Corporal Dum-Dum Dugan, Sergeant Nick Fury's right-hand man in these World War II-era stories. In fact, I wrote a blog about where Stug came from shortly after publishing *Gettysburg.* Check it out here: http://chrispourteau.thirdscribe.com/2014/11/03/stug/.

Last but certainly not least, I want to thank Michael Bunker for allowing me to play in his *Pennsylvania* sandbox. He's always been open to my ideas for doing what I wanted with his world, offered helpful, insightful suggestions for how to improve my stories, and never begrudged me the time when I've needed to ask a question regarding canon or anything else about the world of *Pennsylvania.* Writing these adventure stories is the most fun I've had *to date* as a writer, and that wouldn't have been possible without Michael's generosity, patience, and enthusiastic support. Poppa Bunker seems happy with them, and when the world's creator is happy with how I handled his world, I ain't got no room for complainin'.

Chris Pourteau

May 2015

A Note to My Readers

I *very much* appreciate you, dear reader, and the time you spent reading this collection. I'm still blown away by the idea that people *want* to spend their time—a finite thing we all have, though none of us really know how *much* of it we have—reading my stuff. It feels like a great gift from you to me, every time, so thank you for that. I hope you enjoyed reading these stories and found them time well spent.

I'd like to ask for one more favor. Please consider taking the time to review this collection at the venue where you bought it, and also on Goodreads, if you're a member. Having your feedback helps me know how to improve my craft the next time out. But it also helps other readers, like yourself, decide if they should spend their money—and more importantly, to me anyway, their *time*—on a written work. Providing a review is like publishing a public service announcement for your fellow readers, something you also benefit from when they do the same for you. Please recognize that by leaving a review, you're making a real contribution to the world—and the quality—of independent publishing.

About the Author

Chris Pourteau has been a technical writer and editor for over twenty years. His tales set in Michael Bunker's world of New Pennsylvania have been praised by readers and other writers alike. In February 2015, he published one of the first five novels helping to build the core canon world of the Apocalypse Weird universe, *The Serenity Strain*, a book that has been well received by AW fans. Folks also seem to dig his short story *Unconditional*—a stand-alone tale about the zombie apocalypse from the perspective of the family dog. *The Serenity Strain* has garnered over 50 reviews and *Unconditional* has received more than 40, and each has achieved an average rating of 4.8 out of 5.0 stars.

If you'd like to let Chris know what you think about *Tales of B-Company*, or if you just want to say howdy, feel free to email him at c.pourteau.author@gmail.com or visit his website at http://chrispourteau.thirdscribe.com/.

Chris lives in College Station, Texas.